School for Villains

Bruno Vincent

Illustrated by Jo Coates

MACMILLAN CHILDREN'S BOOKS

First published 2012 by Macmillan Children's Books
a division of Macmillan Publishers Limited
20 New Wharf Road, London N1 9RR
Basingstoke and Oxford
Associated companies throughout the world
www.panmacmillan.com

ISBN 978-0-330-47953-0

135798642

A CIP catalogue record for this book is available from
the British Library.

Printed and bound by CPI Group (UK) Ltd, Croydon CR0 4YY

THANKS

There are several gnarled and dastardly teachers to be discovered in this book, but I don't want to give the impression that they're in any way based on the teachers who inspired and encouraged me when I was young. This book is dedicated to them with huge thanks and, as I say, they're not like the teachers in this book. Definitely not. Not a bit . . .

Simon Potter
Mike Patton
Mike Reeves
George Giermakowski
John Foster

(And I'd like to say thanks to Gabriel Yeowart and Harry Walker too.)

A NOTE

WELCOME TO TUMBLEWATER. A large district of narrow winding streets tucked inside a much larger city. A place filled with the poorest, the weirdest, the nicest and the nastiest of people. And stories – lots of stories. Last year I became the storyteller of this place, recording all the grisly tales I came across – until I found I was in the middle of one myself. My long-lost sister Maria had been kidnapped, and before I could look for her I had to go on the run from the police and hide in the Underground, a special society of fugitives and outcasts. I stick to the shadows, stay out of sight and see all manner of dark things.

Follow me, and together we'll discover some of the grisliest tales, and continue the search for Maria. Don't make a sound and we both might escape with our lives.

PROLOGUE

 freezing wind blew in over the grave-stones.

The crowd shivered and pulled their cloaks closer around them, huddling in small groups near the scaffold. I looked around to check that my friends were still in sight. It was a dismal place – Ditcher's Fields, the muddy graveyard where prisoners were hanged with no trial and then hurriedly buried, usually in some-one else's grave. The crowd, gathering closer now as the moment of execution approached, squeezed between the narrow lines of gravestones, or sat up on the piles of old headstones that had been dug up and cast aside.

I moved uneasily from foot to foot, looking out for other people dressed like me, with dark hoods and scarves to hide their faces. One stood near the gate, ready to help us into a waiting carriage, and two of the others were beneath the scaffold. Only a few minutes to go now.

Glancing at the nearby police officers, looking bored

3

and miserable in the rain, I wondered whether we had any chance of success.

Behind me there was a sudden buzz of chatter in the crowd that quickly dwindled to an excited whispering. A group of men was approaching the gallows, the one in the middle hidden by a canvas sack over his face, and his hands bound in chains. Now there was silence as the men began to climb the steps.

As the spectators swarmed in around me I slipped between them until I was almost underneath the platform. There, to my disgust, I saw a group of children gathered, looking up gleefully as the men's feet creaked across the floorboards above.

The noose swung lightly in the wind as the men reached the platform and began to set about their business with very little ceremony. The executioner did this far too often to give it a second thought. The sack over the culprit's head meant he could not tell what was happening until he felt the rope looped roughly around his neck.

The officer stifled a yawn (it was not yet seven in the morning) as he watched the executioner whip the cloth from the head of the condemned. A scruffy-haired, weathered-looking man was revealed, looking down at the crowd with watery grey eyes. He blinked as the rope around his neck was tightened. Starting to feel tense, I looked around for my comrades and was relieved to see that all five of them were in place.

The officer in charge turned to the crowd and began

4

reading the sentence from a sheet of paper. He got to the phrase, 'I sentence you, Mary Spokes . . .' before frowning and looking through all the papers in his hand for the right one. The crowd laughed and shouted insults at him. Someone clapped loudly, and a chatter started out again among the cold and wet people waiting for their early-morning spectacle. Out behind the graveyard gulls were crying out over the river, and the sound of traffic was increasing – the clattering wheels on the streets, the clanking of engines and foghorns on the river.

At last the officer found the right page and holding it up he began to read it out again with indecent haste.

'On this day,' he sighed, 'the twenty-third of November . . .'

Only a couple of seconds now . . .

People clutched each other as though they were at the theatre and watching the exciting final scenes of a play.

Suddenly the officer stopped. There was a strange creaking sound and a tremor passed up through the wooden scaffold so that all three men staggered to one side, then steadied themselves.

The crowd laughed much louder, really delighted this time, and the officer grew furious. He mumbled the rest of the words as quickly as he could until he reached: '. . . and I now pronounce the sentence of DEATH upon this man—'

A huge snapping sound cut him off. Gasping, the crowd looked to the bottom of the scaffold and saw that it had been sawn right through, and was about to topple.

It swayed dangerously, sending all of the men on it to their knees, before with a resounding crash the wooden support gave way completely.

People screamed and laughed at once as the platform fell sideways, taking the officer and the hangman with it, crunching into the tombstones and splattering into wet earth.

But the condemned man stayed hanging up in the air for a moment – the rope was tied to a high branch of the graveyard's only tree, unconnected to the platform. The untightened noose was still caught around his neck and his hands tied behind his back. The rope caught under his chin – not quite strangling him, but leaving him dangling in the air.

'Twist your head!' I shouted up at him. 'For God's sake, wriggle, turn, get out of it!'

For a second I watched him twisting like a dumb animal being slaughtered and then the noose slipped and he fell with a shocking suddenness and landed in the mud. I was at his side in a moment – freeing his arms from their chains, and then pulling him along with me into the thronging chaos of the crowd.

People were running forward and back, frightened by the crash and excited by it. Policemen were streaming through to help the official and the hangman, not noticing that the culprit had escaped.

The condemned man seemed no less baffled by what

was going on. Gasping for breath as I shoved him into a gap between two piles of old headstones, he asked, 'Who are you?'

I put my hand over his mouth as three more police officers ran past. Then I pulled off my cloak, revealing that I was wearing another one underneath, wrapped the first one around him and pulled the hood over his head. Looking up I could see the way through the crowd to the gate and pulled him to his feet.

'Don't worry about it,' I said. '*Move!*' I kicked him in the behind to emphasize my point.

As we neared the gates I grabbed him around the shoulders and pretended to limp heavily, screwing up my face as though I was in pain. I cried out too, loudly and pathetically, as though I'd been injured by the falling scaffold, and making such a bawl that no one could pass by without covering their ears.

People were streaming out of the graveyard from fear of the police, who were running past us in huge numbers. They ignored me as I approached the gate and I saw my tall friend there waiting, pointing towards a carriage.

'There we go – that one,' I said to the condemned man, pointing to a coach-and-four twenty feet away. Our escape vehicle was so close that the man who a minute ago had been so near to death couldn't restrain himself, but ran across the street towards it.

'Oh no,' I muttered. 'Now he's drawing attention to us.' At once behind me I heard the shouting of police, telling us to come back. I reached the door of the carriage right behind the condemned man and shouted to the driver to get us going. Our tall friend caught up with us, just in time to jump on the footboard and cling on to the outside of the carriage.

'Faster!' I shouted, leaning out of the window.

The driver leaned round to look down at me.

'How clever of you,' he said. 'I hadn't thought of that. Let me know if you have any other bright ideas.'

I looked back as we headed up the hill. The police were streaming out of the graveyard – more than a dozen of them – and jumping in their own vehicles, or stopping other people's and taking theirs. The first of them had already set off and were only a hundred yards behind us and beginning to pick up speed.

Our carriage lurched left as it went around a grain cart and ducked right again to avoid an expensive-looking gentleman's sedan. Suddenly we were at the eastern crossroads and the driver pulled us right, through the stream of traffic, so close to crashing into the passing carriages from both directions that the startled horses started to neigh.

The carriage's wheels creaked loudly as our weight was thrown from one side to the other. Somehow we remained upright and passed under the railway bridge as a train crossed it, its plume of sooty smoke falling over our heads like a thick curtain, and we emerged from the dark cloud driving towards a side alley, straight towards some boys playing with a dog. We shouted as one and waved our arms – the boys jumped back in the nick of time and the dog ducked between the wheels. We all slumped into our seats with relief.

Finally our cobbled back alley came to an end, and we had to make a turning towards the main road.

'Take a deep breath,' said the driver. 'This might get a bit shirty.'

'What does he mea—' said the condemned man, before at the crack of a whip a sudden burst of speed threw him back in his seat. I leaned back out of the window and saw a group of police on horseback following us.

The driver whipped the horses harder and harder, and goaded them with curses. In the confusion, for a second I thought I recognized his voice and it worried me for some reason. But there was no time to care about that as we hurtled down the main road, faster and faster.

The buildings around us grew taller as we neared the court of justice and town hall. The streets got narrower. We were picking up speed, clattering downhill, and what people there were shrieked and rushed out of our way. But one man, a farmer trying to control his pony, was too slow to react. The animal panicked and slipped its rein, and the cart wheeled backwards directly in our way.

I saw our driver panicking too, looking left and right as the cart came closer, until at the last moment he wrenched the reins to one side, and we dashed past just in time as the cart overturned behind us.

A miracle – the cart blocked most of the road and the horse collapsed on its side, kicking its legs desperately. The police horses all reared up and refused to go further, infected by its panic.

'Thank God,' said Uncle's voice from behind me.

I looked at the tall cloaked man.

'Uncle!' I said. 'It *is* you! I hoped it was.'

I looked back. The road was a crush of horses neighing, and men shouting at them to no avail. But even as I thought we had escaped, a single horse leaped over the fracas at a terrific rate, goaded cruelly by a whip which drew blood from its neck.

'Anyone still following us?' Uncle asked.

'Just one,' I said.

'Have this,' said one of the men inside the carriage as he gave me a loaded pistol. I grabbed it, terrified by the jolting of the carriage. I'm sixteen! I thought. I'll probably blow my own head off!

But I leaned back out and aimed the pistol nonetheless, because this was no ordinary police officer who was following us: it was someone I'd seen before. She had the slim figure of a woman and long curly red hair, but weirdest of all she wore a thick leather patch covering both her eyes that seemed to have no effect on her ability to see. To see too much, in fact.

'Use it!' shouted the driver angrily at me as I tried to aim. I definitely recognized his voice, but couldn't think about it – now wasn't the moment to be put off.

A flour cart passed us and as I fumbled with the weapon to get a better aim it went off, exploding a bag of flour in a huge cloud. The farmer yelped and jumped for cover as Uncle snatched the gun off me to reload it.

The horses were tiring as the road forked into three directions ahead of us. This had always been one of the busiest junctions in the town. It was eerie to see it empty, and I felt the driver hesitate at the strangeness of it, and we slowed for a moment. I looked back: the red-haired creature was charging through the cloud even faster than before, and gaining on us.

'Go!' I shouted.

The driver chose at the last moment – when the red rider was almost upon us – to drag the reins towards the left turning. Our horses were exhausted, almost dead from the effort and stress, and couldn't pull the huge weight of the carriage behind them. The front right wheel, weakened by fire, snapped and the carriage bumped for a few yards before we crashed with fantastic force into the scaffolding at the front of a shop.

Our windows were shattered and part of the roof torn off by the impact but our momentum pulled us clear of the wreckage and I leaned out of the window again to see the side of the building, smashed open and suddenly without its supporting scaffolding, collapse downward just as the red rider passed under it. Our carriage screeched to a stop, sliding sideways along the cobbles, and we all turned to watch it happen.

There was a brief scream of the horse as it twisted between fallen planks of wood and then its neck was crushed by a tumbling block of bricks. The dreadful red-haired creature's legs were trapped beneath it and she put out her arms to try and protect herself, but the second wave of falling masonry was much heavier than the first. A wooden beam fell across her chest in a shower of dust and stones, and an instant later a brutally massive stone followed it, hitting the earth with a deep thunderous smash that shook all the buildings around and covering her completely.

For a moment we all looked, wondering if it could be true that we were free, and feeling aghast at the same time – even for the worst enemy, it was horrible to watch such a death. But already the cloud of brick dust was being dampened by rainfall and disappearing.

The driver turned from the spectacle and gently urged the horses so that we crawled forward on three wheels, scraping over the cobbles. We turned off the street on to a path beside one of the narrow canals which slid silently between many of the backstreets of Tumblewater.

We came to a stop with a whistle from the driver, and climbed out on to the pathway. The whistle had summoned a boat from under an arch in the canal, which now stole forward until it was beneath us in the water.

'You men go down to the boat,' said the driver. 'I've got to go back.' We didn't have time to question him as he disappeared back around the corner, we presumed for something he'd dropped. One by one we climbed down into the boat and after a wait of no more than a minute the driver returned, with no explanation, and joined us.

One of the men who had piloted the boat towards us climbed back up on to dry land. He released the horses, and patted their behinds so they ran away.

'What will you do with it?' I asked, looking at the ruined carriage.

Flames were still stealing back and forth over the end of the vehicle. One wheel was missing. He followed my eye and said, 'It'll be a pile of firewood within the hour.'

The boat's captain had already pushed away from the side and we heard these words as the man disappeared behind us into the distance and the gloom. In a few moments a bridge passed overhead, and he was lost to sight completely.

We all sat back in the parts of the boat we could find to ourselves, and looked up at the light between the edges of the buildings above us. Rain spattered on our faces, and the only sound was the rowing of our guide. He turned many a corner, and manoeuvred against currents, and wove a careful course through the silent hidden waterways until he said, 'We're here.'

Above the boat was a rough hole in a brick wall a few feet above water level. Realizing this was an entrance that we were supposed to use, I climbed in and found a ledge I could sit on. The others followed until we were all sat inside in a little room. The boatman handed up his lantern and, bidding us good luck, he pushed off into the stream and was gone.

'Thank you!' I called, and all the others followed my example with a chorus of grunts of gratitude. Then we were all alone. The tall man leaned forward and turned the lamp up so we could see each other.

The condemned man sat back in his seat, and looked at all our hooded faces in turn. Totally baffled, I couldn't even think of a question to ask, until one of the cloaked figures reached out and took his hand.

'Pleased to meet you, sir.' And he pulled back his hood and removed his scarf to reveal – a girl. 'Sally Dolton, at your service.' The condemned man stared at her – as did I. Sally was my friend, whom I had never intended to put in a moment's danger, let alone to allow her to follow me on a life-threatening mission.

Then the two figures next to Sally took their hoods off, revealing themselves to be two other of my closest friends. They introduced themselves as Tusk and Mayrick. Now there was only the tall man, the driver and me left.

I was glad to reveal my face. 'It's good to have you here!' I said. 'I'm so happy to have helped you escape. You don't know me, but my name's Daniel Dorey.'

The tall man next revealed himself with a more sombre air. 'They call me Uncle,' he said, and they shook hands.

We all looked up at the only man who had remained

standing. I thought I even noticed apprehension on Uncle's face as he looked at the stranger. Even though Uncle had organized this raid, he didn't seem to have a clue who the driver was. Now slowly that man pulled his hood back, rolled his scarf down and introduced himself.

'My name's Inspector Rambull of the District Police. It's a pleasure to meet you all.'

TWO DAYS EARLIER

ASPERS & PERI-
WETHER PUB-
LISHING.

Silence in the room. Mr Jaspers behind his desk, flicking through a manuscript.

I sat before him, waiting for his judgement on the collection of tales I had delivered. I had been there rather a long time, and the wait was playing havoc with my nerves.

'Remarkable,' he said, putting the book down, and taking his pipe out of his pocket. He paused, looking at the ceiling, as though a divine thought had just oc-curred to him, then farted quite loudly.

'Cravus, stop that, you foul animal,' he said. The office assistant fidgeted uncomfortably on his stool across the room, and blocked his nose with scraps of paper.

'Wonderful,' Jaspers went on. 'What an imagina-tion. Tell me, what happens next?'

'Caspian Prye is still as mad and dangerous as ever, and still in charge of Tumblewater. My sister is still being held captive somewhere around here, and he is still trying to find her,' I said earnestly. 'I have to find her first – and all I've got to help me is this key.'

'Wonderful,' he said, smiling.

'It's *not* wonderful, Mr Jaspers, my life's in danger! I could be captured and killed by the police at any time! My sister really *is* missing!'

'Wonderful,' he said again. 'I love the way you *inhabit* your stories.'

I sighed and gave up. There was no persuading him, and this wasn't exactly putting me in a good mood. I changed the subject.

'You didn't, ah . . . You didn't object to the character of the publisher?'

He threw himself back in his chair and considered. 'No! Of course not. I mean, it's grotesque exaggeration, of course, and no one would believe that that was what I was *really* like.'

He farted again.

'Cravus, I've warned you before,' he muttered half under his breath. 'That's a disgusting habit. Stop it at once.' Cravus's shoulders hunched at the rebuke, and he screwed the paper wedges more tightly into his nose, and carried on kicking a cracked teapot that was collecting raindrops.

Water dripped from the roof into pots, buckets and saucepans, and the blond boy who sat at the other desk (to whom I'd never been introduced) was holding a heavy manuscript above his head with which he was trying to crush a cockroach that sporadically darted across his desk, between the inkwell and his hat. Every few seconds the book slammed down with an incredibly loud bang.

'So . . . you like it?'

'My dear boy, I can tell already it's wonderful!' He said this in a slightly carefree way which sounded like he hadn't read it at all. 'This sort of book is the reason I became a publisher!' A faraway look came over him again and I pinched my nose just in case. 'Reading this, for a few hours one can forget that one is trapped in a sodden pit surrounded by loathsome crustaceans!'

The blond boy and Cravus exchanged a look at the words 'loathsome crustaceans', not sure whether he was talking about the cockroach, or them. The book slammed down with a WHAM!

I was at least happy there was nothing wrong with the manuscript, or at least nothing he had noticed so far.

As I looked out of the window, a familiar face stepped into the view, and recognizing the tall figure outside I realized it was time to leave.

'Mr Jaspers,' I said, 'can I leave the manuscript with you?'

'Of course. Pop back in a few days and I'll have my editorial notes ready. Really,' he said with a sense of disbelief, as he flicked through the pages, 'I wonder how you come up with this stuff sometimes.'

I sighed. I had told him about twenty-five times that

the adventures were all my own, but he either didn't believe me, or he could never remember. How he could possibly exist within this rain-drenched part of the city and remain unaware of the evil influence of Caspian Prye was beyond me. Leaving him to it, I said goodbye, and waved to the blond boy at the other desk. He gave me rather a sorrowful look as if the only sane person was leaving him on his own, and slammed the book down on the desk harder than ever, as the cockroach scuttled to safety.

'Hello, Uncle!' I said, as I stepped outside.

'You're in a good mood,' answered the tall man, as we began to walk.

'Of course I am,' I said. 'I finished writing the book of tales last night and handed them to Mr Jaspers just now. It's going to be called *Grisly Tales from Tumblewater*.'

'Congratulations,' he said, but he sounded far from happy. I looked up at him.

Over the last few weeks, he had been looking more and more troubled. I hardly ever saw him smile these days, and I wondered whether I would be able to get him to tell me why. Although I was only sixteen, I had found out that for some reason when you asked a grown-up if there was anything wrong, they always said that they were fine (especially if they obviously weren't). There was normally a cleverer way of asking, that would make them tell you everything, but I hadn't yet worked out what that was for Uncle. Poor Uncle was my protector, who had saved me from the streets and found me a home and a job – the job of writing down grisly tales. Except he was not just my protector, but that of every downtrodden family in Tumblewater, helping them escape under the streets into the Underground, a secret society which he was in charge of.

'OK,' he said, taking a deep breath. 'I'm sorry, Daniel, my head has been elsewhere these past few days. Tell me again, just so I haven't missed anything. We don't know where your sister is . . .'

I had told him the story almost as many times as I had told Mr Jaspers – only in Uncle's case, it was fatigue that made him unsure of the details.

'The witch hid my sister somewhere here in Tumblewater, and that witch is now dead. Caspian Prye wants to find Maria and force her into marriage, so I need to get to her before he does. The good news is that I have the only existing clue, the bad news is I have no idea what it means.'

There was one thing that made finding my sister important not just to me, but to us all. Caspian Prye was the most guarded man in the kingdom – so much so, no one was known to have ever seen him face to face. So long as we found my sister we had a chance to lay a trap for him. It was quite possibly our only chance to kill him, and free ourselves from the Underground.

'Let me have a look at this clue,' said Uncle at last.

I pulled the key up on its string from under my shirt. He looked at it closely for a second with deep concen-

tration and turned it over in his hand before handing it
back, looking at me seriously.

'It's a key,' he said.

'Oh, *thanks*. I had no idea.'

'No, Daniel, listen. It could be the key to anything.
A safe, a trapdoor, a chest, a gate, a music box – anything. Even something magical. We have to find out
what.'

'And we are going to find locksmiths to tell us what
it's for?'

'That's what worries me – I'm afraid I've got some
bad news. Tumblewater's locksmiths are in trouble.
The first two I visited recently were abandoned and
boarded up, the windows broken. The last one I went to
was raided right in front of me. The owner was dragged
away by the police and I was nearly caught myself.'

I stared at him. 'What do you think it means?'

'Well, as I watched, the police emptied all the keys
out into the street and searched through them, looking
for one specific key. Then when they didn't find what
they were looking for they set fire to the shop and tore
the walls down with hooks. I'm afraid that somehow
they know what you've got – and they want it for themselves.'

As he told me this he steered us both down a quiet
alley where the only sound was the light pattering of
the rain on the ground. I knew this trick of his well,
when he would guide us away from the main street into
the quietest corners without apparently thinking about

21

it. Then the next moment we would be in front of one of the secret entrances to the Underground, and soon we would be among the warrens of hidden passages beneath the streets. The city below the city, where the illegals lived.

Taking a torch off the wall, he took us to a door made from metal mesh grilles hammered together and let it swing back. Below us was a great spiral staircase made out of cast iron set in a pattern so you could see downward through the holes in it. As Uncle held the torch up I could see the light glimmering down through the holes in the metal and reflecting off steps that went down what looked like forever.

'We're going to visit some people I know – rather out of the ordinary people. The first one lives . . . below.' He pointed to the floor.

After we had been circling our way down the iron steps for a few minutes, we both began to feel dizzy. Our footsteps seemed to clatter away above us and below for infinity, so to take our minds off it we began to talk.

'I know you've been down here once before, Daniel,' said Uncle, 'but what you saw was only one tiny bit of it – it's much, much bigger than you realize. We have schools here. Hospitals, churches, theatres even. We have our own message system which works, we have cooks making food and clothes-repair shops and pretty much everything you could want.'

He suddenly put his hand out to stop me and, feeling a nasty sliver of fear, I saw that the staircase ended right in front of me.

'See beyond the edge,' Uncle said. 'There's a steel rung in the wall. See it?' There it was, about waist high in the flickering light. Our journey downward was not finished. Seeing all that black space ready to swallow me up I quaked, but didn't want Uncle to see that I was scared, so I forced myself to reach out and grab the metal rim.

If there's anything I love then it's climbing so, spooky as it was, I took to the climb easily at once, enjoying the fact that I was going first.

'Where are we going?' I asked.

'People who deal with ordinary locks are obviously no good,' Uncle said from what sounded like a long way above. 'We need some specialist help. And the man we're seeing is definitely less ordinary.'

It was hard to tell how long we climbed but after a while my feet touched the floor, and Uncle was soon after me with the torch in his hand. He waved it around, looking for the right direction. As my eyes got accustomed to the intense darkness some shapes became visible and I saw tunnels around me. They were large and solidly constructed, with looming arches spreading out in several directions. We were now so incredibly far down I couldn't begin to imagine what these tunnels had ever been used for.

'We don't know what this place was,' said Uncle, who seemed to be reading my thoughts. 'Possibly some monks built it and lived here. But it gives me the chills anyway, so let's be as fast as we can. This way.' He led me along the nearest of the caves, where mud squelched underfoot. The curve of the long tunnel's roof and the wet stone wall amplified noise, making our footsteps and our breathing seem very loud.

The tunnel suddenly ended in a brick wall with a single doorway in the middle of it. The doorway led to a narrow stone passage down which came a chilly draught.

'He's in there,' muttered Uncle, stepping forward. He stood in the doorway and cleared his throat. 'Griswald,' he said loudly into the stone passage beyond. 'We want to talk to you.'

I shivered for about the thousandth time that day as I heard a slithering sound coming towards us from the chamber beyond. Then a shape appeared at the end of the passage – a man, cloaked in layers of black cloth.

'Put the light away!' he snarled.

'Sorry,' said Uncle, 'I forgot.' And he planted the torch in the mud to the side of the doorway.

Even in the weak reflected light at the end of the passage I could see that Griswald flinched away from its every flicker, as though the light physically hurt him.

'We've got something to show you,' said Uncle. 'It's important.'

'Show me, show me,' whispered Griswald. Uncle nodded at me, so I walked forward, with more than a little trepidation, into the stone passage. My back blocked out most of the light so I caught occasional flickers of the half-face he had turned to us, which was so pale it practically had no colour at all.

As I got near he reached out a hand. 'Give it to me,' he said, then snatched the key away. I moved aside to give him some light, and saw as he held it up that it twinkled green and purple at different angles as though it had crystals in it. Then it went out of sight, disappeared behind his hidden face, as though he was licking it. When he held it up against the light again the end was shining with liquid. Then he turned so I could see him a little better – one of his eyes flashed pale yellow.

He held the key back to me.

I took it and because he didn't say anything, I asked, 'Why do you live down here?'

He blinked his pale eyelids, so translucent I could almost see the irises through them. 'I see too much,' he said. 'Visions, things I don't understand. They could be from far in the future or in the past. Down here, deep in the earth, is where I suffer them least. But still they come. A white-skinned monk travelling like a ghost through a dead city, only his black teeth showing. Fire-rockets that fall from the sky and destroy whole streets. A huge, fearsome metal engine that runs on metal rails at terrible speeds and belches black smoke . . .'

'You mean the railway?'

'The what?'

'That's the railway. It exists now – I rode on it last

week. It runs above the streets here, and it rides far out across the country.'

He had worked himself up into an excitement as he talked about his visions but now he relaxed a bit. 'Hmm,' he said. 'Maybe I've been down here too long.'

'So what do you think?' I said, holding up the key.

'Of course,' he said, clearing his throat and turning his head to me. 'It's a key,' he said.

'Oh, *thanks*,' I said.

'What is it?' asked Uncle from the other end of the passage.

'He says it's a key,' I replied.

'Oh, brilliant,' I heard him mutter. 'Thanks a million.'

'Anything else?' I asked. I felt I'd been dragged into a grisly circus freakshow for nothing. And then I saw Griswald's wide-open pale eyes snap shut.

'No,' he muttered under his breath. 'It's too ancient, even for me. I don't know where it came from or what to do with it. But . . .' His voice dropped to a whisper. His eyes flickered in their sockets, his back went rigid and he started shivering like he was having a fit. Then, to my terror, his voice changed completely. His pathetic whisper became deeper, urgent and commanding as though someone more powerful was speaking through him. 'She's waiting for you, Daniel. But she says you haven't got long. She needs you to find her soon. Soon! There's not much time!' His voice rose with desperation, and my heart leaped in my chest, but before I could ask any questions of this new incarnation, his body relaxed and he slumped to the floor, unconscious.

I found Uncle holding the torch anxiously at the other end of the passageway. I told him what had happened and asked if we should fetch help. 'No,' he said, 'that's to be expected. It costs him heavily to access his visions. It will take him a while to recover, and then he will want to be in private.' We started to walk away. 'It troubles me, though, that no one can help us with this key.'

'He said it was too ancient for him to see anything from it.' For some reason I chose not to tell Uncle about the strange voice which had sprung from him. Surely much too deep to be Maria's voice?

As we reached the edge of the tunnel we heard an unexpected sound coming towards us – the sound of happy whistling. A lamplight bobbed towards us through the darkness and a girl carrying a basket appeared.

'Halloo there!' she cried in a friendly voice.

'Is that you, Molly Naylor?' asked Uncle. As he saw that he knew the girl he let out a deep breath of relief, and I realized how scared of the caves he really was.

'Hello, Mr Uncle,' she said pertly.

'What are you doing here?'

'Bringing food to Master Griswald, as I do every week, like a good girl.'

'That's a pretty horrible task,' I said.

She smiled and walked past us, and I stared at the

towel that covered the basket she carried. I wondered what was beneath it. Raw fish? Pig's blood? Fresh brains? I saw that Uncle was already climbing the iron ladder towards the surface, carrying the torch, and waving goodbye to Molly I ran after him.

'She seemed nice,' I said when I caught up with him. 'What now?'

'There's someone else I want to consult. And he lives . . .' I followed his gaze as he fell silent, looking up the metal ladder to the surface.

So began our epic climb upward – and a hard slog later, Uncle pushed open a lid and we found ourselves above ground, in a quiet deserted alley between two very tall buildings. Uncle took me by the arm until we were on another staircase up the side of one of the walls. I was starting to feel light-headed at how far we had climbed in one short hour. When we reached the roof and saw rising above us a huge chimney – and circling round it, a metal staircase – I exploded with impatience.

'*Another* one?' I asked.

Uncle was bent double, trying to get his breath back. 'I should have thought this through a bit better,' he admitted.

I'd only been in the city a few months, and the rooftops had always been shrouded in fog and darkness. So what rose above me now seemed majestic and unfamiliar. A round brick chimney wider than a house, that disappeared into the fog fifty feet above our heads.

I ignored the specks of rain that fell on my face as I stared upward but Uncle just marched wearily towards it and began walking up the steps. He stopped before he went out of sight and called down to me.

'We haven't got all day!' he said. 'Well, *I* haven't anyway.'

I hurried along behind him, my curiosity growing with each step. The earth retreated below us, becoming blurry in the mist, until we were walking around in circles among the clouds.

'Here,' Uncle said, leaning against the rail of the staircase.

I tried to disguise my fear as I walked out on the small bridge with only a thin metal grille between me and the rooftops far below – so far below I could just make out the chimneys. But I kept walking until I saw a tower, stained almost black with smoke and age.

As I knocked against a wooden door set in the tower's side I said to Uncle, 'So who are we visiting? Is he like the underground man?'

'He's in a similar line of business,' said Uncle, 'but I wouldn't say they were similar, exactly.'

'Come in!' shouted a voice from within. 'It's quite unlocked.'

Opening the door I walked in and found myself in a circular room which was far and away the cosiest and most welcoming place I had ever seen. A thick Turkish rug lay beneath our feet, all around were deep comfy-looking chairs and sofas, tall cases containing old leather-bound books. Beautiful maps and paintings of rustic scenes hung from the walls between odd-looking musical instruments, hunting weapons and other curios, and the whole scene was lit by the leaping yellow flames of a bright-burning fire in the far wall.

'Who is it?' asked a genial voice and, not able to find where it was coming from, I saw a tiny wooden staircase that rose from beside the hearth to a raised platform about ten feet above our heads. Up there, a plump man with a grey beard sat at a desk. Little spectacles perched at the end of his nose; behind him rested a large artist's easel covered in astronomical charts and anatomical diagrams; the quill in his hand boasted a large feather that arched over his shoulder and swung gently from side to side as though it was gently fanning the back of his head; and the cup by his side contained some hot infusion which let off sleepy curls of steam. As he glanced up at us I saw that the steam had fogged the bottom half of his glasses. I had never imagined that somewhere could feel so full of knowledge and learning, and yet so welcoming too. I was overwhelmed by a sense of happy wonderment at finding myself here.

Having rubbed his glasses with his sleeve, the old man looked at me quizzically for a moment, then saw Uncle behind me.

'Lordy!' he shouted. 'You two look bloody knack-ered!' When he saw me looking shocked he giggled to himself, scuttling down the tiny staircase that looked like it couldn't take a man half his size. 'I get so few visitors,' he said, 'by the old-fashioned route at least. I forget how exhausting it is to make the trip. Jolly nice to see you though, Uncle, old bean!' he bellowed, tottering away through a door and returning with a kettle.

'The *old-fashioned* route?' I muttered to Uncle through gritted teeth. 'You mean, there's another way?' He looked too exhausted to notice.

Yanking the kettle's lid off, the huge man held it underneath a spout that stuck out from the mouth of a stuffed otter on the wall and twisted its left ear so that water gushed into it. Watching me staring, he said to Uncle, 'He needs feeding, eh? Some crumpets, I think.'

Within a couple of minutes we were sat in meltingly comfortable chairs in front of the fire. Before us were two pots containing coffee and tea, and a flask of hot buttered rum – and a huge heap of crumpets, buttered until they dripped. Next to the crumpets were a dozen little pots from which one could choose marmalade, gentleman's relish, lemon curd and a choice of jams that made my head spin.

'Damson, apricot, sloe and apple, loganberry, elderberry, strawberry, blackcurrant and fig. Although if you choose strawberry I shall think very little of you – it is by far the *least* of jams,' he said loftily.

As I rather dizzily took a bite from my first crumpet (covered liberally with blackcurrant jam), our host was already finishing his fourth and saying in the calm voice of absolute authority, 'There is no book, art or

31

science in the history of man which has contributed as greatly to civilization as a well-made tea.' As I ate, I silently rejoiced at the deliciousness of the crumpet, and knew that he was right. Who could do evil after eating such a meal?

'As ever, you are the perfect host, Dr Lapiday,' said Uncle.

'Mister!' the man protested, smiling. 'Don't call me Doctor. It makes me think you'll come to me with a ticklish cough, which I guarantee I can do nothing about. I *am* a Doctor. A Professor too, and a Fellow, a Chair, and all sorts of things. But *Mister*, please.'

'Mr Lapiday,' said Uncle, and smiled for the first time that I'd seen in many weeks. 'I'm afraid I bring bad news. And a request for help.'

So Uncle began to fill him in on what was happening on the ground far below (it seemed the kindly gentleman never left his little turret). The news made him stop eating , frown in consternation, and murmur disapproval. When my own story was mentioned the man's eyes flickered at me and then away, as absently as though he was examining an exhibit in a museum, while his brain put the whole picture together.

'It is very grave and troublesome,' he said. 'My researches take me to the far ends of the earth – through my books and instruments I spend time in the distant frozen forests and the burning sands of the equator, in the innumerable forgotten lands of the past. I had no idea that the situation right here beneath my feet had reached such an awful state. I feel useless,' he muttered. 'Is there anything I can do to help?'

Uncle looked at me. 'We have no access to Caspian Prye, no way of finding him or getting to him. Except for a man we know only as the Apothecary, who has quite disappeared. This is our only clue – show him, Daniel.'

As I held up the key it seemed stranger than ever. Its teeth were intricately arranged like a piece in an ancient puzzle but also nastily curved and pointed, as though they were real teeth belonging to a tiny metal creature that would nip your finger.

Lapiday murmured to himself, turning it over in his hands. He raised his head and thought long and hard, as though trying to locate a distant memory. Then he handed it back to me and watched me put the string over my head and stow it back under my shirt, before speaking again.

'It's a key,' he said.

I swallowed hard and struggled with my feelings before answering. 'This is the nicest tea and crumpets I've ever had,' I said, turning to Uncle. 'So I'm going to restrain myself. But the next person who says that to me is going to get a kick in the knee.'

'Forgive us,' said Uncle to Lapiday.

He chuckled. 'Keys aren't my speciality I'm afraid. But –' he waved a hand over his head and I saw all the bookcases arrayed behind him, packed with thick, decaying volumes bound in dark leather – 'I'll look it up, I just can't guarantee you any results. But it seems to me a *very* old key. Thousands of years, perhaps. It's from a long way away too – the mountains of the Subcontinent is my guess. In this part of the world we never had the ability to make keys like that.

'And it's magical. Definitely magical. I'm sorry to say this, Daniel,' he said, 'but whatever it opens, it's not a lock. Not one you can see.'

'Anything you can come up with,' said Uncle. 'We don't know how much time we have, but this man Prye is desperate. He's got rid of so many people from their homes that Tumblewater is nearly empty. Thousands of us live a desperate existence below the streets, hoping for a chance to return. But Prye hasn't found Daniel's sister yet,' he continued. 'We fear next he might start destroying the whole district – he's mad enough, and has the power to.' Uncle's face fell again into that expression of despair that I'd seen so often recently.

Mr Lapiday met my eye, and I saw that he was as concerned about Uncle's well-being as I was. Adopting a grave expression, he gently took Uncle by the elbow and guided him away. I could only hear that the mutterings from the older man sounded encouraging, but I didn't want to seem to be listening in, so I browsed along the bookshelves.

There were countless volumes by ancient authors in Latin and Greek, and other languages and alphabets I could only guess at. Even though I loved reading it seemed impossible that I could ever conquer as many books as were held here, no doubt including histories, epic tales, ancient sciences and remedies – and I couldn't imagine what else.

As my gaze led me along the shelves I found that I had come under the shadow of the ten-foot-high pulpit which housed Lapiday's desk and instruments, and I was in semi-darkness. Unable to resist looking into hidden places, wherever I was, I explored beyond the bookshelves and found several boxes and chests piled up on one another. Checking to see that no one was watching me, I brushed dust off the top one and tried to pull the hasp open. It squeaked loudly so I let it go, keeping an ear out until I heard the two men again, still talking at the other end of the room.

My eye fell on something large that stood against the wall, covered in a red cloth. It seemed to be a huge painting or a mirror in a fabulously ornate gold-plated frame visible in one corner where the cloth had slipped away. I had to approach it. From what I'd seen and glimpsed elsewhere in Lapiday's apartment, it might truly be a painting that belonged in a great palace or museum overseas, that he had quite forgotten about.

I pulled the cloth back with my hand, but couldn't see anything on it at all. Maybe it was a mirror after all – but then, why cover it? Checking over my shoulder again, I struck a match. The dust I had upset in the air was clouding around me and moving *inside* the surface in peaceful swirls well within the space, and further back than the wall in front of me. I was greedily fascinated by this unexpected portal. The sudden chance to be somewhere away from the rain-drenched mud of Tumblewater was guiltily overpowering. With hardly a hesitation, I stepped through the gap, and felt the red cloth flutter behind me.

From one darkness to another, it took my eyes a few seconds to adjust, while I remained perfectly still. Then I saw I was in a small room clouded with the smoke of cheap candles that were plentifully arranged across a desk a few feet away.

It was a narrow, quiet chamber lined from floor to ceiling with fat old books and thick plump ledgers, so much so that they seemed to choke the room and fill its tiny confines with dust.

Over the desk in front of me leaned a hungry-looking young man, his straggly hair falling down over his shoulders and back. He worked patiently, filling a ledger with tiny neat scratches of his pen, and studying his work in perfect concentration, only breaking his posture for a second to cock his head while he made a calculation. As the daylight through the window faded he took no notice of it – he would go on working forever, it seemed, until he had finished the last page of the ledger. Except at last he stood, and placed the book with care on a high shelf, where it took its place alongside a long row of perhaps forty other volumes, with numbers on the spines which showed that they went back two hundred or more years. Those that bore his signature must have accounted for tens of thousands of hours of hard study from this young man's life.

Within the rules of the portal I had used, I didn't know whether he could see me or not so I remained quite still and for a strange moment drank in the feeling of that curious room. He had work that consumed him so much that he seemed long ago to have become trapped-up in this smoky nest and to have forgotten the outside world. But he clearly felt alive in the calculation of sums – amounts owing, amounts paid, interest owing, interest paid. He glanced to one side for a second and I saw how vulnerable he looked, how young he was to already be behaving like an old man. And I thought I saw something I recognized in those features too. Perhaps he was related to someone I knew, or perhaps I had seen him in Tumblewater, more grown-up than he was now – the ways of magic portals were unknown to me – but my heart went out to him.

I trod carefully back through the empty picture frame without seeing the unhappy young man's head stir even an inch towards me, and let the red cloth fall back to cloak the gap.

'Daniel?' I heard a rather testy voice behind me, and rushed back out from the shadows. Both the men were staring at me.

'Couldn't you hear us?' asked Uncle, suspiciously.

'Er, no, sorry,' I said. 'I was distracted by this amazing book.' I held up the first volume I had snatched off the shelf and looking down, saw it was entitled, *The Junior*

Ornithologist's Guide to the Dietary Requirements of Subtropical Birds of Prey in Temperate Climes by Prof. D Dumble. I gulped.

Uncle looked at me rather dubiously, but Lapiday seemed quite convinced by my explanation. 'It's funny,' he said. 'Boys of your age are normally interested in adventure books.' He pointed to a bookcase and glancing at it I saw the same worn old titles which were in every children's bookshelf across the land.

'I don't know,' I said suspiciously, and thinking how much I preferred my Grisly Tales. 'They're all the same, aren't they? No matter what happens, you know the hero's always going to get through and win in the end.'

Lapiday looked shocked. 'But those are just the *finished* ones,' he said. 'Are you telling me you don't know about the library of *unfinished* books?'

I looked to Uncle but he seemed as clueless as me. 'No,' I said. 'What do you mean?' He was already busy untying a rope from the wall, and letting it out carefully I saw another bookshelf slowly descend from where it had been hanging in the roof. As it touched the floor, I saw it contained only very slim volumes – perhaps half the length, or less, than ordinary storybooks.

'You don't suppose *all* heroes have succeeded in their tasks, do you? That's just the version that adults tell you. No, there are hundreds of tales where the hero doesn't make it, the stories that didn't finish the way they should. Think about the Black Death reaching Europe, think about the destruction of Pompeii, or worst of all – the burning of the great library in ancient Alexandria. Those were all stories that had heroes who were supposed to prevent them happening. They were supposed to have happy endings. The hero doesn't *always* survive, Daniel . . .'

On that chilling note I looked at the slim volumes again and glanced at a few titles – *The Rescue of Julius Caesar*, *The Boy who Saved the Mary Celeste* – and I shivered.

But Lapiday suddenly jumped up, his grave look replaced by one of delight. 'My food! I'd quite forgotten it was time for the delivery.' Uncle and I followed him to the window, which we could hardly see out of because it was almost entirely blocked by an extraordinary instrument that looked like an enormous tuba. Suspended from the ceiling and as large as an elephant, its brass tubes twisted round and round as they got smaller. It had a mouthpiece at head height, stoppered with a cork, and the horn itself poked out of the window and got wider and wider, until it was as wide as a horse is long, and seemed heavy enough to topple the whole tower to one side. It looked like a huge loudspeaker.

'What do you use that for?' I asked. 'To make announcements?'

'No!' He smiled. 'Quite the opposite. It's a very, *very* powerful ear trumpet. Depending where I point it, I can hear conversations all over the city.' He popped out the cork and held what I had thought was a mouthpiece up to my ear. Through that tiny little hole I could suddenly hear a cacophony of voices, so loud that they might have been at my shoulder. He smiled at me again.

'It's pointed at the high street, right into the middle of the market,' he said. 'You'd be amazed at the conversations you pick up.' As he spoke he hauled at a rope that ran over a pulley outside the window. After a minute of listening to the babble of the crowds and not being able to make out a single thing anyone was saying except the shouting of lots of prices, I saw a large basket rock into view on the end of the rope. It was full of food – fruit, a tied handkerchief full of eggs, some butter, fish and meat all wrapped in wax paper, and of course a large box of crumpets.

'In case of guests,' he said, tucking the box under his arm as he unpacked the hamper.

'And what's *that*?' I asked, looking beyond the oversized ear trumpet to a decidedly dangerous-looking contraption beyond it. It looked like a metal-plated rocket, and was almost as wide as a barrel.

'Oh, that's Doctor Whizzbang,' he said. 'I spent three weeks making that a few summers ago. Seeing things explode has always been a hobby of mine. Enough gunpowder in it to blow up a small castle, I'd say. Only I'd have to travel about a hundred miles to test it safely and even then, it doesn't seem fair on the owner of the castle, do you think? Now – want a lift down?'

We both opened our mouths to say no, and then felt the large tea we'd eaten in our bellies, remembered the exhausting climb, and looked again at the basket. It was large and deep – like the baskets I'd seen attached to hot air balloons. Before we knew it we were being lowered down through the clouds – clouds of rainy fog and heavy factory fumes that always hung above the buildings.

'That was an extraordinary place,' I said. 'I hope I have a chance to go there again.'

Uncle said nothing, but stared thoughtfully out into the greyness as we continued our descent, jolting ever so lightly every few feet as Lapiday let out another arm's length of rope.

I spent the downward journey wondering how high up we were, and trying not to peep over the edge of the basket, and before I knew it we were near the ground, and then hit it with a thump.

'Molly Naylor!' I said, amazed. She looked as startled as we were. 'Is there an eccentric person in Tumblewater who you *don't* bring food to?'

'Why of course,' she said, turning away (as the basket was winched back up behind us by Lapiday's invisible hand), smoothing her skirt and addressing us rather primly. 'There's the dead ones. And those in prison. And then there's the Apothecary.'

'*Who*?' we both asked, in unison.

Molly was alarmed and suspicious at our interest, and wouldn't tell us at first. But as her duties were finished for the day and we were all walking together towards the nearest entrance to the Underground, I decided to change the subject, and began to tell her about my stories.

'You write stories?' she said, looking at me again. 'Fancy that! I've never met a writer before.'

'But you've heard of the Grisly Tales that are told in these parts, by so many folks?'

'Of course! I was just never sure what qualified as a grisly tale.'

'Let me tell you one then,' I said, and told her the story of the Boy Who Picked His Nose. At the end she expressed her enjoyment by punching me in the shoulder.

'I've thought of one!' she said. 'Can I tell you, and maybe you'll write it down?'

I bowed (rather pompously, I admit) and said, 'That's exactly the idea – there's nothing I'd like more.'

So she told me the grisly story she liked best (and now I'll tell it to you too), and as Uncle and I listened to the polite, pretty and garrulous girl tell her tale we slipped through the alleyways towards the entrance to our safehold under the streets.

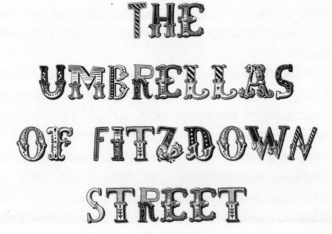

THE
UMBRELLAS
OF FITZDOWN
STREET

On one street at the very most westerly tip of Tumble-water, there was every day a most startling apparition. Otherwise ordinary and forgettable, the brief passage of Fitzdown Street was a short cut between two of the bigger and more important railway stations, that brought thousands upon thousands of smart men in suits from the suburbs to work in the huge offices in the city.

At six thirty sharp each morning a stampede could be heard approaching from around the corner, and then a sudden torrent of black would appear. Black shoes, spattered with mud. Black trousers, splashed with puddle water. And above them, black umbrellas squeaking endlessly against each other, held by hundreds of hands encased in black leather gloves. All the while the rain thrummed upon the umbrellas like someone impatiently drumming their fingers, and the hundreds of shoes rumbled on the cobbles.

These were the many hundreds, if not thousands, of clerks who arrived at the nearby railway station and who, every day, trooped as fast as they could towards their offices in another part of the city. Then at the end of the day they came back in the opposite direction, and the whole procession was repeated in reverse.

A small boy called Liam sat at his window, resting his chin on his hands. Every day this sight filled him with wonder, the stampede of faceless clerks putting him in mind of a crowd of cockroaches or beetles. From behind Liam came the noise of his brothers and sisters (of whom there were twelve or thirteen – he could never keep count), who played and fought and shouted all day long in the next room. His mother tried to keep them under control, or lost her temper, or threatened to have a breakdown by turns. Unfortunately for her the only guaranteed way to get a moment's peace and quiet was, in fact, to have a breakdown, which she did at least once a week. At these times she would collapse on the kitchen table and sob inconsolably. At once all the children would become silent, and ply her with cups of tea, and generally stand around like a sequence of Russian dolls, but looking decidedly less angelic.

Liam was not interested in the violent playing of the other children. A quiet little boy, he preferred watching the world from the window. Below him, all sorts of things happened in the street. Groups of children kicked a ball back and forth. People stopped and chatted to one another. From his high vantage point, he kept an eye on all the families eating their lunch and their dinner, and the sick little boy in the building opposite who lay in his bed day and night, his crutches propped up at the end of his bed. He was on the sixth floor, at just the right height for Liam to see in through his window, and although Liam would often wave to him, to show the little boy he had at least one friend, he thought perhaps the boy's eyesight was affected as well as his legs, because the lad never raised his hand to return the wave.

Sometimes Liam would lean out and look down

six storeys all the way to the ground – the sight of the huge drop made him feel sick and thrilled at the same time and he would lean straight back in again, his heart beating fast. He could spend hours there, happily resting his head on his folded arms, waiting for the excitement of the thousands of returning umbrellas.

One evening, as the procession of umbrellas passed below, bobbing up and down so they looked like the surface of a shallow river bubbling over black rocks, something caught Liam's eye. One of the umbrellas had stopped, so that the others moved either side of it like a stone parting the stream. What happened next made Liam's heart miss a beat. As he watched, the umbrella began to rise, as though it belonged to a very tall man who had previously been stooping over and was now standing to his full height. It rose further and further, so that the figure holding it stood twice as tall as those around him. Its face was hidden by the rim of the brolly and its body was concealed by the long black mackintosh worn by every clerk in the city.

And yet it *still* rose upward, until it was twenty feet or more tall!

Liam looked over his shoulder at the rest of the room. Half to check he was not asleep or in a daydream and half to make sure his sight of this incredible apparition wasn't going to be interrupted by his siblings. His worries were groundless: in the kitchen his eldest brother was chasing four or five of the younger children in circles, imitating an enraged dragon (although making a louder noise than even a dragon would have done) while two of the youngest clung to his shoulders and yelled giddy-up into his ear. As he turned back to the window, Liam heard the sound of his dragon-brother crashing into a chair and tumbling to the ground, accompanied by the excited scream, of half a dozen children, and the helpless wail of his mother.

Ignoring the noise, he focused again on the street below. He couldn't believe it. The figure was still there. It had grown even taller, and now it had leaned over too, so that its umbrella rested against a second-storey window. It was as though the man was leaning in for a chat with an old friend. The other faceless clerks continued to swarm either side of him, as though the bizarre figure was invisible to them.

At this point Liam felt compelled to share this extraordinary sight with the others. He raced to the kitchen door, and excitedly shouted to them to come and see, but they didn't listen, and after he'd repeated it at the top of his voice he saw that he wasn't going to get anyone to hear him. At the same moment he saw too late the charge of his enormous eldest brother (with even more children loaded on his back) coming straight for him, which resulted in another crash and another wail from their mother, and by the time he had wriggled free from the pile of bodies and run back to the window, the strange man had vanished back into the crowd.

He watched the crowd intently, hoping for another sign of the magical apparition, but none came. Within a few minutes the stream of clerks' umbrellas thinned to a trickle and then suddenly as the rush hour came to an end, it stopped. The street became peaceful again.

Shortly afterwards, however, the street seemed to erupt.

Liam was unable to sleep for wondering about the strange figure he had seen – what it could have been, whether it was a type of person his parents hadn't yet told him about, or some strange type of fairy or ghoul which only he could see. So he lay in the bed which he shared with all his twelve or thirteen siblings and fidgeted as voices echoed up from the street below, and the light of torches flickered across the ceiling. He longed to get up and go to the window but he was crushed between his two eldest brothers and couldn't move.

The uproar in the street outside grew and grew – he could hear people knocking on doors, questions being asked, and the crying of various women. Finally his father got up and angrily threw open the window.

'Shut up!' he shouted. 'What are you all blathering about down there?' He leaned out of the window, listening to someone far down on the street. Then he closed the window and sat heavily on the side of the bed. All of the children looked over nervously, waiting for him to speak, as his mother asked, 'What is it, love?'

'A manhunt,' he said. 'A child has gone missing from across the street. Nobody knows how it happened.' A heavy and mysterious silence filled the air.

'What do you mean?' his wife asked.

Liam's father took a careful glance at the children for a moment before answering quietly. 'The boy was asleep in his room, and no one went in or out. The only answer is impossible: that he must have been snatched out of his window – up on the second floor, overlooking the road.'

For the rest of the night urgent shouts echoed along the street, people ran back and forth, and little sleep was had by anyone. Although they all pretended to be asleep, the children fidgeted in bed, wondering that something so horrible had happened so nearby – almost beneath their very noses.

The next morning Liam's dad left for the factory at his usual hour, grumpy and sleepless, and the other children fell to playing 'child-catcher', where the eldest hunted the others around the house in order to catch them and gobble them up. Their mother watched, feeling faint and helpless, worrying for the mother of the poor child who had gone missing, and trying to make lunch for them all without being crushed to death by the stampede.

Meanwhile Liam retired to his usual viewpoint. All day long he watched people visit the family who had lost their child, to offer their condolences. The search by the police continued from door to door, into every nook and corner of the street and up and down all its buildings, until Liam heard the knock on his own family's front door, a few feet away.

When his mother answered it (after taking a couple of moments to hush her children) Liam heard her say to the officer outside that nobody in their flat had seen anyone or knew anything about it. Liam jumped from his chair and ran to stand beside her, looking up into the serious face of the old policeman, done up in his thick black woollen coat with his brass buttons and truncheon hanging from one hand. What should he say? Surely neither his mother nor this terribly serious-looking man would believe what he had to tell them about the strange figure he had seen?

His hesitation lasted too long and before he had found the courage to speak, the policeman had made his polite departing words and the door was slammed shut.

Quickly the children took up their shouting and playing again: they had got bored of the child-catcher now and were playing a version of hide and seek where some of them took turns to hide the baby in ingenious places (such as the coal bucket, the kettle and a sack of potatoes). This game, as it involved making one of her children actually disappear, understandably upset their mother even more than the previous one, but they were so used to upsetting her by now that they really didn't notice.

Liam sat glumly with his chin resting on the edge of the window sill.

*

A few days passed, and the missing boy was not found.

'Missing, presumed eaten,' said Liam's elder brother.

At first the search carried on round the clock, and then, as time went on, fewer and fewer people were searching, and those who carried on looking had a hollow feeling of dread. All this time Liam looked on, feeling terrible for not saying what he had seen. His one consolation was that if he had told the truth, he would have received a beating for his trouble, and been ignored as well.

After three days, with the boy still nowhere to be found, the street was reopened to the crowds of evening and morning commuters. Able to use their short cut once more, they rushed eagerly down the street each morning, regular as a heartbeat, as though nothing had changed. Not one of the black-cloak-and-black-umbrella-wielding clerks ever paused to read the signs that were pasted on the walls, asking for information about the kidnapping.

One evening, Liam stared down once more at the thousands of identical umbrella hoods bobbing and flowing, and wondered about the people beneath them, if people they were. He wondered too for the hundredth time what it was he'd seen that night, whether he had been hallucinating (which he was sure he had not), and whether that strange figure still moved among them.

Then he blinked.

In the middle of the street, as the others hurried on around it, one of the umbrellas slowed, then stopped. A cold feeling of fear pierced him, and he felt paralysed. The still umbrella was, just as last time, in the centre of the lane, right below his window. He had to raise the alarm.

Behind him in the next room his family were playing as they usually did, but with the quarry in his sights he was determined not to take his eyes too far from it. He shouted for them to come. He waved furiously at them from his chair by the window. Although several of them could see him no one noticed, so he shouted again. Any second now the apparition would be gone. Looking down from the window he picked out the umbrella hood again instantly. Hundreds of others were pouring around it, but that single one remained perfectly still. Except – except – it was hard to tell, but as he looked he was sure it began to rise a few feet above the others.

Becoming furious with his family's stupidity, he threw first a stubbed-out candle, then a book and finally picked up his chair and flung it at the open kitchen door. It bounced against the frame, and his second-oldest brother tripped on it, and went sprawling. Two of the girls nearest him burst out laughing and jumped on him, accompanied by much screaming from the others.

Liam turned back to the window and thrust his head out to look down into the street again. In the opposite building he saw the crippled boy trapped in his bed. To his confusion he saw that, for the first time ever, the boy's eyes were fixed on his. A terrible fear gripped him.

Knowing he only had a few seconds, he turned again to his family to scream for help at the top of his voice. He screamed again, and a third time. It was no good – he could do nothing to stop it. No one would listen to him. He spun back to the window and his words died in his throat.

The street had disappeared. He could see nothing but blackness – the shiny black of an umbrella hood, and the individual drops on the waxy surface.

y the time Molly had finished her story she had completely forgotten her reluctance to tell us about the Apothecary, and happily spilt the beans at once.

'He's a very mysterious chap,' she said. 'All I know of him is that he is always moving around, and doesn't seem to mind living in the most dark and horrible quarters, so long as it means no one will come looking for him.'

My heart sank. I was sure this must be the man we were looking for.

'So he was staying secret,' asked Uncle, 'in order to carry on his devious, underhand business?'

'Oh no!' Molly stopped walking. 'Now listen here. Some of the people he has to deal with are strange and unusual enough – underhand, if you will, Mr Uncle, and illegal perhaps – and maybe he himself seems a bit strange. He's so used to living his life in the back corners of the world that he doesn't like to meet your eye, and some people think that 'spicious. But his medicines are proper good, believe you me. My mum was cramped up double with pain and he cured it with one of his mixtures. And my cousin Ruby's husband lost his voice (which wasn't much of a loss if you ask me, with the mouth he had on him), and the Apothecary brought it back in a trice. More's the pity.'

'Do you know where he can be found?' I asked.

Molly was looking impatient now that we had kept her for so long, and was casting glances either side of us down the tunnel, wondering which was the right way home. 'I don't know,' she said absently. 'Last I heard he was in Pruitt Lane, the street they say is haunted. But that was weeks ago and I would expect he's moved by now.' She had become tired with our questions and when we said our thank-yous she moved off without looking back.

Uncle led me along the lane as I wondered what we would do next.

He had been right in one thing: as I began to see more of it, I was totally amazed by the Underground. Streets branched off left and right, whether they were made out of old tunnels built of brick and stone or had been dug by hand and propped up with wooden posts. Everywhere was the proof of how much effort people would make to survive. It almost felt like every house had a ghost of itself under the ground. Stalls selling every kind of clothes, shoes, food, little items such as candles and ink. Every now and then there was even a more established shop that went back into a room-sized hole carved out of the mud, with glass windows and painted signs outside. Coffee sellers stood at the corners, as did 'wayfarers' who gave people directions, and 'shelter agents', men offering (for a price) to find places deep within the tunnels for families to sleep in. As they directed people to and fro, porters ran through the crowds after the better-off ones, carrying large cases on their backs.

'People are arriving all the time,' Uncle explained.

'Why do they stay here?' I asked. 'Surely they can get away through the tunnels to another part of the city and escape? Emerge above ground elsewhere?'

'Ah, but where, exactly? The land of milk and honey?' Uncle asked. 'Besides, almost all the people here have family still above the surface who are in danger. They want to stay close, help them if they manage to escape. Or they've got nowhere to go and are hoping Prye's reign will somehow come to an end and soon they'll be able to go back to their homes. Here,' he said, as we reached a door in the tunnel wall, 'I've got urgent business I have to take care of. In the meantime I want you to enrol in this school.'

'School?' I said, aghast. 'I finished school ages ago!'

He was already a few steps along the road ahead and his mind already on other things, but he turned his face back to me for a moment and in the flickering shadowlight I saw how lined, drawn and withered he looked. He said in a straight voice, 'Daniel, I've been awake for more than three days and there's no sign of sleep for me soon. There are many hundreds of people whose welfare depends on me. Thousands, in fact. I want you to pay attention and learn what you can. This is no ordinary school, as you will see, and they have much to teach you. Now keep your wits about you, and I'll see you very soon.'

And with that, he left, trudging tiredly away. I caught notice of young children in the tunnel around me, shrinking back from the lamplight so they were hardly visible except by the blinking glints from their eyes, and the whispering between them.

I looked again at the door (which seemed quite ordinary) and saw a message scrawled roughly in the mud of the wall above it, as though someone had used their whole hand to gouge out the letters:

RIDLEY GARNET'S SCHOLE for VILLAINS

I turned to the children again and, laughing, was about to make a joke that the school couldn't be that good if it didn't know how to spell the word 'school'. But in that flickering light I saw a dreadful earnestness in the young eyes and realized the children were looking up at me with fear. The joke caught in my throat. The bravest of them, a boy of no more than six, crept a little closer. 'Are you a pirate?' he asked.

'No,' I said. Still not sure what was afoot, I wanted to laugh but his seriousness did not falter.

'A murderer then?'

'No! This isn't actually a school for *real* villains – the sign is just to scare little ones like you away,' I said, and now I did laugh. But the children shrank back instead, as though I didn't know the danger I was in. Their fear began to irritate me, and I turned the handle on the door, a little more roughly than I had intended.

Below me a narrow stone stairwell twisted out of sight. The door closed behind me as I took my first steps, and enclosed in that tiny space for a second, I wondered what any place could be that could strike fear into those children who had lived such a life of horror among the tunnels. My answer came as I reached the bottom step and laid eyes on six older children, half boys and half girls (although it was hard to tell), all wearing masks and clutching daggers in their hands. The masks were carved into twisted gargoyles with scars and boils and grotesque distortions, leering so violently that they made those stone creatures on the walls of churches seem like gentle cherubs. Not sure what to do, I could only watch as one of the gargoyled monsters turned lazily toward me, pulled a dagger from his belt, took aim with it and let it fly towards me.

I only had time to throw myself back against the wall, close my eyes, and think something along the lines of 'This is definitely not the way I was planning to die'. I heard the blade thump into a block of wood, felt no pain in my body, and cautiously opening my eyes I saw a board about a foot to my left with three daggers sticking out of it.

I slowly let out my breath as I realized the dagger-throwers had no interest in me at all. The three who had yet to throw their blades were scratching away at them with little sharpeners, and behind their horrible masks they were moaning to each other about a teacher.

'It's impossible! No one can hit those targets. It's impossible!' one boy was saying as he lifted his mask to blow away the metal fragments from his dagger.

'One of these days someone will hit *him* in the arse with a blade,' said a girl. The target was marked with a piece of paper, upon which had been drawn a gruesome illustration: a cantankerous old man who walked with a stick and whose features were enlarged and contorted to look as evil as possible. 'Then he'll be sorry.' As he said this another boy threw his blade in anger. It spun in the air for twenty feet towards me and hit the picture in the chin.

'Hey you!' he shouted. 'Get lost! You're putting me off.'

I didn't need to be told twice. As I made my way out of this chamber, a crowd of younger children ran across my path, kicking and punching each other as they ran. When the front one slipped for a second, the others piled over him to reach a doorway. I helped him up, then followed the others through the door, finding them gathered at the end of a corridor. A very tired-looking man stood at a small wooden lectern, patiently polishing his spectacles to conceal his irritation.

This old gentleman attempted to take names from a register, but when this proved impossible because the children were shouting so much, he just pulled out a long stick with a paintbrush on it and counted them that way, dabbing each head with a white dot so that he knew he'd already counted it (but, from the look of him, losing count anyway). When I saw the brush approach me, I pushed it out of the way and stood up straight so the teacher could see I was too old to belong to this particular class. Or any class, as far as I was concerned.

At the end of the narrow corridor into which we were crammed there was a door that remained shut, and to which all of the boys and girls kept turning, as though they expected it to open at any moment.

I wondered whether there was perhaps some incredible spectacle beyond the door – some treat such as a wrestling match, a trapped walrus or elephant – or even an execution. Then, as the time grew closer and the children quietened down, I wondered whether it could actually be *school* they were excited to attend.

As I wondered at this possibility, the teacher made his way through the children (boxing a fair few of them about the ears to get them out of his way) until he reached me.

'You are attending the School?' he asked. I nodded, and explained that I had been told to attend by Uncle. I didn't know exactly what effect this would have, but so important was Uncle to the Underground that the name always seemed to have the same reaction: the old man instantly lost his weary suspicion and became eager to please.

'Of course,' he said. 'Do send him my best. Well – the door should be open any minute now – I have no control over it, they can only open it from the inside.'

This revelation gave me a twinge of doubt. 'They?'

Before he could answer, the ringing of a bell came from beyond the door, followed by the clank of a turning lock.

At once all the children were struck into silence. Those who had been wrestling in the mud clambered up to their feet, scraped dirt from their eyes and stared gormlessly as the door swung open.

'Be careful on the stairs,' the old man said as they filed forward. 'And try to behave yourselves.'

Quietly we crowded through the door on to a flimsy wooden staircase that descended into a huge chamber that seemed as tall and narrow as a canyon. For a moment, we might have been forgiven for thinking we had stepped into hell.

The bell had summoned pupils from every direction and they appeared at the top of staircases and ladders, from the doors in the walls and holes in the floor. They swarmed among each other, making a terrible din, carrying all sorts of weapons, from a bent rusty railing to a butcher's hook. Whole groups wore masks, as though they were members of formidable gangs, and looking up I saw children swinging across the gap on ropes, swift and unhesitating like monkeys, with nothing to protect them from the fall. The pupils were mostly male, but those girls that were there joined in even more roughly than the boys, as though to prove they deserved to be here. The law of the jungle clearly held sway.

Some grim-looking men stood in one corner muttering to each other and casting unreadable glances back and forth. The place was lit by a ramshackle collection of lanterns, candles and burning torches which made for bright pockets of light that made the dark shadows between them seem all the deeper, as though they went on forever. As we descended, the iron door clanged shut behind us and looking up I saw a skinny little man push the lock shut. This was indeed an initiation ceremony.

I reached the ground and got swept up in the rush of passing bodies. I tried to hang back from the group of younger children in front of me and keep to myself, but it was next to impossible. We were crushed from both sides and the chorus of voices echoed off the walls into a deafening boom. It felt like passing through the digestive system of a writhing animal, and I could only put my hands by my sides and try not to fall over as I was propelled forward. I soon found myself crammed in among some boys who were muttering in an incomprehensible slang, jumbling English words so they sounded like nonsense. They refused to meet my eye.

Some kind of command must have been called out that I didn't hear above the roar, because at once a ghostly hush spread all the way down the long cavern. As each pupil became aware of it, they went instantly and completely silent, and it was even more chilling to see a sudden and complete obedience fall over them – as though we were in the presence of something much more powerfully malignant. Following their eyes, I looked up and saw a door cut into the dark wall, far above, from which stepped a thin old man, on to a narrow wooden scaffold.

An extra-sharp stillness came over the crowd as they looked up at him, and he shuffled forward to the edge of his makeshift balcony to speak. His face was tired and old, and deep lines criss-crossed it. He walked slowly with a stick whose top pressed hard into his palm as he leaned heavily on it. There was power and knowledge expressed in his smallest movements, even though he seemed neither educated nor grand. In fact he looked no different from a hungry and decaying beggar one might see on the street, using an empty bottle as his pillow. Had I seen him curled up outside an inn late at night, I might have thought he had no more than a few hours to live.

After pausing, perhaps to catch his breath, at last he spoke, and all other thoughts flew from my mind. I had never heard a voice so loud and commanding, one that struck me as cold and sharp as a splinter of ice.

'We have a new class joining us today,' he said. 'There's two points of business we always have to take care of when new ones are in. Threadbenning, the numbers, please.' A chubby man standing to his side, balding and contrite, looked at a sheet and called out:

'Fourteen, Mr Garnet!' Mr Threadbenning had to bellow at the top of his voice, and was still hard to make out compared to the old man.

'Fourteen,' that man repeated, in his penetrating voice. 'That is the number of students we have lost overnight. Seven dead, and seven captured – headed for the gallows.'

Seven dead? I thought. In just one night?

'That brings us down to a total of three hundred pupils in the school. So, new children, understand this.' He leaned over the rail and spoke with concentrated threat. 'You are here to learn, to learn quickly, and not to lark about. We have many thousands of people starving in these caverns around us, and hundreds of police on the streets above who would spill our blood, and will do if we give them the sniff of a chance. The evidence is hanging up there on the gallows this minute.' He gripped the rails, and far above as he was, I saw him bare his teeth, and deliver a final volley that was like being addressed by a great king or emperor of the ancient world:

'You will listen. You will learn. You will become the best damned crooks in existence. Or we shall all perish – GRADY PUT THAT FROG DOWN IN ASSEMBLY HOW MANY TIMES MUST I SAY IT?'

He then flashed an unexpected smile at us. 'Work hard, children,' he said, chuckling to himself, and somehow even that little laugh was clearly audible to us all, far below.

I breathed again, and relief that I was but an anonymous speck in the crowd flooded through me. Then I saw Garnet stop halfway through his door and turn to face us once more.

'I almost forgot. We have here a new lad today who is a little out of the ordinary. Daniel Dorey he is named – he wears a black coat, I am told. Ah yes, there you are, lad.' Surely it was impossible that among all the multitudes of costumes and hundreds of boys his old eyes really could find me? Yet they were locked on mine.

Around me hundreds of heads turned to stare. And still more hundreds craned round to try and make me out from the furthest corners.

'Mr Dorey is to join class 4C. He also has a very interesting secret. Which I dare say you will all discover in a couple of hours.' And then, staring straight down at my utterly transfixed expression, he smiled at me as though we were old acquaintances, and turning to retreat up the stairs, laughed the same deathly chuckle as before. Unable to look anywhere else, I kept my eyes on the old man as he slowly crept away.

The second the door closed behind him, another bell rang and it was again as though all hell had broken loose. Before I could try and work out who or where 4C might be, a hand grabbed me by the scruff of the neck and yanked me into the middle of a group that was rushing past.

'Keep up!' said the hand's owner.

Oh great, I thought, as I caught sight of her. I'm the new boy at the roughest school in the world, and I'm being knocked around by a *girl*.

'I'm Sally!' she said, not looking back. 'Sally Dolton.

First class starts in two minutes. Questions later.'

Lines of children marched up staircases, in through doors in the walls, or climbed ladders to jump through holes into deep chambers that I could see were carved out of the mud and rock. Through some of these holes I saw desks, chairs and boards covered with written instructions while others showed glimpses of machines and tables covered with metal tools. Some gave no sign of what was inside except the ghostly light of the lamps shining off wet bare walls. I hardly had the chance to look, but the boys and girls who went into these darker rooms looked stronger, more toughened, their faces set firm, like soldiers on manoeuvres.

Following the children in front of me up a staircase, I was soon in a room where some chairs were scattered higgledy-piggledy on one side. Each student rushed and took one so I followed suit. This Sally girl seemed incredibly keen and sat right at the front, but I drifted to the back, where I was more comfortable. I sat beside two boys who seemed to be friends – one tall and the other short. They introduced themselves as Tusk (short) and Mayrick (tall) and before we had a chance to make any other introductions, the room hushed.

In front of us a man stood stock still. His clothes were very old and worn, but by Underground standards incredibly clean and neat. He sported an extraordinarily bushy moustache and had a brutal scar that spread across his cheek up to his forehead and made his right eyebrow twist upwards as though it was stuck in a permanent look of sarcastic annoyance. He refused to meet any of us in the eye until we were perfectly quiet, and when he spoke it was with a surprisingly soft voice and a thick Highlands accent.

'My name is Mr Lackland,' he said quietly, 'and we have very little time, as you've already been told. So let us get on at once. You are here to learn the ways of the knife.' Our eyes moved instinctively to the sharp blade that he held in front of him. I felt a shiver. I had never thought even in my most idle fantasies that I could find myself in a room with someone teaching me how to wield a blade. There was a tense excitement coming from the class around me too.

'I want you to have respect for this blade. Not to see it just as something fun, that swashbucklers cut each other's throats with on pirate ships. It can end your life in an instant and in a bloody, painful way. You, come here!' He pointed the blade at a short boy, who got up and came forward.

'When it comes to the blade, the most important thing is to know how to defend yourself against it. So take this –' he flipped the dagger over and caught the sharp blade between forefinger and thumb, so that the handle was offered to the boy. Then he produced another blade from a sling under his arm, and showed the boy how to defend against thrusts from different angles. The rest of us watched open-mouthed as the quiet-spoken teacher made slow attacks that were wide of his body, and easy to defend. Then gradually, as the nervous boy got used to the sound of metal on metal and grew more confident, the attacks came faster and harder: the forward thrust to the chest, the angled thrusts from each side, the sudden wild swing.

Soon the short boy was defending himself against this tall and smartly dressed adult with confidence. He responded quicker and quicker, and Lackland's lunges came faster and harder. The boy was beginning to enjoy himself, we could see, until eventually he dodged out of the way so well he was able to hold his knife to the teacher's throat. Lackland showed no surprise or anger (he didn't even seem to notice the metal against his skin). Instead he stood and said shortly, 'Good. Well done. Who's next?'

Every hand in the room shot up.

Soon the teacher had us all in pairs, taking it in turns to perform the standard attacks (but carefully, so carefully) on our partners, who parried them, and then attacked us in return. It seemed incredible, but within an hour the room was full of swishing steel, clashing blades, and one might have thought it was a young army. Surely a group of youngsters had never learned anything so swiftly. At least that was what I thought, until at the end of the lesson a bell tolled mournfully in the distance among the caverns and we were told to leave through a side door into a dank corridor towards the next 'schoolroom', while more pupils filed in behind us.

There was no running, no shouting. The chaos of

the morning was forgotten. We were *swordsmen* now. No, we walked coolly, studiously (Sally led the way, as she seemed the only one organized enough to have a timetable), our heads buzzing with what we had just learned, going over it again and again in case we forgot. As the next door along in the corridor was opened for us we all looked in, fizzing like lit fuses to take in our next lesson. Disappointingly, all we could see were what looked like gigantic, heavy blocks of iron on the floor.

'In, you lot!' said a little man with a pointy nose and a pointy chin and jet-black eyes. 'Move. Fast. No time. I am Mr Shallows. I've taught seven classes this morning and have another six coming after you.' He snapped the door shut as the last boy shuffled in and smacked at his head with a ruler. 'Move *fast*!' he snapped, and then had us all hold out our hands. One by one, he walked down the line in front of us and flicked our palms with his ruler. We were powerless to protest, and it was worst for me as I was at the end and had to watch him coming all down the line, seeing the wince of pain on each face as he went, waiting for my turn. When it came it was sudden, sharp and nasty. I opened and closed my hand, held it behind my back. What was this for?

He seemed happy for us to hate him, because he stood in front of us, looking as though he'd already forgotten what he'd just done.

'The police are coming,' he snapped. 'Any minute

now. You're cold, wet and scared. But getting this right means whether your friends and family eat tonight.'

'Haven't got any family,' murmured one of the boys, a particularly dirty one with a long, thin face. Considering we'd already been punished for doing nothing at all, I wondered whether this was exactly a wise course of action.

'Ain't got no friends neither,' said the boy next to him, looking rather pleased with himself.

At that, Mr Shallows took a single step forward and the ruler in his hand flashed so fast we couldn't even see it. The first boy to speak had made the mistake of leaving his hand held weakly out, crinkled with pain. Before any of us had a chance to react the ruler cracked down on it, twice as hard as before, and the boy fell to his knees. Then in one movement it came up and struck the face of the second boy, making a whipping sound.

'Stand forward,' said Mr Shallows quietly, retreating to the side of the huge iron box. The two boys were too shell-shocked to do anything else, and as they staggered towards him, the teacher's voice continued quicker than before. 'The police are nearly here. If they find you, they will execute you. Your hands are shaking from cold, and from climbing over mud and brick.' (Now I understood why he'd struck our hands.) 'You have less than two minutes. I will give you three instructions, so listen carefully, and then you will know how to crack this safe. All the riches of the city will be available to you.' He rummaged in his pockets and brought out a key ring on which hung a single key. This he tossed to the boys. The rest of us watched in silence.

'Number one, turn it clockwise. Number two, feel for the clicks – you will feel, or faintly hear, a number of very subtle clicks as you turn the key. Number three, adjust the key to meet the clicks.' The boys stared up at him stupidly, and as the thin-faced boy held it up the key ring jangled because his hand was shaking. Mr Shallows snatched it back off him and briskly showed how the teeth of the key could be adjusted to fit the inner workings of the lock. He handed it back, pulled out a pocket watch, and said, 'Your time starts now.'

The boys jumped to it. The tall one put the key in, turned it roughly until it wouldn't go further, then turned it back the other way, very slowly. The other one kept his ear close to the metal surface. As they thought they detected a click they pulled out the key, adjusted the little metal teeth clumsily and retried it. Mr Shallows had no time to waste on them – he picked two girls, gave them a key, and noted his time on the watch. Then he started another pair on yet another safe, then two more, until we were all feverishly working away at different safe-boxes all around the room.

There was no time to argue, no time to think. We worked as fast as we could, furiously concentrating and then adjusting our keys with delicacy. The occasional loud snaps of the ruler against people's wrists as they failed to complete the task in time only sharpened our attention. In between the pointy-faced Mr Shallows

71

prowled, practising with the ruler against his own palm.

Aside from that there was no noise except for little clicks and clinks. Then came the occasional metal creak as the safe doors swung open and the pupils rested back on their feet, breathing deeply with relief. Once any pair completed their tasks Shallows at once turned them towards a bank of larger dark shapes that stood at the back of the room, like hulks. One by one the pairs graduated to, then dealt with, the larger of the safes, which seemed at first as unbreachable as rock. But we had no choice but to try our hardest, and because we had to, we quickly found we had it in ourselves to get them open.

As I waited at the end for the final few pairs to finish, I looked over the class around me. Out of the whole group, Sally was clearly the one in charge. She was also the closest thing that this school had to a swot – the most earnest pupil in the class, who threw herself at every task with deadly seriousness. The others found this a bit annoying but since she was always helping them out with advice when they struggled, they tended to stay on her good side. What's more, she had the maps and timetables. She seemed a natural leader, but because I hate being told what to do I avoided getting into lengthy conversations with her.

The other two boys I had met were much more like me – the tall, rather gloomy-looking Mayrick and his short friend Tusk, who seemed sparky and agitated, as though he was desperate to get out on to the streets right now and throttle Prye with his own two hands. Whenever there was a quiet moment they would slink into a corner and cast knowing looks all around, muttering sarcastically to each other. I liked them immediately.

At last we were watching the final pairs, willing them to be successful, hating the sight of the hovering ruler, until there came one final click and the huge iron door sighed open, and they joined the rest of us.

Mr Shallows didn't waste a second. He tucked the ruler in his pocket, consulted the stopwatch and, looking at us, said simply: 'Good.'

In the distance a bell sounded again. The faintest of smiles creased at the side of his mouth and regarding the whole group of us, he looked pleased with himself. 'Up there,' he said sharply, nodding at a hatch in the roof reached by a ladder. Our next class. 'Chop-chop!' he shouted, and turned back to stand behind the door as the next group began to file in, looking innocently around themselves as we had done shortly before. Quietly we climbed up and through the hatch. Once more, we were amazed by what we had managed to learn from him in such a short time. But most of all, we just hated him, and hoped never to find ourselves in his room again.

Nevertheless as we gathered in a group above the hatch at the top of the ladder, there was a quiet thrill in the group. We knew how to fight with knives, how to defend ourselves from them too; and we were trained safecrackers. *What's next?* we whispered excitedly.

Our voices faded to silence as our eyes adjusted to the enormous gloomy chamber we were in. The walls were made of thick stone slabs, from which hung lengths of rusty chain. Elaborate medieval instruments – spiked maces, three-pronged spears, curve-bladed axes – rested against the walls. Ropes were tied to metal hoops in the wall, and whips tipped with flesh-gouging claws were curled on hooks. In front of us was a long oblong wooden table fitted with a cranking mechanism – in other words, a rack. Even the last few who'd been whispering shut their mouths when they saw that.

'Call me a silly old worrybag,' said Mayrick gloomily, 'but does this look to you just a little bit like a torture chamber?'

'I'd *like* to say no,' said Tusk next to him, 'but it does bear some of the classic signs.' He picked up a huge double-bladed axe, its edges stained with a dried brown substance. The three of us looked at each other.

'Now what exactly *could* that be,' asked Tusk, 'except blood?'

'Could be rat's blood,' I said.

He propped the axe up at its full height – it was taller than his head. 'I'm not saying you're wrong,' he said, 'but I get the feeling that killing rats probably isn't the main thing it was made for.'

'I don't think they're very likely to actually torture

74

us,' I said. 'Not if they're training us to be on their side.'

'Boys, put that down, please,' said Sally, passing by. 'Class is about to start.'

Mayrick turned to me. 'They might not torture *all* of us; it could just be one or two, to show the rest how it goes.'

'Well, if that is the case, I hope they pick her,' Tusk said. 'She's so damn cheerful.'

We heard a clicking noise and turned to see a tall man staring at us. This new teacher (at least we hoped he was our teacher and not a psychopath who had strayed in through the tunnels) stood next to the rack and looked us over one by one, with a most disparaging expression. He was very thin with wild wiry hair and huge eyes that looked almost amphibian, like those of a frog, as though he had been below ground almost all his life. He ran his hands through his hair constantly in a distracted manner, and his whole attitude was so demented and arresting that we couldn't help but pay attention.

'Welcome, ladies and gentlemen,' he said, in a doom-laden voice. 'Today we are here to learn flower arranging.'

We stared at him in absolute silence.

'Really?' asked a voice from the back.

'No, not really,' said the teacher. 'And we're not here to use the gymnasium either.' He gestured towards the torture equipment. 'My name is Silas Crone. You!' He pointed at the small chubby boy called Wharton, who

75

had been the first to be picked out for sword-practice too. He stepped forward, looking a bit less nervous than he probably should. Mr Crone handed him an expensive-looking leatherbound envelope, thick and heavy.

'What is it?' the boy asked. 'Is it an exercise book?'

'Look inside,' said Silas. The boy popped it open and we all craned forward as he removed a large, fluttering note.

'A five-pound note!' cried someone.

We gawped – this foreign object seemed so flimsy, so like any other sheet of paper, yet it was six months' wages, or more, to most ordinary people.

'The object Wharton is holding,' said Silas, 'is a gentleman's pocketbook, where he keeps his money. Now put the note back in,' he snapped, 'and put the book in your inside pocket.'

As though he was handling an ancient scroll, Wharton folded the note with extreme caution and placed it back within the wallet.

'Now,' said Silas, standing at the other end of the room. 'Walk past me.'

The boy blinked and set off, deliberately averting his eyes from the shock-headed stranger walking towards him as though there were a thousand sights and distractions to catch his eye rather than forbidding walls of stone. As he drew level, Silas Crone seemed to lose his concentration – he swayed and bumped into the young Wharton very lightly, and put a hand out to steady him. Wharton walked back to the rest of us, looking mystified as to what the exercise had achieved, until we all saw Mr Crone at the far end of the room, holding the wallet in his hand.

'What I just did is easy,' he said, unfolding the five-pound note and rattling it in the air in front of us once more. 'By the end of this lesson you will all be able to pick each other's pockets without any difficulty. And any boy able to take this five-pound note off me . . . can keep it.'

Now he made us face the front, and got Wharton to steal the book from him – clumsily at first, but in only ten passes he had made the timid boy perform the switch so subtly that it was quite invisible – we saw no movement of his hands at all. The idea of such a nervous little boy getting the five-pound note made us jealous and spurred us on. We knew it could be done – and there was hardly any time to practise.

But before he would let us try it ourselves, Crone raised a crooked finger of warning as he gave instruction. 'This is only one of many crimes we will teach you down here that, above the surface, can be punishable by death,' he said. 'But this is the one that youngsters like you get caught for most. So pay attention, it might save your life. The trick is this: when you knock into someone, to do it gently, almost as though you are brushing past them and have made a little more contact than you expected. You meet their eye – this is essential – and apologize sincerely.

You put out one hand to steady them, and in the same instant your other hand is swiftly moving inside their coat. When your hand touches their arm, the tips of your fingers are on the top of the pocketbook. Then, to show that you mean it, you *squeeze* their arm to say sorry and to make sure they haven't lost their balance. That's the moment when the pocketbook is lifted out of the pocket. Then both your hands return to your side in what looks like a perfectly natural movement. And you continue on your way, walking as normally as possible. You carry the pocketbook in your hand as though it's your own and you do *not* place your hand into your own pocket straight away.'

At first we were all terribly clumsy – people got their hands stuck, or even accidentally punched each other. But as we tried again and again, a few pupils started to exhibit a real flair for it. The pocket watch Crone placed on the rack (and which none of us dared to steal) ticked round until there was scarcely any time left in the hour. And it was like learning a magic trick: without really understanding how we had acquired the skill, by simple practice we had become good at it – and would soon be perfect practitioners of the art.

As the hour bell chimed and we headed through the door, I felt a nudge and turned to see Tusk with an excited look in his eye. I saw his hand inside his jacket pocket, holding it open so I could see the piece of paper within – during the many swappings of the different wallets between us, he had managed to sneak out the five-pound note. Trying to keep my smile to myself, I climbed the stairs. Soon we came back out into the main cavern, and made our way along a pathway carved into the rock.

There seemed to be no end to it as we wound through these narrow caves, with more rooms to discover at every turn. I glanced through doors as we passed, wondering what the next lesson might be and whether there was a chance (as I thought there must be) that one of us might actually end up dead. It didn't seem unlikely.

In one room I saw rows and rows of thin, studious-looking pupils, perhaps thirty of them, hunched over and hard at work. They seemed to be doing drawing of some kind, using extremely delicate pens and paint-brushes, working away with painstaking carefulness and a mysterious intensity. Each wore a jeweller's looking glass clenched over one eye and as I passed, one of them, a girl, looked up and saw me. Her eye was hugely magnified, making her look repellently ghoulish, so I hurried on. It was only then I recognized what the piece of paper was that she had been working on.

'Did you see that?' I asked Tusk, who was behind me on the ledge.

He nodded, taking the five-pound note from his pocket and tearing it into shreds. 'Never guessed they'd have their own bloody forgery department,' he said bitterly. As he tore it up I wondered why I didn't care – it was, after all, a very convincing forgery. But then

79

I realized, down here in the Underground, what use would it be? You couldn't buy your way out, after all: we were all stuck here together. Going above ground meant risking your life, however much money you had, fake or otherwise.

Then something else caught my eye. Hardly visible in the gloomy cavern below, you could just make out a hole in the centre of the stone floor. A master held out a glittering object of shiny metal and dropped it down the hole, then stood back and consulted a pocket watch. At once the boy at the front of a queue stepped forward, dived headfirst through the hole and there was a splash. What class could that possibly be?

We were all a little tired now after the exertions of the day, and our energy was depleted further when we saw our next lesson was to take place in what looked like a traditional classroom. Slowly and with reluctance we took our seats as a wrinkle-faced woman fiddled with a lamp at the front of the class until she had managed to turn it up to full exposure, and then we saw that the walls around us were covered with maps of every size. Some were scrawled on scraps of paper, some drawn so neatly they might have been printed on a press, and they were all shaded with dozens of different colours. Lots of the maps were weirdly long and twisted, or very, very wide and intricately detailed, and some of them looked hundreds of years old.

'Quiet please, children!' said the woman, clapping

her hands. 'My name is Miss Slade, and we've got a lot to get through!'

I looked at the books and pencils in front of me. 'Lots of what exactly?' I asked, feeling suddenly rebellious.

The woman looked absent-mindedly over the top of her glasses. 'Geography,' she said.

'But I *know* geography!' I complained.

At this, the old lady pushed her glasses up her nose and although until that moment she'd had the gentle look of a benevolent aunt, she now glared at me fiercely.

'Oh really?' she said in a quietly menacing voice. 'Then perhaps you can show me the location of Hobster's Corner on these maps? Where it's said that desperate medical students kidnap people and eat their flesh.'

'No,' I admitted.

'Or the Singing Well of Sidchurch, that swallows boys whole, of its own free will? The Emberstone Mine-shaft, that emits gases so horrible they kill people by the nastiness of their smell alone? The Sharp-Toothed-Rat-Ridden Cave of Absolutely Certain Death, which needs no further explanation?'

I shook my head weakly, and at the same time she pulled at the corner of a huge cloth so it fell away from the wall with a huge *woomph*, sending up a cloud of dust. It revealed the largest, most complicated and confusing diagram I had ever seen. It was as high as the ceiling and twenty feet long, with lines shooting off everywhere, crossing each other, going round in loops.

'We are here, children, to learn the geography of the Tunnels. Now pay attention, because I will teach you to draw this map and understand the dangers that surround us – knowing it could prove the difference between life and death.'

'That's what they all say,' muttered Tusk, who was still in a grump about his lost fiver. He looked up to find her face about an inch from his.

'Well,' she said, 'they're all ... *correct*.' He flinched.

For one hour, Miss Slade made sense of the enormous map by taking us through the other smaller maps and allocating each pupil one of them to copy out. There was one map that showed where food was stored, how it came into the tunnels and was distributed. There was one for escape routes and emergency exits and another that showed the most dangerous parts of the Underground: tunnels at risk of collapse, others ruled over by gangs of bandits and murderers, those which had flooded or where people regularly went missing for reasons no one knew. Another map showed where you could find candles, firewood and matches wrapped up in waterproof leather pouches, so if you found yourself alone you need never be trapped in the dark.

Then there was the map of ghosts. If there was any terror to be found in the ancient places of the Underground (and there were many – diseases, rats, cannibals and even rumoured crocodiles) the one that people feared the most were ghosts. Looking at the map it seemed almost every tunnel, stairway, chamber or waterwell was haunted in some way or other, whether by silent apparitions, howling banshees or phantom animals that would invisibly lick or nibble your hands. Some vengeful spirits would try to scare you to death, said one description, or lead you astray into dangerous places. Others were simply so mysterious and terrible, they could not be described by those who had seen them – next to these were just written chilling warnings. Some were comical or even friendly – they might walk the passageways warning you about other, evil spirits that lurked nearby. Here was one map I could have studied for hours if I had the chance.

There were maps that showed the plumbing; the areas controlled by gangs; where doctors and hospitals could be found; gardens and cemeteries; shoe-repairers; gentlemen's clubs for the more refined outlaw; palm readings; coffee and tea shops; porters' lodgings; wine & ale merchants; locations of the poorest and most starving people; disease hot-spots; and a curious map of curses and incantations that no one, not even Miss Slade, could make out.

Each of us was given a sheet of white paper on to which we could copy our allocated map. As we passed our work to each other near the end of the hour, we saw thirty brand-new maps, that we could take away with us to help us understand the whole system ourselves. At the end of the lesson the teacher pulled me to one side.

'You're Daniel Dorey, is that right?' I nodded. I

expected her to give me a hard time for being difficult at the start of the lesson but instead, checking first to see all the other pupils had gone, she giggled and punched me on the shoulder harder than I could have expected. 'When you catch up with Caspian Prye, kick him in the arse for me!' She followed this up with a kicking gesture that was practically a somersault.

'I will!' I said, and staggered slightly as I ran out of the classroom, but caught up with the stragglers as they dawdled at the top of a staircase carved out of the rock so steep that I chose to close my eyes and feel my way with my hands rather than look down.

At last, it seemed, the day was over, because glancing through the doorways in the next tunnel I saw what looked like dormitories that were quickly filling up as boys and girls came back from their lessons. It seemed that whole classes all slept in the same place as well as taking the same lessons together. After walking far beyond the dormitories of the younger children, we ducked into a side tunnel and headed towards an enormous gaudy poster with drawings on it of a strongman with a curly moustache and a dancing bear. The poster was advertising a huge circus which was coming to town for one week only, on a date which had passed more than twenty years ago. Without pausing Tusk pulled up the bottom of the poster, exposing a hole in the wall, through which the boys crawled. When it came to me, he insisted I follow him.

'Come on!' he said. 'Come and see where you're staying.'

A cluster of boys and girls were eating what smelt like tasty stew around a table. Other children were studying by candlelight, leafing through books and maps, and testing each other. In a far corner, a very fat and fretful boy was attending to several large pots of stew which bubbled on top of some decidedly unsafe-looking fires. He had a handful of younger helpers who darted around him and between his legs, chopping things and bringing him the ingredients for him to add to the stews. One boy stood atop a little ladder and scooped out servings into bowls that were held up by a second boy. If he didn't hold it up in time, the ladleful of soup splashed on to the floor, provoking a shout from the cook and a bop on the head for them each with the ladle.

Nearby a few boys and girls were playing a game where they hit a rubber ball against the wall with their hands. A few others were playing a board game on the ground beside them and a little further on a game of skittles was noisily going on. It took me a little while to realize what was missing from this picture. Then I got it – adults!

'What is this place?' I asked.

'It's where we live,' Tusk said happily. 'Those of us who are orphans.'

Reluctantly at first, a warm feeling began to spread

through me, a complicated sort of happiness. There was no one who challenged me, who asked me what I was doing. Here was a place where I wouldn't have to worry constantly about my possessions, or look over my shoulder for someone carrying a knife.

'Welcome to the Circus,' said Tusk. 'We named it after the sign outside, but really it's because we all wanted to run away one day, to the circus – and now we have.'

We sat at one of the tables and someone appeared with bowls of stew for us. At that moment there was a heavy bump and the whole table bounced as the cook sat on the bench, taking off his hat and wiping his brow with his wrist.

'Tusk,' he said urgently, like a sailor reporting on the condition of a sinking ship, 'we've no more nutmeg. I've not enough ginger to last two more days – not a pinch of oregano, turmeric or paprika. And after to-morrow, no meat! How will I make my lamb tagine!' I thought he was rather over-dramatizing to get attention, until I felt the taste of his stew on my lips. It was heavenly – meaty and spicy, with a thick gravy that was also delicately delicious. Every mouthful made you crave just one more.

Tusk was saying reassuring things, but the chef was anxiously looking around and not listening. 'No meat,' he was saying darkly, 'but perhaps . . . one of the younger boys will do . . .' He realized he had said this out loud and then saw the looks he was getting from the rest of our table and giggled nervously. 'Of course, it was a joke! Ach!' We noticed that he had been running his finger along his sharp knife, and had pressed too hard, because he had drawn blood. He sucked his finger, and looked away.

'So, Daniel,' said Tusk, hastily changing the subject, 'I think it's high time we heard your tales of Caspian Prye. Have you actually *met* the man?'

All eyes were now on me. Taking a deep breath, I related my experiences – how I had come to the city just an ordinary orphan who only knew that he'd had a sister once upon a time, who had gone missing. How I'd become the victim of tricks and spies, how I'd been chased by Prye's corrupt police force, because Prye thought I knew where my sister was hidden. I saved the best bit for last – the moment when, hiding in a dark and deserted shop, I had come face to face with a shadowy figure looking in through the misted window that I was sure was Caspian Prye himself – the great villain who lurked above us all.

At the moment when I described how Prye's face appeared, one of the boys had grabbed another's arm for comfort. Embarrassed, he now let it go.

'But that's just one story,' I said. 'I've got lots of others equally as horrible that don't concern Caspian Prye. But listen! Much more important than that – I need to hear *your* grisly tales. I know you must have hundreds of them, and I want to write them down.' And I explained to them how I had got my role as a story-writer, and that as far as I was concerned, it was their duty to tell me all the tales that they knew, so I could write them down. All at once a babble of excitement rose around the table, and the next thing I knew, the cook was being shuffled along the bench towards me.

'Get off!' he was shouting, and, pulling a particularly heavy-looking rolling pin from what looked like a holster around his waist, started bopping boys on the head with it to get them off him.

'Tell him Baby's Hungry!' they kept saying, as they backed away from him.

'Ah!' he said, immediately calming down. 'That's what it is. You want to hear that story again?'

'Yes! Yes!' they cried, and turning to me they assured me that it was the most revolting story I was ever likely to hear. And on reflection, they might be right.

BABY'S HUNGRY

Every Wednesday morning Constance Bunch would step out into the streets of Tumblewater to spend the morning visiting her friends for tea. It was far and away her favourite day of the week and she smiled as she heaved herself on to the omnibus with a jaunty swing, and did not notice either the alarmed look of the conductor, or the fact that the bus lurched from side to side as she got on.

Within a quarter of an hour she was sitting in the front parlour of the rather spindly Henrietta Hogspittle, and a platter was laid before her of sixteen freshly toasted crumpets, shining with the oodles of butter that had melted into them.

'Oh, I *mustn't*!' she declared, turning her eyes away from the buttery treats. Her stomach growled as loud as a dog in protest, and she pressed her hand against it to keep it quiet. To Henrietta's disgust, she saw the hand disappear for a moment between bulges of fat.

'Really, Constance,' said Henrietta in a bored voice, as though she'd had to go through this a hundred times before, 'I insist. They'll only go stale otherwise.'

'Well . . .' pondered Mrs Bunch, 'seeing as I've not yet had a bite today, I suppose it would be irresponsible not to – in my condition.' Of course they both knew Mrs Bunch had in fact breakfasted more heartily than a garrison of soldiers not more than an hour before. Indeed, there was a telltale speck of egg yolk on her nose and a flake of kippered herring in the hairs on her chin that was hard to ignore.

'After all,' she said, patting her belly softly, 'Baby's hungry.'

Mrs Hogspittle couldn't suppress a shudder of disgust at this phrase, but Constance didn't notice because she already had two crumpets squeezed together in her fingers, and was digging a spoon around in the jam pot.

Once her hunger was sated and the plate was empty, which took no more than two and a half minutes, the two women carried on their conversation, which mainly consisted of gossiping about their friends in a decidedly mean and uncharitable way. All too soon it was time for Constance to go, and getting up out of her chair (a little heavier and shorter of breath than before) she bid Henrietta goodbye, and stepped once more into the street.

She bobbed from side to side with each step, puffing and sweating a little as she went along, and thinking to herself that at least she was working up an appetite. For her friends were so generous that she was sure to have more food put in front of her at the next visit.

She was a little put out, therefore, when a few minutes later she found herself at her friend Eliza's house, pressing her buttocks into one of the rather undersized chairs, and settling down to a chat, and not a single snack in sight. She fidgeted uncomfortably, insofar as she *could* fidget without breaking off one of the arms of the chair, and she couldn't concentrate at all. Her stomach rumbled threateningly.

Poor Eliza had once been a lady of great standing in society, but had fallen on hard times and was dreadfully short of money. That was why her house was so bare, and small, and located in this dismal part of Tumblewater. It was rather trying for Constance to come to such a dirty hovel in the first place, but to have to put up with Eliza's long face and miserable stories without a thing to eat was more than she could bear and her stomach set up a howl of hunger.

'My dear,' cried Eliza, 'are you all right?'

'Quite, quite, my love,' said Constance, smiling. 'Baby's hungry, I suppose.'

Eliza glanced nervously into the kitchen. 'Of course,' she said after an uncomfortable pause. 'How rude of me. Let me get you something to eat.'

Eliza returned after what sounded like a rather desperate search of the kitchen, with a small and rather dried-out-looking cake, cut into slices. At the promise of being fed, Constance's stomach once more relapsed into silence, allowing the two ladies to sit back and have a nice friendly chat.

Constance could pay attention even less now the cake was on the table, so instead she muttered something vague and then leaned forward and began to devour it mercilessly.

The first slice vanished like a flash. The second and third were wolfed at a still great speed, as though she was settling into her stride. The fourth slice she lingered over pleasurably, bite by bite. The fifth she munched through with grim determination, like a weightlifter straining with effort. All this time she nodded, and mmm-ed and ahhh-ed along with what Eliza said, not paying the slightest attention and making occasional remarks which were very hard to make out, as her mouth was full of cake.

By the end of the fifth slice her stomach was as thick and dense as a sack of wet sand, and her eyes had taken on a somewhat bulging appearance. There was a light sweat on her forehead, and her hands gently ran up and down her sides, as though she was checking for further pockets of room, and finding none.

There could be no doubt that she was finally, incontrovertibly full.

Though she was now so full that she was dizzy, Constance decided it was time to go. Five slices of cake was probably enough for now. Besides, there was none left, so she might as well make her way home. She would leave her dear friend to her poverty and cakelessness.

Eliza thanked her for coming, and pretended not to notice as Constance struggled to get out of her chair. She had to turn away as Constance briefly stood up with the chair still wedged around her enormous backside, and finally freed herself with a slight *pop!*

As she stood at the door Constance patted her friend on the arm and tried to make one last kindly and cheering remark. Unfortunately, she still had a mouthful of cake which she could not swallow, so when she tried to say:

'Don't worry, my dear, I'm sure that soon everything will be much better!'

What she actually said was:

'Borfleworflaw, singworflogglug. Floor vair fledge uttah!' (Gulp, burp.)

With that she waved her hands and waddled off down the street as fast as she could go. Eliza stared after her for a few seconds, quite baffled, before closing her door.

As she let herself into her apartment building, Constance leaned back on the door and breathed hard. All those steps to climb! She couldn't face it just yet; the sight of them made her head spin. For some reason the staircase seemed to be narrower than it used to be, and these days she had to squeeze between the banisters and pull herself upwards along them like a mountain climber. What's more, this morning's treats were heavy inside her and all she wanted to do was to collapse into a comfy chair.

Hoping for a distraction to let her get her breath back before she mounted the stairs, she saw that the door to the ground-floor apartment stood open an inch, and an eye was peeping out. There must be a new neighbour, after the flat had stood empty for all this time! At once she took on the noble and superior air she tried to give herself in company, and advanced to the door, giving a little wave.

'Hello there,' she trilled grandly. 'Do I espy a new

friend has moved into the mansion?' No matter what she said, the building was most definitely *not* a mansion, and the ground-floor flat was a particularly squalid affair, crammed in beneath the stairs and overlooking the dank patch of overgrowth that was their tiny 'garden', no doubt swarming with rats. But her attempt at flattery seemed to work, for the door squeaked open and revealed a small female figure.

Constance struggled to make out the lady's face in the shadows. But she could see that the lady nodded in greeting, and said, 'I believe you are Lady Constance Bunch?'

Constance's heart swelled as she heard herself promoted to the status of a lady. Here was a good, sensible and intelligent friend. At last, a worthy neighbour!

Constance bowed. 'I bear that name,' she admitted, 'and may I know yours?'

'Oh, my name, my name,' said the little woman, turning and retreating inside, 'is of no consequence. It is not a name to boast of, let's just say that.'

Constance stared in through the doorway after the eccentric woman with no name, feeling rather intrigued. She stepped cautiously inside, assuming that she was meant to follow, and let the door close behind her. In a few steps she found herself in the door of a little sitting room. The woman was placing a battered kettle over a fire in which a meagre handful of coals glowed. There was a curious aroma all through the room – half pleasant and half not-so-pleasant, like an exotic perfume. She saw that it came from a red candle that glowed on the mantelpiece opposite.

'Please sit down,' said the little woman, but Constance, hardly able to bear her own weight, was already slumping heavily into the only comfortable-looking chair. She thought she detected some kind of accent in her neighbour's speech, perhaps from a far-flung land, but her host spoke very precisely, and it was hard to tell where she might be from.

'I am pleased to meet you,' said Constance. 'It is so nice to have a new neighbour – these rooms have been empty for so long.'

'Ah, Lady Constance!' cried the lady, and the reason for her intense and nervous appearance suddenly became clear, for she burst into tears, and covered her eyes with her hand. 'The last tenant here was my husband! Do you remember him?'

Had Constance's stomach been empty (which it almost never was), it would have turned over in horror at these words. Instead it erupted in a short burst of explosions, like gas escaping through hot mud, making a sound which distracted both of the women for a moment and made the hostess insist that she fetch some food.

'No, please . . .' said Constance, for truth be told she was still so incredibly crammed full that she hadn't yet been able completely to swallow all of the food from the morning's feasts. There was still one last mouthful that she was discreetly chewing, and there were at least three more lumps of cake stuck halfway down her throat.

And yet, at the mere the mention of more food, her colossal digestive system rumbled back into life and in the same way that you suddenly notice that a horribly over-stuffed suitcase still has room for one more sock, she felt the tiniest amount of space appear in her belly. Unable to resist, her protests turned to a feeble whisper.

The strange little woman was already fetching cutlery and making a rather extraordinary-smelling pot of tea from the whistling kettle. As she did this she told Constance the story of her husband.

'He wrote me letters when he first came to this country, sending me money and saying that he was working hard, but he said that some people hated him for no reason – just because he was foreign. Can you believe it, Lady Constance, some of them lived in this very building!'

'*No,*' Constance whispered dramatically.

'Yes!' said her new neighbour. 'And they hated the colour of his skin so much that they decided he must be a criminal, and when a crime was committed on this street, they reported him to the police. Who would do such a thing?'

Constance would have shifted uncomfortably in her seat if she was able to move in it at all. Instead she clutched her belly somewhat nervously. 'I can't imagine,' she said, struggling to sound kind and sincere.

Her host handed over a cup to Constance which

didn't at all look like any tea she was used to – it was clear and golden in colour, and smelt a bit like cinnamon.

'He was innocent,' she went on, not noticing Constance's discomfort.

'Oh, I'm sure,' said Constance, who looked quite unsure of anything at all. In fact, she was going quite red, which luckily for her wasn't visible in the murky light.

'If I ever found the person who did it . . .'

'Revenge,' whispered Constance, unable to control herself.

'Ah no, Lady Constance,' said the little woman, bringing down from a high shelf a little plate covered in a white cloth. 'Revenge would be to do something just as bad back. What I would do – if I found them, of course – would be to do something *much worse*.'

Their eyes met for a moment, which was broken by a gargantuan burp from within Constance's tummy.

Her neighbour's expression changed to a smile. 'But let me not speak of these horrible events! Here you are in my rooms, a proper Lady, and I talk about curses and such things! Please forgive me – allow me to fetch you something to eat. This is a rare delicacy where I come from, and only served to special guests.' She withdrew the cloth from the plate she was holding and beneath it was a curious-looking little treat about the size of a golf ball. It was quite impossible to tell if it was sweet or savoury.

'It is only small,' said the woman, 'but it has a con-suming appetite.'

It was a rather strange phrase. Constance thought that she meant the morsel would remove her appetite, but she decided not to correct the woman.

'Well...' she said slowly, almost to herself, '... Baby *is* hungry...'

Reaching over her huge belly she picked it up and popped it into her mouth. As she did so her neighbour caught a horrible glimpse. The inside of Constance's mouth was coated with chewed food, like a cave covered with wet moss, with only a narrow hole down the middle for her to push the morsel through. Yet the poor little woman showed no signs of disgust. She watched with perfect calm, and saw the fat lady out of her apartment a few minutes later.

That night Constance did not sleep well. Something troubled her stomach and she kept waking up to dread-ful groans and rumbles. She slept on her left side, her right, her front, her back, the floor, but nothing was comfortable. And she sweated too – sometimes horri-bly hot and the next moment deadly freezing, as though she had a terrible fever coming on.

For a moment she pondered the strange delicacy she had been offered by the kindly neighbour, which had been soft and mushy with some sort of bean or seed at the centre. But it was far more likely that her stomach pains were caused by the seven cups of tea, the entire box of biscuits, the basin of soup, rack of ribs, jam roly-poly and full cheeseboard which had followed it.

At one point she got up and walked around, holding her stomach in her hand like a tubful of dough. With a start she realized that the discomfort that tore away at her insides was . . . She was starving! Could it be true?

I've never been hungry in the middle of the night before, she thought. The idea was worrying, and she went straight back to bed and tried to force herself to sleep. But her stomach just wouldn't lie still, and rumbled and bubbled and squeaked more violently than she had ever known. And yet it wasn't exactly painful – and certainly not indigestion.

'It's like someone's knitting in there,' she said aloud. She lay in the dark a long while, wondering what was wrong with her insides, before eventually falling into an uneasy sleep.

In the morning Constance went out into the street feeling somewhat light-headed. As she walked along she felt a rather ticklish feeling in her stomach, which she tried to ignore, and concentrated on the list of things she had to buy.

As she loved shopping for food so much, instead of allowing her cook to order all of her supplies, each day Constance went to a different kind of food shop. On Monday she had gone chocolate shopping, on Tuesday afternoon she'd ordered some live lobsters to be delivered packed in ice, startling the cook who had never been asked to cook something that was still alive before. Today being Thursday, Constance made her way to the delicatessen, where she bought lots of different kinds of cheese, slices of cold meat, pots of olives and jars of pickles and sauces. As the shopkeeper placed the last of the paper packages in a pile, Constance noticed him looking surprised at how much she had bought, and then was startled to notice it herself. It looked like more than a whole family could eat in a month. Why did she need so much? But an angry rumble from her stomach stopped her sending any of it back.

Instead she laughed girlishly at the shopkeeper and ran her hand over her stomach. 'Baby's hungry,' she cooed.

He raised his eyebrows and turned around to add up the price. The rumble in her stomach suddenly grew worse, and she felt a sudden nasty pain there, as though she had swallowed a pair of scissors. The blood rushed in her ears as the food was packed into paper bags.

'Always good to have your custom, Mrs Bunch,' the man was saying. 'I'll have this delivered after lunch.'

'NO!' shouted Constance uncontrollably. Everyone in the little shop went quiet, and the little man turned to give her a cautious look.

'Pardon me,' she said, 'but that won't be necessary. I shall carry the things home today.' Handing over a pound note, she snatched the bag away from the man, and rushed outside, hardly knowing what she was doing.

Walking along the street again, she quickly darted into an alleyway, the sort of dark, dangerous place where muggers would lurk. Ignoring the revolting stench that stuck to her shoes, she tore the wrapping from a lump of cheese and crammed the whole thing into her mouth. Next came a package of sliced ham that she scrunched into a ball and stuffed in after the cheese, which was already half swallowed. She chewed and gulped urgently, but her throat was very dry, so she upended a jar of apple chutney over her mouth and drank it like lemonade.

She leaned against the wall, breathing hard, and wiping her mouth, as she heard footsteps from further down the alley. Two men were approaching – thin, sly characters in muddy clothes and hungry smiles. As he came closer one of them brought a short blade from his pocket.

At the sight of the knife the blood rushed in her ears and something deep and primal took over her. Instead of running she watched them until they were only a few feet away. Then she opened her mouth and let out a vicious animal snarl, as deep as a tiger's roar. The men slipped over each other in the mud to get away and she was alone again, and able to compose herself.

A minute later, daintily touching the corners of her mouth with a hanky and trying not to look startled, Constance stepped back on to the street. The empty paper packages lay torn apart in the mud. She walked fast, trying to block the suddenness and strangeness of the episode from her mind.

In the afternoon she felt a little calmer and decided that it would be best to get some air in her lungs, so she went out again and after walking for a while, found herself in front of a butcher's shop.

'But it's Thursday,' she told herself. 'Butcher's day isn't until tomorrow.' Yet she couldn't tear her eyes away as the butcher hacked at a sheep's leg with his cleaver. A familiar feeling was stirring in her stomach, a kind of heat rising in her throat and hunger forcing all other thoughts from her mind. And now in her belly there was another, even weirder feeling: a horrible wriggling, almost as though some spindly creature was writhing over and over.

Before she knew it she was inside the shop and standing at the counter, in front of her a bowl of freshly made raw sausages. The butcher meanwhile patiently cut away at a rack of lamb until it was reduced to a number of delicious-looking chops. Then he piled them into a bowl and turned see if customers were waiting. He saw there was one – a rather well dressed (if incredibly fat) woman, with her back to him.

'Madam?' the butcher asked. 'Can I help you?'

She shook her head and made a sort of moaning sound. Her shoulders were shaking as though she was crying and he noticed that whichever way he looked she turned away, avoiding his eyes. The butcher frowned.

'Madam?' he asked again. 'Are you quite well?'

She shook her head again, more firmly this time,

and waved him away. Again she made a muffled sort of moan as though she was saying no, but it sounded like there was something in her mouth. Becoming suspicious, the butcher stepped round the counter.

'Excuse me?' he said, leaning round to see her face. She twisted again in the opposite direction but too slowly, and he caught sight of something sticking out of her mouth. It was a raw sausage that she was hurriedly trying to chew and swallow!

Looking at the counter, he saw that a whole string of sausages he had left in the bowl on the counter had gone. Slowly, she turned round to face him. She was still struggling to swallow, and her eyes were wide open – whether out of guilt or madness, he couldn't tell.

The lady gagged and coughed as she tried to speak, then opened her purse and dropped much too much money on the counter. She rushed to the door and pulled it open, and at the same time seemed to realize what she was doing. She stared at him for a moment, clearly unsure what to say.

'Baby,' she muttered, gasping for breath. She said 'Baby' as though it was something she was frightened of, which bewildered him. But she was out of the door and running away before the butcher could think of anything to say in reply.

Early next morning Constance lay in bed, stock-still and terrified. Having devoured those sausages and much else besides, her stomach felt empty again already. It wasn't possible! And the noises it made – it wasn't just rumbling like a normal stomach any more, but making much more terrible sounds. Growls, grunts and snarls filtered up from her insides. And when she got hungry it didn't just make her long for food. It hurt, and hurt badly – like the inside of her stomach was being nipped.

What's more, her dogs, Spoony and Mr Pickles, had taken against the animal sounds coming from within her and had done nothing but yap and bark since she had got home. It was so distracting that she'd had to shut them in the pantry to try and get some rest.

Now, she had woken up from some strange and disturbing dreams to find the barking had stopped at last.

Her head and limbs ached and a terrible foreboding hung over her that she didn't understand. Just for this minute the hunger was slightly less than before, but she knew she wouldn't sleep any more so she decided to get up and dressed. As she did so she thought of the poor dogs trapped in the cold larder all night. Poor creatures!

Constance trotted from her bedroom through the hall, the drawing room and kitchen, to the pantry door.

As she placed her hand on the handle something, she had no idea what, caused her to stop. The doom-like feeling that had hung over her head since she woke up suddenly got very intense and locked in a tight headache around her skull.

'This is ridiculous!' she told herself. 'You've had a bad night's sleep, that's all. Now take Spoony and Mr Pickles for a nice walk and get some fresh . . .'

But still her hand hesitated on the handle, and she had to force herself to twist the lock, and snatch the door open.

There were no dogs sitting on the floor. Nor hiding among the shelves. It was a large, dark cupboard kept nice and cool (as every good pantry should be) and it took a few seconds for Constance's eyes to focus on what was inside. Her thoughts were distracted then as she noticed that the floor was horribly dirty. It was smeared all over with a terrible muck, as though a rag had been dipped in mud and swabbed all over the floor. A most appalling mess . . .

How could the dogs possibly have got out? Had she got out of bed and unlocked the door in her sleep? A little grumble in her stomach told her that all was not well. She felt a little movement as though the spindly thing in her dreams came alive, and she felt that searing heat in her throat again.

It was not muck on the floor. It was blood. Lots and lots of blood. The two dogs' bodies were nowhere to be seen. Her head felt light. There was no room in her mind to feel horrified or scared because her whole attention was taken over by one sensation.

Hungry. She was hungry, *hungry* . . .

'Baby,' she muttered, her stomach churning as she lurched towards the front door.

When she got to the top of the stairs she knew she must have eaten something large in the night, for at last the moment had come which she had feared: she could no longer fit between the banisters. She stood looking at them wildly for a second, then lifted the sides of her belly up like wings and resting one on each handrail she leaned forward and slid down the stairs with plummeting speed.

She crashed off the end of the banisters just as two of the ladies who lived on the floor below were holding the front door open. Bouncing off the floor on her sturdy legs at lightning pace, she raced through the door past her friends, who both screamed.

'Baby!' she gargled as she sprinted past, now quite out of her wits, and the two astonished neighbours watched as she shot out into the street, running narrowly between two carriages crossing in opposite directions. As they stared on, amazed both at her speed and that she hadn't caused a road accident, they stepped out on to the pavement to watch. Reaching the other side of the street, their neighbour curved to the right and sprinted into the distance, as though chased by a devil. People leaped out of her way all along the pavement until she found herself outside a sweetshop where she screeched to a halt, swung her shoulders and threw herself bodily through the door without pausing to open it. Shouts and screams came from within.

Now quite terrified, the two women moved back inside and shut the door, so that no one on the street would associate them with the dreadful commotion going on outside. The taller lady wondered what on earth this behaviour could mean, and they both shook their heads in dismay. Then the shorter lady asked whether there had ever been signs of madness in their neighbour Constance.

'No,' considered the taller lady, pausing on the third step of the staircase (and refraining from touching the banister because it seemed to be coated in a repulsive sweaty smear). 'But she was always making that absurd remark about "Baby" being "hungry".'

'Oh yes,' said her companion, who looked sick at the thought. 'That was horrible, wasn't it? She's sixty-five if she's a day . . .'

'I *know* . . .' continued the taller lady, and as they both shuddered at the thought they rose up the stairs until they were out of earshot of the hall.

There below, unseen by the stair-climbing ladies, sat the quiet figure of the neighbour Constance had visited a few days before. She was sitting on a stool outside her front door, knitting a lady's scarf that lay in her lap, for the light in her flat wasn't good enough to work by. She knitted patiently and slowly, and showed no interest in what the ladies had been discussing.

Over the course of the next few days, as the little woman sat there, and gradually worked her way closer to finishing the scarf, she saw the comings and goings of the other people who lived in the building. She saw them meet upon the stairs and chat in the doorway, and without being in the slightest bit nosy, she couldn't help hearing what they told each other.

It appeared that, with no explanation whatsoever, the poor Mrs Bunch (not Lady Constance, as the little lady now silently corrected herself) had gone quite mad. A most terrible and undignified business – she had been arrested as she attempted to escape the sweetshop where she had apparently been trying to eat all the sweets.

'Don't exaggerate, Alice,' corrected the tall lady, once more pausing on the stairs as she heard the vulgar details.

'I'm not exaggerating, Martha,' the other insisted. 'She was trying to eat *all* of them. And got more than two entire boxes of gobstoppers inside her before she was apprehended.

'What on *earth* is a gobstopper?'

'I'm glad I've no idea, it sounds perfectly awful.'

The policeman who arrested her had needed five other officers to help lift her into a police wagon. By that stage, the rumour went, she was trying to bite their hands, their ears, and even the leather of their shoes.

The quiet neighbour knitted for hour after hour and day after day without so much as setting foot on the street, but piece by piece the story filtered down to her. Who knew if it was true – certainly the little neighbour didn't. She carried on knitting the little scarf that would keep her warm in the winter months in this cold northern land, and listened placidly. In this she was probably alone, because no one else who heard the grisly end could help but be appalled.

It appeared that Constance had begged for food, and complained of stomach pains as she was led to her cell. When trapped alone there, she had let out blood-curdling screams but the police had seen this sort of thing before. They had assumed she was merely drunk and needed to sleep it off, so they left her there. In the middle of the night the screams became truly dreadful, and reached a crescendo before suddenly stopping.

When the officers opened her cell door in the morning, they were confronted by a macabre sight as bad as any murder. Constance's dead body was there, but instead of being the corpse of a hugely fat woman, it was a shrivelled shell that weighed almost nothing. There was blood everywhere and smeary blood-marks up the walls to the prison bars, which had been bent apart. A bloody trail led down the wall on the other side, and ran to a sewer opening, where it ended. Something or someone had escaped.

Constance's cause of death was quite mysterious. Or rather, it wasn't: there was a gigantic hole in her side, as though something enormous had been torn out of her. Something almost man-sized, some said. The police surgeon performed a post-mortem on the body, the results of which were kept secret. But rumours, as ever, sneaked and whispered back into the house, and fell from the stairs to the little woman's ears. Rumours that the hole in Mrs Bunch's side had borne *teeth-marks*. No one knew what to make of that.

All the while as this information (or gossip, or speculation, we should call it) gathered around her, the little woman sat, patiently knitting, and showing no sign that she even heard or understood the words. People on the stairs began to talk about other things, and at length she finished her scarf, and made herself a hat to go with it – you couldn't be too careful in these winters, after all. When it was done she tried it on for size, then took it off again and folded it under her arm. She went back into her rooms, where she quietly packed up her belongings, and then in the doorway placed the hat on her head and the scarf around her neck and carrying a small hessian suitcase went out into the street, never to return.

hen the cook had finished, there was a hush around the table and, caught up in the grotesque tale as I was, I realized that almost all of the children in the cavern had come to listen. They were crowded around the table so tightly there was scarcely room to breathe, and I worried that if one of the larger boys so much as coughed, a few of the smaller ones might be crushed out of existence.

Luckily Sally's loud voice rose above the murmur of the crowd to shout, 'OK, ladies, that's enough for one night. To your evening tasks, please! And I have to show our guest his sleeping quarters.'

She spoke with an impressive authority for someone who was younger than me. The others all murmured disappointment as they got up to go about their chores and I watched, amazed that they were going. This whole place seemed like some kind of paradise for children, where they could do pretty much all they wanted, away from the eyes of adults. So it made sense that all they had to do was a few jobs each day, and they could keep it that way.

'I see you're a reading man!' said Sally, pointing

at my pocket. 'What tome is that?'

I had completely forgotten there was a book in my pocket, and when I pulled it out I found myself holding a copy of *The Junior Ornithologist's Guide to the Dietary Requirements of Subtropical Birds of Prey in Temperate Climes*. As ever, Sally's rather domineering manner put me on edge, and made me look around for Mayrick and Tusk, but for now they were nowhere to be seen. Slightly desperate, and not knowing what else to say, I showed her the book and said, 'It's my favourite.' Her eyebrows shot up.

'Oh . . . How, how jolly interesting. Good for you,' she said unconvincingly, before changing the subject. 'But to answer your previous question, yes, we're a gang. One of about twenty underground. Some of the gangs are outlaws. *Proper* outlaws, I mean, outside the control of Uncle and the Underground. Those kids are insane. They'd kill you if you so much as walked on to their patch by accident. So we don't.'

'Where do the other gangs live – in places like this?' As I asked the question I realized I had said it too loudly. A few boys nearby who were swabbing the tables and sweeping up rubbish looked at me like I was mad, and the cook (who was scrubbing the inside of one of his enormous pots with murderous energy) stopped to stare and then spat viciously on the floor.

'No,' she said under her breath, guiding me by the elbow to the side of the cavern discreetly. 'Look here,' she said.

She lifted a metal lid that hung between two rocks and we both peered into the gap. I could see through a hole in the rock to get a good view of the cavern below which, on first glance, appeared to be a glimpse into hell. I saw beatings taking place, horrible initiation games (where boys had to eat some disgustingly inedible substance, or perform some other dastardly challenge, in order to be accepted), bullying, tortures, younger boys being forced into trials of strength or endurance (through further beatings) by sneering older boys. There was screaming and unhappiness, and for a second I was reminded of my earliest days at the orphanage, and the horror of being powerless, with no one to help you.

Sally let the lid fall shut with a clang which made me jump. 'That,' she said, 'is called the Doldrums, where the main five gangs all live, and fight among each other all day and night. Those boys are the stupid ones. They account for most of the casualties above ground, because they don't pay attention and don't know what they're doing. Here in the Circus we know we're risking our lives and breaking the law, so we get it right: we work in teams, share our knowledge, train each other – and survive. Mostly.'

'Who . . .' It felt like a stupid question, but I had to ask it. 'Who looks after you?'

She stopped and turned round to me, looking offended.

'*We* do, Daniel,' she said. 'We look after each other,

because no one else will. Now, let me show you your sleeping quarters.' She led me to the rear of the cavern. There were hundreds of prison-style beds, going so far up the wall it made me feel giddy. Ladders reached to the first twenty or thirty beds and beyond that rope ladders had been hung from higher ledges, or, nearer the top, simply ropes with thick knots. From some of the higher outcrops of rock, more spindly home-made ladders could be seen extending up into the dim flickering darkness. Children had stuck candles to the side of rocks around their beds with molten wax, and could be seen lying down and writing letters by their light, or sitting with their blankets around their shoulders and reading well-thumbed and damp-stained books.

'You see that empty bed, near the top? That's where you'll be sleeping,' said Sally.

It was so high up it was only just visible, in fact. But I swallowed my fear of heights and thanked her. I wondered if I would fall out of bed in my sleep.

When evening tasks were done, there was a conspiratorial atmosphere as all the children gathered around the fire. It blazed fiercely for the first half an hour or so, drawing more and more pupils down from their ledges and from every corner of the cave. By the time it died down to a warm and companionable crackling, a huge crowd had gathered.

The cook (his name was McCrummock) spent an hour preparing another speciality of his – hot chocolate. I only knew it as a drink which posh ladies drank, and couldn't believe my eyes as I watched him prepare it. Firstly, twenty pints of milk. Then seven huge ladles of rich black cocoa. He heated and stirred, heated and stirred, as the crowd around us grew. Then went in another seven heaped scoops – of sugar.

Sugar! It couldn't be!

The tin he poured the sugar out of vanished as soon as it appeared, flung among the legs of his scurrying servants, and between the boiling fires and roasting tins. For a moment, I wondered about all the people I knew who would kill to get their hands on some sugar. And yet I had just caught sight of a great big *tin* of the stuff, as large as an umbrella stand. Now I was privy to this secret information, I felt protective about the Circus. Death, capture, police, torture, yes yes yes, but – *sugar*! That was worth keeping a secret for. I watched the cook with awe as he sprinkled cinnamon into the mixture too. The smell that wafted over was mouth-watering, to say the least.

The cinnamon was followed by – could it be – *cream*?

At long last, he handed me a steaming metal cup, and I took my first sip.

The sweet, rich, beautiful flavour swam through me and I couldn't help closing my eyes as my spirit took flight. I sat there for several minutes, savouring the heavenly concoction and feeling the flicker of the flames against my legs. I hugged the cup between my knees and took the final sips, making them as small as possible, to prolong its deliciousness. By the time the cup was empty, I was full, and not just with chocolate – with happiness, and gratitude, and desire to help these kids however I could.

Sally was the first to throw the dregs of her cup into the fire and head to bed, cheerfully telling the others to do the same.

'Otherwise you'll all be tired and grumpy tomorrow!' Everyone ignored her, but she pretended not to notice, whistling her way towards her bunk. Shortly afterwards most of the others followed her example, and I realized they'd only waited so it seemed like they were doing it of their own accord, rather than following her advice. Tusk and Mayrick remained beside me, however, and together we watched the red glow of the dying fire.

'Daniel,' said Tusk after a moment, 'Mayrick and I would like to introduce you to a secret. You have to promise you won't tell anyone.'

I nodded. 'Of course.'

'For the security of this camp, it's essential that Sally doesn't let anyone risk their lives by going above ground. That's why we are protected by that chap –' he pointed to a bespectacled youth who now took his seat on a chair by the door. 'We call him Martin the Sound Boy. Each night he has to stop anyone sneaking out. And after all, they *are* training us to slip unseen through the night and perform crimes, so we have to watch very carefully that nobody gives in to the temptations and goes above ground.'

'I understand,' I said.

'Nobody, that is, except for us. Most of all, we want two things. First, to provide Cook with enough ingredients to keep making his his amazing stew. And second—'

'To be the best,' said Mayrick. They were both looking at me intently. Mayrick went on. 'In secret we've been going out at night on raids. We've been honing our skills – at breaking into buildings, at stealing and taking what we want, at eluding capture and leaving no trace of our presence, and bringing the stuff back here. That's how we're able to eat so well in the Circus. That's why not one child here goes without shoes, while hundreds and hundreds of others in the Underground do.'

'And that's why we've got an armoury of guns and knives, probably better than the police's, stolen out of the empty houses and abandoned shops. And why I've got a collection of priceless watercolours buried here in the Underground,' interrupted Tusk. 'But that's another story. No one knows about all this except us, and now you.'

'What about them?' I said, gesturing to other small groups, who were talking among themselves.

'What we don't know we can't tell others, so those other chaps may or may not be organizing raids of their own, but we won't ask. See Buxton and Cornish over there, with that disgusting dog that follows them around? – Boggins, I think they call it. Don't go near him, he'll be sick on your foot. Well, they're as innocent as anyone, as far as we're concerned. But then, we have a mysterious supply of bread – buns, cakes and lots and lots of waffles – that I can't account for. Then there's those two, Hamish and Andy. As harmless as you like, officially – so's their dog too, Fred he's called – but then how do we account for our endless stock of things like pants and socks? We've even got a stock of *shoehorns*, that we couldn't possibly ever need. But all these things are useful for trading with other people in the Underground.'

'Shoehorns,' tutted Mayrick. 'That Hamish is . . . a bit eccentric, to put it nicely. He's *obsessed* with shoehorns. And they both refuse to wear trousers on a Friday.'

From the other side of the fire, Boggins let off a giant fart which caused an orange gush of flame in the fire and made everyone look at each other embarrassed for a moment, before carrying on with their whispering.

'So you're inviting me . . . to come with you? That's flattering, but why? I haven't got any of the skills that you have,' I protested.

'You might think that,' said Tusk. 'But you've eluded capture for as long as any of us – and with the police on your tail. From now on there's a third reason for us to go on raids: you're the only person in the whole of the Underground who's seen Caspian Prye and who has a way of finding him. If there's anything we can do to help bring him down, no matter how dangerous, we will do it.'

I let out a sigh of relief, and leaned in closely to whisper. 'There *is* something we can do. There's someone I desperately need to find,' I said. 'It could make all the difference.' I showed them the key.

'This belonged to a witch, Gora, who was killed right in front of me. She used to work for Prye – and hid my sister away from the world on his jealous orders. But when Gora and Prye fell out, she hid my sister from him too. Prye would do anything to get this key – which holds the clue to my sister's hiding place. But the frustrating thing is, we don't know what it's for. There's only one man who might help us. He is named the Apothecary, and has a birthmark across his face.'

The boys looked at each other.

'Well, that's something to go on.' Mayrick shrugged. 'I'll see what we come up with.'

Tusk slapped my knee. 'Come on, let's get some sleep now. If we do get a tip-off we'll need all the sleep we can for the next few days.'

We wandered tiredly to the rear of the cave and I climbed up first the wooden ladder and then the rope ladder and then the knotted rope to my bunk, and when I got there I lay and thought.

It was impossible to sleep at first and I fidgeted, throwing the blankets off and pulling them back on again, unable to find any comfortable position. Above and below me, and on the opposite wall, the lights were winking out one by one, almost as though I was in the sky, and watching the stars go to sleep. Gradually, by stages, I drifted off and dreamed of myself trapped in stone, and my faceless sister searching helplessly for me through empty streets.

The sound that woke me was a horrible metallic clanging. Sally Dolton was far below, hammering the inside of a huge, rusty bell. Quickly I jumped up and began pulling my clothes back on, seeing boys and girls clamber down the walls like insects rushing from a nest.

Nearly a hundred of us descended on the dining tables at once, and before we knew it breakfast was being handed out at every table. The chef had clearly been working for hours already. Bowls of bread (only slightly dry and crispy) were dropped in front of us, then huge heavy pots of tea spilling through their spouts, then tureens of hot porridge and jugs of milk. There was a fervent display of hungry breakfasting, with children dipping bread in their porridge, milk or tea, and slurping their drinks in a few seconds flat.

Minutes later, still trying to wake up and take a sip of tea, I was one of the only people left at my table. I saw the chef glance up and, noticing the crowd was thinning, start to relax and untie his apron. Then he wandered out from the serving area and came over to me with a frying pan in his hand.

'There you go,' he said quietly, and dropped on to my bread a couple of rashers of bacon that were glistening with fat. 'Don't tell anyone, they'll all want it,' he said under his breath, moving off. Then he turned back. 'You'd better kill Caspian Prye,' he said, holding up his frying pan, 'or I'll bash your head off.'

'It's a deal,' I said. Looking around to see if anyone had noticed, I quickly folded the bread over to make a sandwich and stuffed it in my pocket. I quickly joined Tusk by the gate and soon we were on our way to school.

Our first class was in lock-picking, which was different from safe-cracking, but many of the principles were the same, which gave us a useful head start. After ten minutes of lightning-fast training, we were dropped one by one into 'The Warren', a maze in which we had to pick one lock after the other to find our way out and escape, with only darkness and the sound of keys clicking quietly in other locks for company. It was close and nail-biting work, even worse for those who hated confined spaces. The sheer fear of it was supposed to help us learn fast, and under pressure. It worked, and one by one we opened the last door with a gasp of relief and joined our friends.

There's no fear like being trapped underground in a space not much larger than a coffin, and having to use your wits to scrabble to safety. None of us spoke afterwards about what that experience had been like.

We left the class feeling as we always did, wiser, tougher, a bit more indestructible. Tusk led us towards the next lesson down a hall. We were all too weary to care what class came next, but after a while we took notice that there were flashes of light and sprays of sparks coming out of the doorways.

'These are the factories,' Tusk explained. 'The boys and girls here work all day smelting, and building machinery – all the things that we might need.'

I saw sweaty and oil-stained children come out carrying armloads of spades, saucepans and scientific instruments. When we saw a boy with several guns in his arms I stopped and stared. He was about eleven, and took no notice of us, stomping off down the corridor without looking back, the pile of rifles teetering above his head.

Tusk looked at me, surprised that I didn't know about this already. 'They are training us in all forms of combat,' he said. 'What did you expect?'

Further along the hallway we heard gunshots in the distance and soon we were alongside the shooting galleries that resounded with blast after blast. In the confined space the noise was horrendously amplified, so loud it hurt our ears. It was a terrible effort to walk past these galleries without peering in eagerly, or stopping by the door to watch – which every one of us wanted to do. We had to tell ourselves that in a couple of days, maybe only a couple of *hours*, it would be us in there, taking aim with live ammunition.

'It's on for tonight,' whispered Tusk in my ear. 'We have a lead on the Apothecary and we want you to come with us.'

I nodded and carried on walking, trying to control

the wellspring of hope that his simple remark had released within me. I couldn't help but imagine that later tonight, by some outrageous chance, my sister might be free, and I might be getting to know her at last. But I knew at the same time I must prepare myself for disappointment.

At that moment we were stopped by a huge cart being wheeled in front of us. If he could have seen it, the cook would have died and gone to heaven. Pallets of fresh fruit and vegetables were piled on top of racks of steaks, sausages, ribs, skinned rabbits, a whole goose, beneath which was a pail of cream . . .

'Where's *that* going?' I asked.

'That's for the D Crews – the Destruction Boys,' Tusk said. 'You know, the groups of larger boys, who are built like bulls and do all the most dangerous lessons? They eat four times what anyone else does in the Underground, and they exercise all day long. To build up their strength.'

'So . . . they destroy things?'

'No,' said Sally, who was listening in. 'They go above ground and, in secret, they *build*. The city-in-a-city that we've made on the surface didn't spring up by itself. There is a hard-working genius who plans our routes through the buildings, where it is safe for them to go, which walls or ceilings or fireplaces or floors we can knock through so that the hole can be made invisible afterwards. There are teams working all the time to make this happen, inching forward house by house,

124

smashing away at brick, chipping at plaster, digging great holes under streets and then carrying away all the dirt so that no one will know that it's there. It's terribly dangerous work, and very tiring. They're our real heroes.'

'Golly,' I said quietly. There were two classrooms in front of us and Sally and the boys disappeared rapidly into the left-hand one, while I couldn't resist lingering to peer into the other. Inside this perfectly ordered and very well-lit room were five rows of boys sitting at easels. I blinked and looked away before taking this in a second time. I took a step inside to look closer at what appeared to be on the canvases, and was open-mouthed at what I saw.

A field of sunflowers. A still life, showing a bowl of fruit. A watercolour of a large country house on a summer's day, its walls covered with ivy.

There were others I could see, and every last one was simply an old-fashioned painting, that might hang over any mantelpiece. The teacher, a rather airy-seeming fellow, walked casually around the classroom giving earnest advice to his pupils, suggesting a darkening of shade here, and perhaps an extra bit of detail there.

'What the—'

'Come on, Daniel. This way,' Tusk caught my arm from behind. I was still open-mouthed.

'But . . . what the . . . ?'

'Painting class?' he asked. 'Think about it. The

Destruction Crews would be useless without the painters – we'd leave signs of ourselves everywhere we went. There wouldn't be a single secret tunnel or hidden entrance that wasn't obvious. With every crew that goes out – of, say, eight Destruction Boys – at least two painters go with them, armed with paints, and a plasterer too, so they tidy up behind them. They have to be able to copy almost every type of wallpaper there is, quickly and convincingly.'

After all the classes I had seen the previous day, I had become accustomed to the idea of learning violence, or more delicate crimes, such as forgery – I'd never thought there would be tasks which weren't criminal or in any way dangerous, and were harmlessly enjoyable. Following Tusk into the next-door classroom, I wondered whether our next class would be enjoyable too.

The first thing I saw was a dead body laid out on a slab of stone. And the second thing I saw was an old man with a beard and enormously bushy eyebrows chopping a hole in the body's chest with an axe while the children stared on, horrified. My hopes faded somewhat.

'No time for pleasantries,' barked the teacher, who was wearing a white smock to keep the blood off. 'You! Come here.'

He pointed at me and with more than a little reluctance I walked up until I stood over the corpse. It was that of a man, perhaps thirty years old, and there was a distinctly unpleasant smell rising from it.

'Don't worry about the whiff,' he muttered to me under his breath, handing me a needle and thread. 'You'll soon get used to it. Now!' he said, addressing the whole class. 'Listen up, you little brutes. I know each of you has been taught how to burgle, how to safe-crack, how to generally carry on like a little crime wave of your own. Good for you, you little brats! But tell me THIS! What happens when you're up there, doing a job, and one of you gets hurt? If you want to survive, your only chance may be to operate yourself.'

Oh no, I thought.

'I'm Dr Bludger,' he said, clapping me on the back, 'and first off we have to show you how to stitch up a wound, you little blighters.'

I looked down at the body again. No one had thought to close its eyes. The gash in the chest which Dr Bludger had merrily hacked a few moments before was perhaps ten inches long, and the edges of it pulled back from one another so it didn't seem as though the wound would ever close up neatly.

I could only assume that this would be like mending a hole in a jumper or shirt, which I'd had to do often enough in the orphanage. With great care I pressed the needle against the flesh at one end of the wound, which was like tough wax, until the point pierced it and slid through easily. Then putting my fingers into the wound, I pulled the needle from the inside and pushed it through the underside of the flesh on the other side, pulled it until it became tight, then returned to the first side again and repeated the procedure.

'You see?' said Dr Bludger. 'He's a natural. Just like lacing a boot, once you've forgotten what it is you're working on.'

Finally I finished and tied a knot in the end, keeping my eyes closed as I bit off the surplus string. Dr Bludger congratulated me with an inappropriately loud shout before taking a swig from a stone bottle with a label reading 'MEDICAL SPIRITS', having a brief coughing fit and wiping tears from his eyes with the blood-stained cuffs of his surgical coat. After we had watched him in embarrassed silence for a moment he straightened up and, without saying a word, raised the axe above his head and chopped a brand-new gash in the body's stomach.

There were lots of green faces as they came forward one by one, and a bit of discreet retching in the corner (including by Dr Bludger after another coughing fit). They got the hang of it quickly enough, and by the time they had finished the body was almost completely destroyed by Dr Bludger's surgical weapons (he alternated between axe, scalpel and ice-cream scoop). Next we were on to setting bones.

'This is a temporary measure,' he explained. 'If you set someone's bone with a splint they will still be in a lot of pain, but there's a good chance they will be able to escape the scene with you and get better treatment down here in the Underground.' He showed us what sorts of materials were ideal for making an emergency splint: a short sturdy stick for smaller bones and something thicker like a chair leg for broken arms or legs. We tried, and found this job much easier, although soon enough we were running out of bones in the poor corpse to break and falsely reset.

'This chap's nearly useless to us now,' Bludger was saying regretfully. 'He was a good friend and a terrible poker player. I'll have to wait for another corpse to come along.' At that moment a boy entered the room and whispered gravely in Dr Bludger's ear.

'Great!' he said. 'I'll bring them in at once.'

We followed him in through the door to what we now realized was the Underground Hospital. It was crowded with people and noise and pain, and a scattered group of sixteen-year-old doctors were rummaging through boxes of not-very-clean tools, looking for what they needed to tend their patients.

'Now pay especial attention,' said Dr Bludger, 'because this is quite different from what you've experienced so far.' We stood around the bed of a man whose finger had been chopped off, and who was writhing in agony.

'Observe, he is not staying still,' said Bludger.

'Oh, please,' said the man through his teeth. 'It does bloody hurt . . . please . . .'

'Also, he speaks. And blood. There's *lots* of blood.' Bludger grabbed the man's butchered hand and ripped off the bandage to show it to us. At once a jet of blood came shooting towards us and we all ducked, except for Sally, who was decorated by the red splatter, but didn't seem to notice or mind, so hard was she concentrating.

Tentatively we raised our heads to see that the patient's eyes were rolling around madly in his sockets. 'P-please!' he gibbered. 'Help me!'

'Don't worry my fellow!' said Bludger, for some reason yelling as though the man was going deaf. 'We'll have you right as rain in no time! HAVE SOME ANAESTHETIC!' He bit the cork from his bottle of medical spirits and upended it on the bleeding man's injured hand.

'This cleanses the wound,' he said to us, grinning manically. Politely I observed that the bottle was empty.

'Typical!' he bellowed, examining the wound himself so that the jet of blood temporarily veered away from Sally's face and into his own. He grabbed another bottle from a shelf and poured it liberally over the finger and into the patient's mouth. The patient gargled briefly, and then went quiet as the spirits hit his stomach and made his head swim.

'Here we go, Doctor,' said the same attendant as before, presenting him with a pudgy finger on a metal tray.

'You see?' said Bludger, taking the man's hand and plonking the severed finger on the end of the stump. 'I'll have this stitched back on in a jiffy. Now you just lie back.'

'But that's not my finger!' yelled the patient, newly

alert and wriggling madly in Bludger's grip. 'That one's got a TATTOO on it!' Some of the boys around me were starting to faint clean away while the doctor peered at the finger with a mildly interested air.

'Does it?' he wondered aloud. 'Ooooh yes, so it does. Now, my dear Mr Butler, you're quite sure your finger *doesn't* have a tattoo, you're sure of that?' As he spoke he wagged the severed finger at the patient, as though admonishing him.

This seemed to be more than the poor man could take, because with his good hand he now reached up, clutched Dr Bludger's lapels and yanked him off his feet, until the doctor's face was level with his own. The patient was now short of breath, sweating profusely, and looked quite insane.

'YES!' he said. 'Yes, I'm sure! I've had that finger for absolutely ages and it never had a tattoo on it before. So find my correct one or I'll . . . I'll . . .' and he collapsed back on his pillow in a swoon, his hand falling to one side and another jet of blood shooting across the room, making us all (apart from Sally) duck once more.

'Daniel Dorey, be a good fellow and find out what happened to Mr Butler's real finger, would you?' he said as he stared at the patient and he carefully poured more spirits into his mouth. As I ran off to find an orderly I heard him say, 'Now, children, you'll find a great deal of your effectiveness as a surgeon depends on what we call your *bedside manner* . . .'

*

131

At the end of the day's lessons we had trooped one by one back into the Circus, and as we came in walked wearily towards the tables for a bowl of the cook's delicious stew.

'Get ready for us to go up to the surface,' Tusk said into my ear. 'Not just yet though. First we've got to pretend to go to sleep.' As we walked I saw Martin the Sound Boy coming down from one of the bunks, sleepily scratching an armpit and looking as though he was just waking up.

'Good luck on the watch tonight, Martin,' said Tusk happily as he went past. 'I hope you have a ball.'

'*You're* a ball,' said Martin groggily.

'It's fine,' Tusk said under his breath. 'He always drops off to sleep soon enough. He knows we sneak past him all the time but he can never stay awake long enough to catch us. It would be easier to bring him in on the whole thing, but it's more fun not to.'

We were all so tired that soon the stew was devoured and we were trudging towards our bunks, some of us already nodding. Within a couple of minutes I was in bed, trying not to fall asleep. The lights went winking out one by one until there was darkness in the enormous cavern, and the sound of distant snores.

As I lay there in the darkness, for the hundredth time I fantasized about what it would be like to have a sister after all this time alone. She could tell me what my parents had been like, we could eat our meals together, and I could tell her the stories I had collected, and she would be proud of me. Yet it seemed so hope-less – far above me a vast city of empty houses, gutters and roofs streaming with water, gangs of police roaming the streets. And hidden among them a single man of magic – someone whose profession it was to remain invisible to normal people – who might be able to help me find my sister.

After counting the long hour in my head, I climbed quietly out of my bunk. I could just make out two dark shapes, and when Tusk whispered my name I made my way over to him. We crept past the sleeping form of Martin the Sound Boy, with his book leaning against his chest and his glasses askew on his face. As quietly as he could Tusk unlocked the gate, and we all slipped outside.

As we reached the main road of the Underground for some reason I was surprised to see it looked the same as during the daytime. What did I expect – that they would put all the torches out at night and plunge everyone into darkness? But what amazed me was that it was even busier than ever.

'Of course!' said Tusk when I mentioned this. 'What's the main traffic in the Underground? Escaped people coming down from above, and our people going up to steal what we can under the cover of darkness.'

As he spoke I saw a bedraggled, bewildered-looking group of people standing at the crossroads. I soon realized they were a family of ten, ranging from a baby in the arms of its mother to an old man who carried three heavy bags on his back.

'They just keep coming,' muttered Tusk at my side. 'They don't realize that they're escaping from a prison into a dungeon.' Now I noticed that the huge canvas bag Tusk wore on his back weighed heavily on him, and was packed with heavy implements – tools and weapons, I supposed. They were strapped tight so as to make no noise while he walked through the streets above ground, but up close I could hear the gentle sound of grinding metal.

'Ho there!' called one of the guards, stepping out from his hut. He carried a rather damp-looking torch that spewed out more smoke than light. There was a blackboard above the hut on which were scrawled all the free spaces that were available in the various tunnels nearby.

As the guard talked to the new arrivals, boys kept arriving from every direction and speaking into the ear of a bearded gentleman with a ruined top hat who sat in the hut. As he received messages he made constant changes to the board above him with a piece of chalk tied to the end of a snooker cue, crossing out names, adding vacancies, and presently taking another cue, with a wet rag attached, and rubbing out a whole tunnel and its contents. All the time he called out where beds for the night could be found, to anyone who would listen. Tusk shivered.

'A tunnel has collapsed,' he said. 'It happens now and then. I only hope the people can escape through the other end.'

The guard with the smoking torch gathered the family together and led them off towards a grim-looking tunnel in the distance. Behind them, two more families had already gathered. We moved on until we found one of the main transport tunnels, an abandoned sewer, where we could walk most of the way towards the surface, so long as we kept to the sides, out of the way of the huge horses that clumped up and down, dragging goods and timber, and the crowds who tramped in each direction.

When we had reached the next storey up we stopped by a fire where stools were laid out and a woman in rags offered round a huge wooden cup of buttered rum.

Tusk turned to the pair of us. 'Now, this is where we part. Mayrick, you know where you're going. Use the Clarence Street access to get up and go through the house-tunnels until you're beneath the shop. When you've got what you need, you only need to get it to two houses along and there's a plummeting point beneath the hearthstone of number twenty-four. Throw the coffee beans down last, and then jump after them. They should be soft enough to land on. Meet us by the Finchers End Corn Exchange exit at no later than two a.m.'

'If I'm still alive,' said Mayrick, 'I'll see you then.'

'What was all that?' I asked, watching him slip into the crowd.

'Mayrick's going to raid the larder of a restaurant that's used by the police. Then when he's done he'll

135

smash the windows before he leaves, to make a commotion.'

'Right,' I said. 'Because . . . ?'

'It's a diversion. To distract the police from what
we're doing.'

'And what *are* we doing?'

'Wait and see,' he said, and before too long he was
saying, 'Here,' and we ducked through a low mud-
hole into a brightly lit canteen crammed to the gills
with people in every direction who leaned over the
low tables, eating ravenously and having every kind
of conversation – shouting, laughing, crying, playing
fiddles, fighting with fists, declaiming from religious
books. It was mayhem.

'SOUP!' bellowed a voice from the kitchen, and
behind the counter a dozen staff scurried about yelling,
'Soup! Soup!' and getting piles of bowls together.
A door in the far wall was flung open and a huge urn
was brought forth and set down on the ground, its lid
clattering from the steam, and in a moment a dozen
bowls were filled and being held up to the counter.

Within a few minutes a moment of relative calm
descended as most of the patrons became engaged in
eating, so the three of us squeezed between the tables
to find a free spot at the back.

'There he is,' said Tusk. We sat and looked at the
other occupant of the table, who was huddled in the
corner with a cap pulled down hiding his eyes.

'Jimmy,' said Tusk.

136

The figure looked up lazily, saw us and looked down again. He held out a limp hand which Tusk shook, and then withdrew it again straight away.

'Who's he?' he asked quietly.

'He's Daniel, Jimmy. Daniel Dorey. Says he's squared up to Caspian Prye.'

'Yeah?' said the man, and looked up at me from beneath his cap. His lips turned slippery in a sneer. 'He don't look like much.'

'He doesn't know yet, Jimmy. We haven't told him what we're doing tonight.'

I looked at Tusk, beginning to think I'd been more stupid to trust him than I'd realized. He ignored me, and said, 'What have you got for us, Jimmy?'

'Well now, maybe I'll tell our new friend,' he said, leaning forward, and smiling at me. He wasn't much older than I was but there were no teeth in his mouth, just slimy gums. 'Let me tell you what I am,' he said. 'I'm an informant. I talk to the police up above, and sell them information so they can find things. And catch some of our people, so's they can hang them.'

Now I smelt the breath from his mouth too – it was foul, as awful as a cesspit. I shrank back from it, and tried not to show my disgust.

'You know why I do this?' he asked.

Trying not to breathe, I shook my head.

'So they gain my trust.' And he smiled again, showing me the full range of his horrible slime-ridden gums. 'And then,' he said, 'I get to be near them, and hear what they say, and come down here and tell my good friends like Tusk here.'

His sick-smelling breath puffed at me. I put my hand to my mouth as though I was thinking about what he had said, but it was really so I could bite my thumb to keep from feeling sick. I shuddered.

'What about the people who you . . . you betray?' I asked.

He stared at me for a moment longer, his eyes alive and his mouth still open, watching me like he was going to bite me with his gums. Then inexplicably he slumped back in his seat, and pulled the cap back down over his eyes.

'CHOPS!' screamed a voice from the kitchen out the back. There was another surge as people leaped out of their seats to grab plates from the counter and return an instant later, chewing tiny lumps of meat from fatty bones and slurping up the thin gravy.

'Jimmy Cap only sells the police information that we know won't hurt us,' Tusk muttered, as the chaos died down around us. 'We only give them people who are putting the Underground at risk – cowards. Or we give them information and then make sure we rescue our people in time, so that they know that Jimmy's information was accurate and they can trust him. You see?'

I sat back in my seat feeling miserable all over again about how Caspian Prye's evil was infecting everything in Tumblewater, like a bad wound turning a whole body putrid. So many people betraying each other all the time – it was terrible.

'But I was going to tell you what I got, Mr Daniel,' said Jimmy's mouth from beneath the rim of his cap. 'The word among the police tonight is a raid they're doing at midnight. They're going somewhere called the Cobbles. I don't know it. None of them want to go there – they say it's haunted. But it's orders from above. They're going to arrest someone who Prye wants. He doesn't have a name, they just call him the Apothecary.'

I stared at Tusk.

'I've been hearing whispers about this Apothecary character,' Tusk explained. 'Lots of people seem to want him. After you mentioned the Apothecary yesterday, and his connection to your sister, I knew you had to come along. Let's leave now – we haven't got long to get there.'

We got up and I turned to say thanks to Jimmy, but his cap was pulled low and he showed no sign of hearing me. In a few minutes we were trudging up the lonely tracks to the upper tunnels near the surface, where the only people around were those who had to be there, or who didn't care for their own safety. The bustle of the lower levels was gone, replaced with a tense quietness. With Tusk giving directions from his maps, we took many turnings until finally we were standing at the bottom of an iron ladder. As we were so close to the surface we had to avoid speaking if possible, in case we attracted the attention of people above ground.

I climbed the ladder and at the top pushed up a heavy metal grille. All was quiet. Climbing out I held it up so Tusk could follow on behind me. No matter how many times you came out from the Underground, it was always wonderful to feel the fresh air and spattering rain on your face after the dank closeness of the tunnels. We found ourselves in a narrow passageway between two buildings which were oppressive with quiet. It was as though a thick blanket had fallen between here and the outside world – not one peep of the hubbub of city life made its way through to us. Instead, a close and watchful silence wrapped itself around us like a blanket. Peeping round the corner, we quailed at the grim sight of the street beyond.

We were looking out from a row of tiny, ruined cottages, several of whose roofs had fallen in. They led to a cobbled courtyard above which loomed two gaunt buildings more like prison blocks than tenement houses. We might have stepped through a portal into another city, for this place felt utterly abandoned and forgotten, as though no human had set foot here for hundreds of years.

At the end of the lane, where the outside street should be, was a high brick wall. I stopped, confused, and looked the other way. In the other direction the street ended in another wall, this one even higher, and looked like it was part of the original design. This place was completely closed off.

'The plague, Daniel,' said Tusk. 'Two hundred

years ago the plague came to this place, where many hundreds of the poorest people lived. They were all diseased and dying, and the other inhabitants of the city feared it would spread. So they took a terrible decision, and bricked up this place, leaving the invalids to die inside.' For about the hundredth time that day, I shivered.

'We'll have to split up,' Tusk continued. 'Jimmy Cap's information says that the Apothecary's hiding from Caspian Prye in one of these buildings. Remind me what I'm looking for?'

'I haven't seen him myself but this is what I heard. He's thin and tall, his face looks weathered and old but he's as athletic as a young man. He wears a sheepskin bag on his back in which he keeps his potions and a brown cloak wrapped tight around him. He has a long craggy nose – and a blue birthmark that stretches across his face.'

Tusk nodded. 'OK,' he said, and steeling ourselves, we each turned to our respective doors.

nside the building, I walked slowly to the nearest room and looked in. Dust lay on everything as deep as settled snow – or, given the sickly history of this place, like a thick layer of mould that had grown up from the ground itself. No sign of the Apothecary – and it was the same story in every room.

The cavernous silence was so heavy it made my ears throb as I walked up the stairs to the first floor. As my foot touched the landing, I heard the first sound.

A low wooden creak. My heart wanted to burst in my chest, but I stayed still. The sound came again, and then again, rhythmically. A long, low creak, the sound that a wooden door makes when it wishes it could speak like a man, and say, 'Oh, I am tired.' It could be the sound of a floorboard, or the sound of a rope straining with the weight of a body.

Slowly I followed the noise into a room. Before me was a rocking chair. And in the chair was a little old lady. Her hands worked at the knitting in her lap, and as she heard me clear my throat awkwardly she looked up. Neither of us spoke, and with the glimmering light catching the ghostly wrinkles of her face, she smiled, put down her knitting and held out her hand. In it was an orange.

She didn't speak, but her rocker gently went forward and back. In a place famous for being infested with ghosts it was deeply unsettling to see her there, smiling so calmly. Sure that I had stumbled on the first of the phantoms, I nervously took a step backwards and retreated into the darkness of the passageway, leaving her with her arm outstretched.

I crept up another flight of stairs and lit a match. The air here was distinctly colder and it prickled my skin – the flame flickered in a slight breeze. The first thing I saw was a candle in a holder, and gratefully I lit it with the match. At last some steady light. Holding it up, I saw that I was in the attic of the house, a great long room with a pitched roof, and ducking beneath a low beam, I walked down it, trying to see my way to the end. There were a few wooden stools cast to one side, and some shelves on the wall, but I was surprised when I reached the end of the room and into the candle's sphere of light came a plain brick wall. I turned around.

In front of me, on either side of the trail of footprints I had just made in the dust, there now knelt a number of small boys. Eight, perhaps ten, of them. They were all praying, their heads turned downward, all facing towards me. And they were glowing softly.

Steeling myself with a single shaky breath, for a few long moments I forced myself to remain calm. It was the single hardest thing I'd ever done.

'Hello,' I said, taking a step forward, but none of them moved, and now I saw they were mouthing silent words. I don't have anything against them, I thought. There's no reason for them to hate me. They can't kill me. I know they can't.

I stood stock-still and closed my eyes. Maybe there *was* something they could do to me. What would I feel in a few seconds' time – a chilling coldness, a swirling dizzy spell, a bite?

The horrible silence was eventually broken by a long, crazy, stupid, ludicrous, wobbly fart. My eyes shot open. All of the boys' heads had turned towards the noise as well. It seemed to come from a cupboard at the side of the room.

Through its closed door a glowing shape appeared, limb by limb, until he stood in front of us: it was another phantom boy, fatter than the others, holding a ghost baby in his arms.

'I'm sorry, boys,' he said. 'I couldn't stop him.'

'Rumpy, you idiot!' bellowed the boy nearest me, jumping to his feet. 'You ruined our haunting!' The other boys all slowly withdrew their hands from the praying position, and took on another aspect entirely, that of a vengeful gang, rubbing their hands together with glee as they advanced on the tubby ghost.

'It wasn't my fault!' protested Rumpy. 'You taught him to make that noise, how can I stop him?' The baby in his arms grinned and gurgled, and the tubby boy carefully put him down on a chair and retreated to the window, waving his hands. 'Please!' he said. 'No! Not again, it's not fair!'

He disappeared in a cloud of flying fists and boots. 'Help!' he shouted. 'Ow! Get off! That HURTS!'

'Shut up, Rumpy,' said one of the others. 'You're a ghost, you can't feel anything!'

'Get off, it's not fair!' he shouted, nonetheless.

I walked over to where the baby sat on the chair, glowing gently like the rest. It giggled up at me, and waved. Bemused, I bent and picked it up. It weighed nothing, but sat in my arms happily. I offered it a finger and it bit down as hard as it could – I didn't feel anything at all.

'You're such an *idiot*, Rumpy,' shouted one of the boys. 'You spoil everything! Our first person to haunt in a hundred years and you mess it up with a farting baby!' The others started beating him up with renewed vigour as he whimpered helplessly beneath them.

I cleared my throat loudly. The boys laid off the punching for a second and looked up at me.

'Oh yeah,' said one. 'I forgot about him.'

'Hey, why are you holding my baby brother?' said another. 'Put him down!'

I stared at them. 'Who *are* you?' I asked.

At this, they let go of Rumpy, who fell on the floor with an inaudible thump, and stood in a row, facing up at me. 'Who are *we*?' said one. 'Who are *you*? This is our home!'

I couldn't help looking around at the rotted rafters

and the dusty gloom, and thinking what a miserable place this place this must be to call home.

'I'm Daniel Dorey,' I said cheerfully. 'Pleased to meet you.'

They stared at me.

'What?' said one. '*The* Daniel Dorey? As in, Daniel Dorey the writer?'

Dumbly I nodded. 'But how do you . . . ?'

'Boys!' the little ghost said. 'Show some hospitality to our guest!'

He clapped his hands and at once two of the ghosts had fetched me a chair, and the others were sitting around me, looking up with rapt attention. This was almost as disturbing as when they'd been trying to haunt me.

'Let's introduce ourselves,' said the outspoken lad. 'My name's Oates, this is Wrigglesworth and Featherstone.'

I blinked. 'Er . . . what fantastic names. Are they very old?' They all nodded solemnly. 'But wait a minute,' I continued. 'How do you know about me? My first book isn't even published yet!'

'Word gets around,' said Oates. 'We ghosts tell each other everything. Poltergeists, invisible spirits, night terrors, incubi, we share the lot. Everyone's crazy about the idea of you being in Tumblewater.'

'What do you mean?'

'Huh!' said Wrigglesworth, as though I was stupid. 'How many writers do you think there are round here?'

'None,' I said. 'Because hardly anyone in the district can read or write.'

'*Exactly*,' he said, as if I was the stupidest oaf he had ever encountered. 'How can we get famous as ghosts if no one will write about us? There's no publicity!'

'I see,' I said quietly, looking down and noticing that the ghost baby had gone to sleep on my arm. 'Well, I'll write about you, with pleasure. With only one condi—'

'And make us fearful?' interrupted Oates.

'Dreadfully fearful,' I promised.

'As frightening as Grudge, the chain-dragging monster downstairs?' he asked.

'As frightening as him,' I promised, grateful that I had avoided an encounter with Grudge. 'Even,' I went on, 'as frightening as the ghost woman with the oranges,' I said.

They all looked confused for a moment, then shared a look among themselves, and started sniggering.

'What?' I asked.

They saw I was annoyed, and it made them laugh more.

'*What?*' I asked. 'Do you want me to write about you or not?' By now they were falling about on the floor. Oates was the first to recover, and wiped a ghost tear from his eye.

'Did the nasty Mrs Seagrave frighten you?' he said. 'The nice, normal and completely alive woman?'

Now I felt a little bit stupid.

'Did she offer you a nasty orange?' said one of the

others, before collapsing back on the floor, and rolling around on top of his giggling comrades. 'A horrible scary orange?'

I sighed and looked down at the baby as I rocked him. 'They're very silly,' I said to his sleeping face.

'Listen,' I said after a giving them a few seconds to get control of themselves. 'I'll write that you're a bunch of darling little cherubs who pick flowers and read poetry if you don't help me.' That got their attention, and then I explained my position. I had to find the Apothecary, and had been told he was hiding somewhere in the court. 'I've only got a few minutes to find him,' I finished.

'Well, he's not here,' said Oates. 'Our only living resident is Mrs Seagrave.' One of the boys started giggling again at what I had said before, and Oates cuffed him over the head. 'The Apothecary is in the other building. But, Daniel, I'm sorry – I think you're too late . . .'

He pointed out of the window and down below, to where a smashing noise came, followed by the chuckling sound of bricks falling to the ground. There was a second smashing noise and the wall that contained the court suddenly collapsed.

'Here they come,' I whispered.

Bricks scattered across the courtyard and there was a tramping of boots. The ghosts all crammed together around me to get a better look, and we saw policemen gathering there: ten, twenty, thirty of them. They stopped in rigid formation below us, standing stock-still as though they were waiting for something. I wondered what they were doing, until out in front of them walked a thin, athletic woman. She had wildly curly bright red hair and an eyepatch, and wore a man's long coat with a sword by her side. There was something almost inhuman and lizardlike in her stealthy movements that caused me to shiver – and although they couldn't feel the cold, I saw the boys gather close to one another too, at the sight of her. The Tumblewater police who were in the pay of Caspian Prye were mindless thugs, but in her I thought I saw something more intelligently evil, and capable of crueller torture. I noticed with a start that her eyepatch covered *both* her eyes, and yet she seemed able to see perfectly.

'It's all right,' said Oates, looking out. 'They're not coming this way, just going into the other building.'

But that's worse! I thought. That's where Tusk is, and the Apothecary! I watched the men trooping in through the front door at a run, their boots rumbling on the wooden boards like rhythmic thunder.

There was a commotion inside the building, the policemen shouting that they had found something, and that something, when it appeared, was the Apothecary. Although I'd never seen him with my own eyes I knew at once it was him. He was old, his skin weathered, yet he was lean and muscular from decades of travelling. Even so, as he was brought down the steps towards the Eyeless Creature he writhed and tried to get away. Six men had hold of him and forced him right up near her. I saw that even her men looked away from her. She leaned in as though she was speaking into his ear. He must have known he would be executed the next day, like any other prisoner, but perhaps she whispered him the promise of some specially terrible punishment, for his head lolled, and his swarthy features turned pale. Then he was roughly hauled towards a carriage visible beyond the hole in the wall, struggling harder than before, and thrown inside. The only man who might know where my sister was hidden – now in the hands of the police.

The ghost boys, all gathered near the glass, shivered as one. In the courtyard below the policemen trooped back out of the doorway opposite as fast as they had gone in, and piled up into the carriage. As we watched the Eyeless Creature walk towards them, I began to breathe again – at least Tusk hadn't been captured. But the breath caught in my throat because the Creature suddenly spun round and seemed to stare straight up at the window.

The ghosts yelped and tumbled off the window ledge, but I didn't move. There was no way that she could see me. Aside from her eyepatch, it was the middle of the night, and dark, incredibly dark, with rain and fog, and I had pinched the candle out with my fingers. And yet I felt her intelligence roaming through the darkness, searching for me.

Looking down at her I whispered to myself, 'What are you?'

She turned away again, walked to the carriage and leaped on to it as it began to drive away.

'We don't know who she is,' whispered one of the little ghosts. I turned around to find them all looking up at me fearfully, and realized that although they were two hundred years old, they were still little boys. 'We don't know who to ask about her. What we said earlier about all the ghosts in the area wasn't strictly true,' said Wrigglesworth. 'Truth is, there hardly are any ghosts here in Tumblewater any more.'

I suddenly thought of all the stories I'd heard in the Underground, of spooks and spectres and phantoms. 'That's not true,' I said. 'I hear there are hundreds of ghosts below ground.'

'Of course they're down *there*,' Wrigglesworth replied. 'That's what I'm saying. It's up here that there's none left! Hardly a couple of dozen in the whole place, I'd say.'

I looked out from the window. We were high up enough to see out over the rooftops of a few nearby streets. 'How many should there be?' I asked.

'How many people have lived and died in Tumblewater?' mused Oates. 'Hard to tell. Could be ten thousand, perhaps, or twice that, you'd never know.'

'Plus the little ghosts,' added Wrigglesworth. 'Ghosts of dogs, haunted wardrobes, phantom stenches, that sort of thing. There's an alleyway near here used to be haunted by the most horrible fart smell you could imagine. Every time you got halfway down there, there it would be. Not any more though. They've all gone.'

'Except for the wardrobe,' I said.

He stared at me. 'Yes. Obviously.'

'Why have they gone?' I asked.

'To escape the changes.'

'The changes?' I said gently, sitting down on the chair again. 'Slow down. Explain.'

'There's something new in Tumblewater. This man who's taken over the district. What do they call him . . . ?'

'Caspian Prye,' I said.

'That's it. Well, he's got some *very* rum characters coming to town. The word is, he's been trying to use magic.'

'He has,' I said. 'He's using magic to find my sister, who's hidden here somewhere. And he's failed, so far. That's why he wanted the Apothecary.'

'Oh, he's failed *so far*,' said Oates. 'So now he's getting even worse. He's inviting sorcerers, shamans, mystics, satanists, any magician who'll come from around the world to help him. Witch-doctors, occultists, the weirdest, most dangerous and powerful humans to be found. And those who have come are helping him cook up something terrible and evil. There's something brewing here, something that's being brought to life with an awful energy. *That's* what's disturbing the ghosts, and sending them to the Underground.'

'So why haven't *you* left?'

'Us?' asked Oates contemptuously. '*We're* not scared.'

'No! AAAAAAARGH!' One boy showed his fearlessness by charging at me, screaming and smashing his head on my knee. I didn't even feel the merest breath of wind but he bounced off and went careening across the room into some chairs, where he collapsed unconscious. The other boys gave a polite smattering of applause, as though they had just witnessed a good shot at a cricket match.

'I get your point,' I said. 'No need to brain yourself.'

'This place was famous among humans for being haunted. But the truth is, it wasn't – until today no other ghosts ever came here except for us,' explained Oates. 'There were no humans to scare, you see? Apart from Mrs Seagrave, and she's our friend. Now the wall's come down, that might change. Maybe we'll go underground . . .'

'You'd certainly fit in,' I said. 'There's tons of weird things down there.'

'. . . but until now we were quite happy playing up here by ourselves, so it was perfect. Caspian Prye's wizards didn't scare us because they never came here.'

'So that woman with the eyepatch,' I said, 'she could be one of these evil magicians?'

'We think so,' said Oates. 'She could be a wizard, someone powerful in magic. Or –' he looked around the room and lowered his voice – 'she may not even be human at all. She could be a spell. An incantation. Just a body under the power of someone else's magic. Imagine the strength of one who feels no pain, and has no thoughts.'

'She's even freakier than the Monk,' said Wrigglesworth.

'The Monk?' I asked weakly.

'You really are new round here, aren't you, son?' asked Featherstone.

'Easy!' I said. 'I'm older than you! Oh, actually, I suppose I'm not, really . . .'

'The Monk? You mean you've been writing down all the most frightening stories from Tumblewater you can find, and no one's tried to scare you with the tale of the Monk?'

'From the sound of it, I should be grateful no one has.'

'Until recently he was just a rumour. He was said to walk these streets in the Middle Ages. There are nursery rhymes about him and lots of different tales told. He was only ever glimpsed late at night, on a nearly deserted street, and there would always be a death soon after the sighting. They say he last appeared at the time of the Great Plague, two hundred years ago – he is known to appear when this place is in danger and the people are weak, and can be devoured in secret. Just like now.'

'That's all we know about him,' Wrigglesworth went on. 'We don't even know if he was a real monk – just that he wears a grey robe with a hood like a monk's cowl, and when he opens his mouth, his teeth are covered in blood. Now we're hearing that Prye's meddling with deadly magical forces has woken him up.'

I listened in awe. Here was something even more frightening than Prye himself, or his blind servant. Something that could destroy more than your physical body. Wait a minute: Prye . . . the blind servant . . .

'My God!' I said, jumping up. 'My friend is still over there! I've got to go.' The boys all looked at me, disappointed.

'But we didn't get to show you all our tricks!' Oates said. 'How scary we are!'

'Another time,' I said. 'If this is true about the Monk, then this place isn't safe for you either. Come and find me in the tunnels of the Underground. There are lots of ghosts there who'll make you at home, and I promise I'll write you up as the scariest little ghosts in the city!'

With that I was running to the door and they were shouting goodbye after me. I sprinted down the stairs, past the doorway with Mrs Seagrave inside, and I shouted through:

'Sorry to be so rude!'

'That's all right, dear,' she said back, as I ran down the last set of steps and out into the courtyard.

The first thing I saw was Tusk, looking exhausted on the top step of the doorway on the other side. I ran up to the bottom step and said, 'Thank God you're OK!'

He looked dejected, and didn't show any sign of noticing me. Then he slowly got up, came down the steps and together we walked back to the shadow of the alleyway we had hidden in when we first arrived.

'What happened?' I asked.

'I didn't get to him in time,' said Tusk miserably.

'I know, I know, but how did you escape the police?'

'They weren't interested in me,' he shrugged. 'All they wanted was the Apothecary. I failed. I'm sorry, Daniel – it took me too long to find him.'

I swallowed. 'But you *did* find him?'

'He was sleeping beneath a blanket at the top of the house.'

'What did he say?'

'He asked me if I was Daniel. The sound of the police footsteps was already on the stairs and when I explained that I wasn't, but that you were nearby, he said, "I needed to speak to him."'

'What happened then?' I asked.

'As they dragged him away he just said one thing, quite calmly.'

'What was it?'

'"Rescue me,"' said Tusk.

'Which there is very little hope either of you will have a chance to do,' said a dark voice, and two hands came forward out of the shadow, and grabbed our shoulders as roughly as could be. As he leaned forward his face was revealed. It was Uncle, looking fiercer than I had ever seen him.

'Daniel,' he said darkly, 'you've got no idea how angry I am with you.'

or the next half an hour, we were taken deep underground as fast as we could travel. Uncle was not alone. Two other men were with him, who manhandled us below the surface and down the tunnels without much concern for whether they knocked our heads off in the process.

'Ow!' I protested as one of them threw me down a mud-chute. I came tumbling out the bottom end, bruised, only to be grabbed by Uncle again.

'I watched it all, Daniel,' Uncle said into my ear. 'How you didn't get captured I don't know. And I bet you brought your key with you too. What a stupid risk to take!'

My stomach felt hot and wobbly, like it hadn't since I was in trouble at school as a little boy. I was bitterly indignant that he had been watching me, which meant he didn't trust me, and that he had caught us when we had so nearly saved the day. But much worse than that, I hated that he knew I had betrayed him, after everything he had done for me.

He was marching me forward along a tunnel as other Undergrounders turned to look at us. Although I knew we were in the wrong I couldn't help my temper spilling over.

157

'Just because you've thrown me in with the other boys at school, I'm not a *kid*,' I said. 'I'm sixteen.'

'You're not acting it,' he said. 'And you're not exactly encouraging us to treat you that way. And you know exactly why you're in that school – you're learning things there that not might, but *will*, save your life.' We were in one of the deserted upper tunnels and the others were far ahead of us when he spun me round with a rough hand on my shoulder and looked closely into my eyes. 'This is *not a playground*,' he said. 'You were nearly arrested and killed. And then where would we all be!'

'You don't understand,' I shouted. 'That was *him*. It was the Apothecary! We were trying to rescue him!' All at once he changed. The fierce anger went out of his eyes and a troubled frown descended on his brow – the look I had got used to seeing him wear these last few weeks.

He turned away and kept us both walking fast along the tunnel. 'OK,' he said eventually. 'I can understand that. But your friends should not have led you into that danger . . .' He paused, and added quietly, 'Maybe it's my fault. They couldn't know how important you are to us.'

'All I knew was that I was trying to rescue my sister, and that was the only thing that mattered to me.'

At once he became angry again and grabbed my shoulder incredibly hard, so his fingers dug agonizingly into my muscles.

'Let me go!' I said.

'You see these people?' he asked. He gestured to the couple of families who were lying by the side of the passage, some of them trying to sleep, some of them getting a good eyeful of my humiliation. Then he swept his arm further down the passage. There was a crossroads just a few yards on, and a wayfarer's cottage, out of which a rather drunken wayfarer was walking with a lantern, leading a family of eight or nine away to a distant tunnel where they could be housed, as three or four other families stood in line, trying to keep their pride. As he passed the corner on the other side of his cottage, a swing of the wayfarer's lamp lit up a cave dug out from the mud, in which dozens of girls and women sat in rows, silently sewing, struggling to see their stitches by candle flame and with heaps of cloth all around them – piles of rags waiting to be sewn, and stacks of finished garments. The wayfarer's lamp passed round the corner and the women disappeared back into a glimmering semi-dark pierced by twenty dots of candlelight.

I saw those people, and I felt sorry for them. I nodded. But deep down I hated them – even if they died now, they would at least have known what it was to have a loving family. Here was I, trapped under the earth, who didn't even have the memory of a family. And I was supposed to give up my attempts to find Maria?

'Our battle against Prye is not just for *you*, Daniel. It

159

is for every last breathing person who lives here under the earth. With every risk you take you don't just risk her and your own skin, but *all* of ours.'

I nodded again, and rubbed my shoulder. I knew I had been bad, and I wanted him to like me again. But I didn't trust myself to speak.

'You know that now, I can see,' he said, his voice softening. 'I'm sorry I shouted.' He put his arm roughly round me for a second and gave me a hug. Then we were marching again.

'That doesn't mean you're out of trouble,' he said quietly, but I knew the first fire of his anger had burned out. He was already thinking, as I was, about the problem of what we had to do next. As we turned down another tunnel he said, 'Every night I have to spend several hours overseeing all the missions above ground. Tonight I'm going to have to plan our most dangerous mission yet.'

He strode so fast I struggled to keep up.

'What's that?' I said.

'The Apothecary said, "Rescue me." So that's what we're going to do.'

In a few minutes we had decamped to a stone chamber far beneath the streets. With wall-torches burning fiercely across a ceiling already blackened by flames, it looked like the headquarters of a devilish mastermind rather than someone trying to save thousands of lives. There was a big desk for Uncle to sit behind and a row of chairs for the people who came to see him.

First coffee was brought in a steaming jug and set on one end of a long table. A tall, nervous, bespectacled man came in with piles of maps and blueprints, pinning them down on the table with little stones. He was clearly unhappy to be distracted from some other important work (whatever that was) and gave short and petulant answers to Uncle's questions, until he was informed of what the plan actually was.

'You're mad!' was his reaction.

'Don't worry,' replied Uncle. 'It can be done.'

'You'll kill yourself!'

'I tell you not to worry. Just give me the maps . . .' And the conversation repeated itself six or seven times, until at last the irritable man in spectacles grabbed his papers and retired. I had been pretending to snooze in a corner so as not to attract attention but as he rose to go I looked up and saw an incredible map of stains up and down his shirt – coffee, food, ink stains, circles of grease rubbed from his spectacle lenses.

'That man is a true genius,' said Uncle after he left. 'Everything we have is thanks to him. We call him the Anti-Architect.'

He didn't have time to tell me more because at once several men came in through the door with urgent messages and questions, and I retreated to my invisible position, with a newspaper over my face. Presently Uncle sent them away with replies and instructions, and as they left I heard two women come in. They must

161

have been in charge of disguises because I heard Uncle making comments on the designs in front of him, ordering changes to be taken in at once.

More people came and went throughout the night, asking questions, delivering notes and passing on news. I realized this must be how every night progressed, and with a shock I saw what a staggering amount of crime had to go on every night to keep everyone in the Underground clothed and fed. No wonder fourteen pupils could be killed or arrested overnight. Raiders arrived back from nightly excursions to tell what they had got; men and women came from the store to tell Uncle which items had run out, and of which there was a surplus; and teams of burglars came forward to ask what was needed, where other raids were happening and therefore where they should go.

Uncle promised all the support he could, even to those who seemed half-witted or argumentative. He never once raised his voice or exerted his authority in any way, but continued the job with an unflinching diligence. At one point during the night, after the news of several burglaries that had failed or been 'rumbled' by police, the room emptied out. Uncle chose this moment to speak to me, removing the newspaper from my face.

'Sometimes I think about what would happen if Caspian's men came for us, with dynamite, with dogs and guns. Because surely they must know we're down here – they can't be that stupid. But then I think, what about the other way round? What if we went for *them*? If we all just walked above ground, thousands and thousands of us, all risking our lives at the same time, and overthrew them? That's our last hope, if it comes to it, and maybe our best one.'

His attention was soon diverted by more people coming in, with news of further raids above ground. I dozed off after that for a long time until I heard my name mentioned. Looking up, I saw a group of hard-looking men gathered around the table.

'We have Daniel and Tusk to thank for this informa-tion,' Uncle was saying, and for a moment the eyes of the whole group turned to me. Then he went on: 'It's as simple as this – if we succeed we might topple Prye, and if we don't we might all be killed. For this reason, I'm not going to order any man to participate. I will only accept volunteers. Which brings me to my next point: we need six volunteers, but it's important that each man doesn't know who the others are. Then if he gets caught, he can't divulge the identities of the others. I'm going to leave the disguises on this chair by the door so that those interested may pick one up on their way in or out of this room. The six volunteers must be at the Manser Street entrance at five o'clock this morning.'

I could think about nothing else but whether I would be allowed on the raid, and had had no other thought all night. I was far from being in Uncle's good books, and I didn't want to make more trouble for him by asking.

He gave no sign of what was in his thoughts all night, except for at one point when a boy brought in a letter addressed personally to him. Turning the envelope around in his hands, he questioned the boy about who had given it to him (the boy had been asked to deliver it by a stranger), and when he read it he went quiet for a moment, and his expression turned dark. After that he brooded over maps for a while, and I didn't dare ask what it had said. But he wasn't left to his own thoughts for long. After a few short minutes the circus resumed with the arrival of more people who needed his attention and advice.

At last, I was woken by his voice, asking my opinion.

'What?' I said.

'Come here,' he said sharply, and before I had a chance to tell what was going on he threw a cloak over me and pulled the hood over my head. A band of cloth stuck awkwardly over my eyes and I was left feeling foolish as he rearranged it so that it fitted over my nose and mouth, hiding everything except my eyes, and making me look like a bandit.

They stood back and looked at me in the candlelight. It was exactly like the moment when Uncle had first brought me to the Underground, and had me disguised. I saw in his eyes that he remembered it too. His look softened, and he smiled.

The two women smiled too, reviewing their handiwork. To my amazement, I recognized one of them – the woman who had first given me a roof over my head in Tumblewater, and who had disguised me so I could safely walk the streets.

'Nuala!' I said. 'It's you!'

She jumped. 'Daniel?' she asked. 'Good God, the cloak definitely works, I'd never have known you. Don't *slouch* like that, stand up straight!'

I pulled the hood back, and came forward to give her a hug. Even Uncle had forgotten his woes for a moment at this reunion.

'What are you doing here?' I asked. 'Don't you live on the surface any more?'

She shook her head and pointed at Uncle. 'Not any more, thanks to him, that useless lump. The police know him too well, and saw him coming to my house. We got the tip-off that they were coming for me and we only got out just in time.'

'Josephine!' I shouted, seeing the other woman was not a woman at all, but Nuala's young assistant. She wasn't quite as shy as before, and had clearly taken on duties alongside Nuala in the Underground. She gave me a knowing look.

'So it's you two boys getting us into trouble again,' she said. 'And keeping us up all night making repairs.'

It was a delight to see Uncle his old self as he chatted to Nuala, thrown into confusion by her (and Josephine's) affectionate rebukes.

'It's good of you, so good,' he stuttered, 'to help us. These cloaks –' he cleared his throat, regaining his composure somewhat '– are perfect. Six more of them, please, as soon as possible. I need them ready in good time before five o'clock. And I'll see you more than re-paid in food.'

Both of them looked pleased, as though they'd just concluded a clever piece of bargaining, and Josephine gathered the cloaks up from the table to take away with them. Nuala smiled at Uncle, and touched him on the tip of his nose with her finger.

'I forgive you,' she said. 'They'll be ready.'

Uncle's eyes settled on me helplessly until the ladies had left, then I watched as his thoughts returned and his feelings vanished and were replaced with his weary frown.

'Why am I trying this on?' I asked. 'I feel like a high-wayman.'

'That's pretty much what you're going to be,' he answered. 'I know what I said about you not coming above ground, but this is different. The Apothecary at least knows Prye by sight. And it's you he needs to talk to, Daniel. If we fail to rescue him but you're able to talk to him even for a few seconds, that might be enough. It's too dangerous to risk *not* bringing you.'

Once again I saw the vulnerability in Uncle's eyes. Even if the Apothecary somehow knew where my sister was hidden, and helped us find her – what then? How would that help us defeat Prye? We were simply trying our best, trusting that something would come along, some ray of hope.

*

It seemed to take forever for the hour to come round but at last it arrived. Although I was still wearing the one I had tried on earlier, on Uncle's instruction I took an extra cloak, put it on in a quiet side-passage and made my way to the Manser Street entrance, whose location I had memorized from the map. When I reached it, I found myself in a small chamber beneath a ladder. As so often, I had to sit in darkness, and scrabble in my pockets for matches before any light could be produced. How I hated those first few moments when entering a room! Every time it grew worse. You might have thought you'd get used to the creeping fear of being in an unknown, darkened place. But it got worse rather than better.

One by one, other cloaked figures appeared and we sat there, avoiding any unnecessary talk. Only Uncle revealed himself in order to take the lead – in any case, we were all familiar with his unmistakeably tall and narrow form. When he saw by his pocket watch that it was time, he climbed the ladder, knocked on the underside three times and the metal lid was lifted.

We were in a small cobbled courtyard overhung by empty grain warehouses, and a single tree in one corner, lonely-looking and leafless. Together we were six shapes, as sinister in our long cloaks as the Grim Reaper himself. Uncle ran over the plan three times, five times, ten times, until every word was drummed into our heads.

Eventually checking his pocket watch (which, now

I noticed it, seemed quite refined and expensive for an outlaw's) once more by the candlelight, Uncle looked round at us and said, 'It is time to move.'

We all nodded as one, and walked out to the street. At once we broke up, and went our separate ways, to rejoin each other in a few minutes' time at the grave-yard.

What happened next, in all its terror and excitement, you know already. (Remember that bit, back at the very start?) Despite what looked like impossible odds when we reached Ditcher's Fields, the cemetery and place of execution, the Apothecary was soon safely in our hands. And then, defying the pursuing agents of the police, we reached our hiding place, where we were to remain in absolute secrecy, hidden from everyone, for twenty-four hours, until the police search had calmed down. There was no escape, and nothing to do but rest, and hope.

So we pulled our masks from our faces. The first three to reveal themselves came as a huge shock to me – sensible Sally, Tusk and Mayrick had followed me on this mission and put themselves into terrible danger. All of a sudden I knew that here were great friends whom I would know for the rest of my life. Yes, even Sally. But who knew how long the rest of our lives would be? For the last masked figure to reveal himself was the man I most feared beside Caspian Prye himself: Inspector Rambull, the chief of the police force, whose one purpose was to capture me.

Uncle and I stared at him for three, four, five long seconds, and then looked at each other. All of our excitement and jubilation died away in a breath, and our eyes travelled in unison to the metal trapdoor above our heads.

Rambull chuckled, watching us, his paunchy, blotchy face wobbling away. Sitting on the bench at the end of the tiny room, he leaned against the wall, pulling half a stubbed-out cigar from his top pocket.

'Does anyone mind if I smoke? There is ventilation, after all.' Without waiting for us to answer he held a flaring match up to the end of his cigar.

'Seeing as we're stuck in this little place for a while, and there's nothing we can do about it,' he said, holding the cigar away from his face and blowing smoke at the burning end of it to ignite the embers, 'why not have a story? You're a gatherer of tales in this town, I hear, Daniel.'

He watched me stutter for a few seconds, and then put his hands behind his head and puffed the cigar thoughtfully before taking it out again.

'All right, let me tell *you* one,' he said. 'It's called . . .'

THE ACT

As he waited in the wings, Mr Finch fidgeted, sweat ran down his back and the puppet in his arms felt unbearably heavy, as though he'd been carrying it for a lifetime. He moved nervously from foot to foot as he waited to go on. He did his act eight times a week – every day and twice on Saturdays – but the nerves never got any better.

At last the three actors on stage finished their performance of *The Murder in the Red Barn*, threw their props into a box and bowled off the stage. They had stirred the crowd into a frenzy, and the spectators were clapping, shouting, laughing and throwing handfuls of bruised fruit and rotting meat on to the stage. Just as Mr Finch was about to step on stage, the lead actor, who had played the hero, the policeman, the heroine, the heroine's mother and a rogue piano tuner bounded back on to the stage for an encore. He placed the hero's top hat on his head – the crowd roared approval. He replaced it with the policeman's helmet and they jeered. Then the bonnet of the heroine – they wolf-whistled and whooped with glee. At last he slipped on the flat cap of the villain, and adopted his crafty smile. The audience howled with hatred, and a mouldy cabbage hit him in the face, nearly knocking him over. Finally he reeled off into the wings, wiping his face and laughing as other projectiles landed behind him.

Mr Finch counted to five to let the crowd calm down. A last few blackened carrots bounced across the floorboards and the laughter died away. Finch's heart gave a final bu-bump, and he stepped out into the light.

As usual, the audience were instantly struck silent, for he cut such an odd appearance. A tall, hesitant man with a nervous smile and wide eyes, he looked at first like someone who had simply wandered on by accident. Then they noticed the puppet in his arms.

It was quite large, about the size of a five-year-old boy, and its legs hung over Mr Finch's right arm. On its cheeks were painted bright red circular spots, such as would never appear on any real boy's face, and its eyes were perfectly round and much too large to be lifelike. And so, when the puppet blinked, and looked up at Mr Finch, the crowd gasped.

'Go on!' squeaked the dummy. 'Talk!'

Mr Finch started, and looked down at the dummy, as though its coming to life was the last thing he had expected.

'Speak, numbskull!' cried the dummy again. 'What are you dithering for?' The crowd began to titter.

'Look at him!' bawled the dummy, gesturing at the embarrassed-looking man. 'He doesn't know what day it is!' Mr Finch continued to open and shut his mouth as though lost for words.

'I'll have to introduce myself, if this halfwit can't do it!' said the dummy. 'My name's Mr Boyster, and I'd be one half of a successful theatre act if I wasn't stuck with him!' Here he jerked his head derisively up at Mr Finch, who looked rather hurt.

'Oh, don't be like that!' Mr Boyster cried at him.

'We both know what you're like. He tried to go fishing last week and got the hook caught on his own collar. Thought he'd caught a whopper – reeled himself in and knocked himself out with a club before I could stop 'im! Glad I caught him in time or he would've fried himself up for supper and served himself with chips!'

Mr Finch began to relax into his routine. Another five minutes of Mr Boyster insulting him, and then they would sing a famous nursery rhyme together. Mr Finch would forget all the words and the dummy would insert increasingly horrible insults between the sickly-sweet lyrics. Finally losing his temper, Mr Boyster would pull his hand from his pocket revealing a toy gun, with which (accompanied by a bang on the drum from the orchestra pit) he would shoot Mr Finch. Shot to death, the man would then stagger offstage, the dummy still singing in his arms. It was the best part of the act, and always got a round of applause.

Feeling for a moment that all was going to plan, Finch felt a swell of relief and broke his cardinal rule. He looked at the audience. He saw the outline of a man sitting perfectly still three or four rows back and thought (it was hard to make out in the gloom beyond the gas lamps at the foot of the stage) he saw a figure sitting in his lap, a figure staring back up at him with wide, round white eyes. Mr Boyster temporarily forgot his words before the ventriloquist's attention snapped back to his routine. He concentrated fiercely after that, and didn't give another thought to the audience.

*

As he came off stage with the sound of the clapping behind him, Mr Finch dropped into a chair, exhausted.

'Well done, darling,' said one of the dancing girls who queued up next to him, 'You were marvy.'

He nodded his thanks and smiled. The combination of tiredness and excitement made him for a few minutes light-headed and happy. He clumped down the rickety stairs to the dressing rooms and, drawing his curtain behind him, pulled the dummy off his arm so he could stretch out and get the feeling back.

Instead of throwing the dummy to one side as he would like to, he forced himself to walk into the shadows at the end of the room and place it carefully in its special oak box. There were other boxes piled up around it, overspilling with the abandoned costumes of dead and forgotten acts, and dusty cloaks hanging from hooks that loomed over him. As he turned away from putting Mr Boyster to rest he always felt a little shudder. The theatre is a terrible breeding ground for superstitions of every kind, and at this moment every day Mr Finch had the same sharp sense of terror – that Mr Boyster would speak to him, from his box.

Back in front of his mirror, Finch washed his face from a fresh basin of water until all the make-up was gone, and then slipped out of the dressing room to join the dancing girls, the actors, Dr Sinarius the snake charmer and Eric the Enormous Imbecile in the bar.

Accepting a goblet of vinegary wine, he settled back

175

to listen to the happy bubbly conversation of the others. As the first sip of wine tingled on his lips (it might very well actually *be* vinegar, he thought) he noticed an odd sight: that of the theatre manager, Mr Treacle, in earnest discussion with another fellow. Although only the back of his head was visible to Finch, the sight of this man tickled him with an uneasy recollection that he couldn't quite place: he was just a very ordinary-looking bald man who carried a bulky object in his arms.

Have you ever had that feeling that you think you recognize someone at a distance, but aren't quite sure, and instead of calling out, you simply try to move and catch a better look of them? But no matter how you twist your head, with some kind of magical intuition they turn to keep their features hidden from you, until they finally disappear leaving you more frustrated than ever (and leaving your friends looking at you as though you are slightly mad)? This is exactly what happened to Mr Finch in the small, crowded bar at this moment, and yet he had no notion why he thought he knew the man. Telling himself he was quite superstitious enough already without starting to attract funny looks in public, he resolved to forget about the stranger.

Instead he sipped his drink and listened to Dr Sinarius and Eric the Enormous Imbecile argue about their wages, as Sinarius's snake slithered around two of the dancing girls' shoulders, dipped its head to the bar and lapped with closed eyes at its nightly tipple of port.

When Mr Finch reached home at midnight, he found his landlady sitting on the stairs, waiting for him. She was a miserable-looking woman with a face that looked like it was made from porridge and a body the shape of a bowling ball. And for some reason she hated Finch even more than her other tenants. This was possibly because he was timid, and she could get away with being horrible to him, as that's just the sort of person she was.

'Oh, it's you, Arnold,' she said in a tone of disgust. 'Home late as usual. My God, you look awful.'

This was probably true. For the act he performed nightly at the cramped, flea-pit theatre, Arnold Finch earned barely enough to pay his rent and feed himself. And the nerves he suffered ate away at his figure so that he always seemed pale and emaciated. Naturally timid, he blushed furiously at being insulted in this way, and had no words to say back. His landlady, sensing that she'd hurt his feelings, leaned over the banisters to peer at him.

'I see you're carrying that . . . that *thing*.' Speaking with a sneer that was half disgusted and half fearful, she pointed at Mr Boyster, who rested on Finch's arm.

'I am not a *thing*, Mrs Futtiker,' muttered the whiny voice, through his wooden smiling mouth. 'And you need not talk to Mr Finch in that way. He's paid you your rent, has he not?'

'Don't make him talk to me!' said the landlady,

retreating behind the banisters with queasy horror. 'Don't do it, Arnold, you filthy beast! You know I hate it!' She stood up and went back up the stairs, huffing with the effort, to the landing above.

'But, Mrs Futtiker,' said the dummy reasonably, as Finch began to walk up the stairs towards her, 'what can you possibly have against me?'

She stared down at him as he came up slowly, step by step. She met the dead eyes of the dummy, and she quivered for a moment before overcoming her fear. 'I'm just waiting for the chance,' she whispered. 'The second you don't pay your rent you're *out*. You understand me? You theatre folk are all the same – drunks, immoral, feckless. God knows there's no other boarding house that'll have you, and then you'll *starve*! It's what you deserve!'

'Just try it,' suggested Mr Boyster in a cold and measured tone. The landlady leered at them both for a moment and then barged away down the narrow corridor, her flabby hips knocking clouds of dust from the banisters.

Finch watched as she went out of sight, and her door slammed.

Mr Boyster twisted his head to look up at Mr Finch. He nodded at the door behind which she had disappeared. 'Fatso,' he said quietly.

As he went up the seven remaining flights of stairs to his rooms, Finch saw the other guests were at home, just as they usually were. There was Claude, the drunken chef, who had left his door wide open and snored so loudly it sounded like a cobble rolling down a corrugated iron roof; there was the Reverend Shanker, who smoked opium in his dressing gown and dictated poetry to his cat (who took not the slightest bit of notice); there was a frail and pretty girl called Petulia, who sat looking out wistfully from the third-floor balcony, grieving for her latest love affair and dipping her fingers in candle wax; there was a band of musicians practising some terrible racket in the room below Mr Finch's, and an enthusiastic troupe of actors rehearsing *Titus Andronicus* on the roof above.

As he reached his room Finch checked to see if there was any cold porridge in the saucepan. His heart sank. There was not. He'd have to wait until morning to eat now. He sat on the small bed and faced the mirror. Alone again, he couldn't help his worries returning. It was true that if he was thrown out of here, there was nowhere else he could live – all the other boarding houses were too expensive for him. His theatre was the only one in Tumblewater, and he knew it was of such a run-down and lowly character that his act would never be good enough for anywhere else. And there was no other job he knew how to do. Every night this same doubt beset him – that should anything cause him to lose his job, he was dead.

That was why, even though he had performed it thousands of times, just before he went on stage every night he was attacked by a terrifying fit of nerves.

And that was also why he now forced himself to sit up straight on the bed, fetch Mr Boyster into his arms again, and practise his act, over and over, making sure he had it perfect, until at last, some time after two in the morning, he succumbed to tiredness, and fell asleep where he sat, the dummy slipping down to sleep like a cat, curled up in his lap.

When the daylight fell on his closed eyes early the next morning, waking him up, Mr Finch crawled under the covers and tried to sleep some more. But it was no good. He screwed his eyes shut tight and tried to force himself back to sleep but the nerves had already set in, and he was already worrying about tonight's perform-ance.

He got up and put a handful of oats in the saucepan with a splash of rainwater from the tin he left outside his window. He could not afford a stove so he lit a can-dle and held the saucepan over it, stirring the mixture, until at last (after an hour or so) porridge was formed. Then he opened his window, perched carefully between the sprouting weeds that grew out of the grit between the bricks, and ate his breakfast. He saw people hur-rying to and fro beneath him on the street, and so he chewed the tasteless porridge, tried to work out for the thousandth time how he could spend the day without spending any money, and without worrying too much about his act.

*

That evening people bustled back and forth at the back of the theatre. The dancing girls were nervously wishing each other good luck and making adjustments to their costumes; Vladimir the knife thrower was absent-mindedly sharpening all the blades in his case, one by one, in a way that didn't exactly soothe people's nerves.

Mr Finch climbed down the steep staircase to the row of tiny dressing rooms, then stopped in dismay. His dressing room was the one small space in the crammed and hectic passageways where he could be alone, and concentrate. The one rule of those narrow cubicles was that if the curtain was drawn across they should never be invaded. That was sacrosanct. For over three years Mr Finch's had been the fourth one along. And yet now, its curtain was drawn.

A few actors came tumbling down the stairs and ran past him, tripping over some boxes and laughing, and an opera singer leaned disapprovingly out to bellow a famous aria after them in a Latin tongue. Mr Finch moved his head close to his curtain. Now the opera singer had calmed down, he couldn't hear the tiniest sound from within. It was very tempting to draw it back, but so strict was the rule among the people of the theatre, he couldn't do it, even though it was supposed to be his dressing room.

Casting looks back over his shoulder all the way, he retreated up the stairs, through the busy backstage and slipped into the theatre, where the audience were already in their seats. He sat down, resting his bag under his seat, and hoped not to attract attention to himself before it was time for him to go on stage. In fact, as the bustle grew around him, so did the warmth of the room, so that, leaning back in his seat, soon he found it hard to keep his eyes open and felt the tiredness of the day pulling them shut, and his head spinning with the first delicious moment of dreaminess before sleep.

He woke with a gasp some time later, wondering where he was. People around him were laughing, and he could only see a brightly lit stage, on which a man was performing with a puppet. He turned left and right in his seat, then realized where he was.

On stage was a bald, pale man in a dark suit who carried on his arm a porcelain dummy. The dummy was a little girl, just the same size as Mr Boyster, but with a patterned dress, bigger eyes, bigger red spots painted on her cheeks – and freckles too. It was this little dummy that was doing all the talking. She was singing, in fact.

He shook his head for a moment to rid it of his sleepy confusion, and then felt a cold feeling in his stomach. Mr Finch realized it was the song that *he* normally sang at the end of *his* act – or rather, that Mr Boyster did.

'Come on, idiot!' squeaked the dummy at the bald man, as he forgot a line.

'Keep up, fool!' it bellowed, to the crowd's delight. 'You'd forget your own brain!'

But that's *my* joke, thought Finch. That's what *I* do! Seated among the laughter, surrounded by it, Finch saw what a good act it was. It was clever, ridiculous, silly, absurd – everything that the crowd wanted! He couldn't look at the stage any more, and grabbing the bag with Mr Boyster he fumbled along the seats past the knees of the laughing people, and then rushed backstage.

None of his fellow performers seemed to notice the horrible crime that was being committed right in front of them! In fact, no one noticed or spoke to Mr Finch at all. He even had to jump out of the way of the girls on their way up to the stage for their performance. Normally they would wave and say hello, invite him to kiss them on the cheek for good luck. Now it was as if they didn't even see him.

Mr Finch's anxiety was back, but this time it was different, more biting, more intense. The only thing he owned – stolen. He wouldn't be able to perform his act ever again! His jokes would feel like poison on his lips now he'd heard them on the lips of the thief. Mrs Futtiker was right. He would be on the street in the morning – or by the end of the week, anyhow. He put his hands over his eyes to try and push the unfairness of it all from his mind, until he heard a couple of steps and a swishing sound behind him.

The noise came from his dressing room, and he saw now that its curtain was moving slightly. Instinctively, as though gathering a friend close to him, he pulled Mr Boyster on to his arm and stole over to the curtain. There was the shuffling sound of clothes being removed, and the thump of an object being set down, then a sigh like someone relaxing after a hard exertion. Finch became certain this must be the man he had just seen on stage.

At that moment, his eyes fell on the case of Vladimir's throwing knives, which had been left in the corridor. A grim and overpowering compulsion overtook him. No longer thinking for himself, but only with his towering fury, he picked up a knife and pushed the curtain back with its tip. Walking inside he let the curtain fall back behind him, and saw, as he expected, the bald man sitting at the chair in front of the mirror, his scalp illuminated by candlelight.

The sight of the knife-wielding Mr Finch must have transfixed the bald man, because he did not move or flinch as Mr Finch's image grew larger and larger in the mirror before him. The terror of the knife struck him so still that he didn't even blink.

'That's right,' growled Mr Boyster, from Finch's arm. 'Now you know what the consequence is, of stealing another man's livelihood.'

Still the other fellow refused to speak or move.

'What do you say?' muttered Mr Boyster. 'Defend yourself, man!'

But the bald man made no move, and with his temper flaring Finch stepped even closer. He looked once more into the mirror and saw again the bald man's clear, guiltless eyes, and finally gave into his abominable anger.

He leaped forward, Mr Boyster's mouth clicking

open and shut with a ghastly cry, and as he stood back again, he saw the dagger stuck between the other man's shoulders, right up to the hilt.

His anger suddenly gone, Finch listened keenly for any noise outside the dressing room. Far away, he could hear a roaring crowd in the auditorium. One of the comedy acts must be on stage. It was quite possible no one had heard Mr Boyster's cry at all.

He looked again at the knife, and a hundred thoughts flashed in his head. The chief and most dreadful of these was: how *easy* it had been, to murder a man! The knife had slipped in as easily as though it was cutting through straw. He leaned forward to retrieve it now, and even as he pulled it back he realized how stupid he was being. He was bound to get blood everywhere, and tell-tale stains on himself.

But he watched in speechless surprise as the knife came free in his hand, and the bald man's body tipped forward and leaned against the desk. Not with the heavy slump of a dead man, but quite stiffly, as though rigor mortis had set in at the moment of death. Feeling a weird curiosity, Finch stepped forward, closer to him. He could see the man's eyes were *still* open, and wondered if *his own* eyes could be deceiving him.

Then he looked beneath the desk, and saw the man had no legs at all.

There came a fluttery rustle of fabric from the corner of the dressing room, like a cloak falling off a peg. Finch swivelled his head. He could see nothing back there except the ever-present pile of garments that overshadowed that corner of the room.

And the bright, round eyes of the little girl dummy, shining out.

The eyes blinked at him. He dropped the knife and it bounced near his feet, quite without the merest trace of blood. And from the shadows a shape cautiously stepped forward.

The whole ceramic dummy seemed to dangle in mid-air, and yet stare at him with human eyes, in an utterly terrifying manner. But two feet shuffled forward on the floor, in shiny gentleman's shoes. And two legs, in smart trousers.

Finch couldn't speak, couldn't think of a single word. Mr Boyster rattled on his arm as he shook. Because now Finch saw the legs and the face belonged to each other – they were connected by a horribly twisted spine, so that the face was only at arm height. And he saw that, while the arms and legs of the puppet were made from white porcelain, the face was that of a real woman, caked in make-up so thick it looked like china.

Now the face, which was painted in a smile, turned to a scowl, and the make-up cracked like a shattered mirror. Finch could not stand it any more. He turned and stumbled out of the room, and as he ran he dropped Mr Boyster – and saw his porcelain head smash open on the stone floor. He tried to cry out, in horror, shock and sadness, but he couldn't – he just pulled the curtain back, and ran out into the night.

hen he had finished the tale, Inspector Rambull took up his cigar again, which he had allowed to go out. His sense of gloating enjoyment had lasted well into the story, when it had been replaced by genuine excitement at his tale.

Not for the first time, I wondered if there was anyone in Tumblewater who wasn't a natural teller of horrible tales. And I reflected still more ruefully that this was one I would gladly include in my second collection, if I lived to have a chance to write it, which seeing as the Chief of Police was here, was very unlikely.

Except . . . something about our situation didn't add up. I couldn't work out what it was, but as jubilant as he had been at first in crowing over us, Rambull now seemed to settle into a relatively sombre mood. In fact the fat man seemed content to sit there in silence forever, without explaining anything to us at all.

It was Uncle who finally broke. 'I don't understand it. The only people I told about the disguises were our most trusted men, our inner circle. So you have penetrated even that. My only question is, why have you waited so long to capture us – and why put yourself at risk among us like this?'

Rambull let the silence continue a while, and then put his hands inside his cloak – and I thought, this is it: I've brought all four of my favourite people in the Underground to their end. But in his fingers was no weapon, just another cigar. With his spare hand he flicked a match alight and held it up until the cigar was lit. Certainly, this man knew how to play it cool.

'I would say that you are indeed in an amount of trouble,' he said, and coughed, and cleared his throat. 'I don't know that I've ever seen a group of people in so deep. Your chances are –' he puffed on the cigar – 'slim. Maybe I should explain how I came to be here with you.'

The fat man sat up slowly and Uncle and I returned to our seats, watching him. Rambull blew smoke rings out over the canal water, and coughed some more. The others had in the meantime found their hunger and unfurled the canvas sacks we'd brought with us. They were handing out chunks of bread and cheese and ham, and passing round oval canteens of water and little bottles of rum.

Rambull tore his portion of bread in half with his teeth and started explaining, while chewing through what looked like half a loaf. His huge brown eyes fell on me as he ruminated.

'You've seen that Creature, the red-haired one?'

I nodded. 'How could I have not seen her?'

'She was brought in by Mr Caspian Prye with one purpose and one alone: to catch you.'

I felt a cold, dead feeling run over me, as though I had just heard my own sentence of death. 'But why would you warn me?' The second I spoke the words I regretted it, because it begged the answer: It doesn't matter, you're hers now anyway.

But Rambull surprised me. 'I'm not a gentleman, by any stretch. The law is tough and you've got to be tough to enforce it. I'm sure it makes its mistakes, but where we would be without it? Well now, I'm getting from my point.' He mopped his brow with the back of his hand. 'I suppose I'm saying I've been no gentleman when it comes to treating criminals, and I've felt no need to repent for that. You lot don't like me and that's just the way it should be. But these last months I've seen innocent families killed in the name of the law. A good man can be led astray and do bad things, and he will deserve punishment. But there aren't crimes enough in this whole city for the number of people who've been executed. The law is tough, as I say. And life is tough too, and unfair sometimes. But even me – even I – I get my grammar mixed up. I've had no learning...'

I saw that he wasn't stuttering over simple language, but was trying to conceal his feelings. And I felt the most unexpected emotion I could have imagined – I felt *sorry* for this terrible brute, as he tried to cover up the sadness he felt. He blustered over words, and coughed, and relit his cigar, and at last got control of his voice, and went on.

'At the end I had to admit I watched people hanged

who had done nothing wrong. And saw how I had helped it happen.' He went quiet again; we all watched him. 'I couldn't stay,' he said. 'I had to escape. But not just escape – it's wrongdoing I hate, and if they have been doing wrong, the police . . . well, then I have to stay, and help stamp out that wrongdoing.'

For all his physical might and his gruffness, he had delivered his explanation humbly. I guessed it was as close to an apology or a confession as he would ever come, but it moved us all. And, in the back of our minds, it made us stronger in our mission – that he, who had been such an implacable foe, knew we were right. A tiny victory against the massive force against us.

We all thought about these things, and in the silence Rambull explained how he had found us. 'I began planning to come down here. I knew from my informants that there was some sort of society underground. I could never have guessed at the amazing things you have down here. Just yesterday I had a haircut and got my shoes mended better than they were when I bought them.

'I went missing from my job; I lay down in dank holes among the rats, and went without sleep and food. My only need was to remain completely unknown. But by and by, talking to the tramps and street vendors, I couldn't help running into old criminals I had arrested. To my amazement, instead of wanting to kill me, the act of seeing me brought so low made them friendly and welcoming, as though we had something in common. It was something I had never wanted from anybody before, but on this occasion it moved my heart to see that – well, maybe criminals are ordinary persons too, and don't necessarily mean to be bad. It may sound like a simple thing to you folks, but was quite a revelation to me.

'So I started to keep with my old contacts and hear news from around the tunnels. When I heard about this raid, and a chance to get back at those who are doing wrong in the name of the law, I couldn't deny myself that privilege. And now I'm here, among you,' said the fat man. 'This is where I live. And I'll do anything I can to help.'

We ate and we waited for the quarantine period to finish, when Uncle decided the first urgency of the search would be over, and it was safe for us to emerge into the tunnels. We drank the rum, exchanged stories, argued and played cards on the little table. Not a single minute passed when I didn't look through the layers of pipe-smoke that filled the room at Inspector Rambull, and wonder at the sight of him, shrouded in his cloak like a black iceberg, and the change in him.

It felt incredible to be at last in the presence of the Apothecary, a weathered, swarthy-faced man of deep and serious demeanour who looked on edge in the company of other people. He had a much softer voice than I had expected. Between the games of cards we tried to explain to him about the Underground but somehow he seemed to know a lot about it already. Even so, as we described how big it was, about the schools, the hospitals, the fact it was a whole society, he became impressed.

It killed me not to be able to talk to him about Maria. Of course I wanted to desperately, but even the smallest whisper echoed annoyingly in our strange little chamber. I was far from trusting the ex-Inspector Rambull and could do nothing anyway until we were out of this room, so I pushed questions about the key and Maria out of my head until I could speak to the Apothecary alone.

The evening and night crawled past, followed by a dull hollow noise as the metal lid in the ceiling was lifted away. Nuala's smiling face peered down at us.

'They said you'd done it,' she said. 'But I didn't believe them.'

'Stop chinwagging, woman, and get a ladder down here!' bellowed Rambull, and her face disappeared as quickly as it had come, only to be replaced by the instrument he had asked for, which came down so fast it nearly hit him on the chin.

In a minute we were out of the hole and walking the tunnels, Nuala and Uncle talking together behind us and Josephine up ahead, almost skipping with glee.

'You won't believe what's been going on,' she said. My thoughts were so taken up with my sister I had no idea what she could mean, or why (aside from the rescue of the Apothecary, which as far as I knew had been kept absolutely secret) she was so happy. I vaguely remembered overhearing Uncle remark that our rescue of the Apothecary, whether successful or not, would be a major diversion, and almost every other crew in the Underground would use this opportunity to go on raids. It turned out these had *all* been successful. 'There's never been anything like it – no one needs to go hungry tonight. I think there's going to be a party . . .'

As she said this we reached the mouth of a tunnel which looked down on a large thoroughfare that led down to the deeper places below. I was confronted with a sight I hadn't seen before in the Underground. The whole road was packed from side to side with huge numbers of people travelling downward, and all of them in the highest of spirits, children skipping in the gaps between the adults and songs being sung by whole groups, many of whom carried crates and hampers over their shoulders or, in the case of the heavier loads, over the shoulders of six strong men and women, in the style of a coffin.

Josephine climbed down the ladder to join the throng, calling up to me.

'Fruit! Jam! Bread! Meat! Wine!' she shouted. 'Toys, clothes, sweets, books! BOOKS!' And she was so happy that she disappeared dancing into the crowd and left us to find our own way.

It was indeed quite a fantastic feeling. The ordinary mood of the Underground had been totally turned upon its head, and from every side more people poured down from other chambers and hidden places, like blood pumping fast through the veins of a body out of sheer joy.

The whole group from the kidnapping assembled at the bottom of the ladder and then set off in the same direction as the crowd. The mood around us was almost dreamlike, yet it was as weird as a happy dream can be, if a happy dream could ever take place in such a strange and dark place.

I had mixed feelings, now that my relief about Rambull was wearing off. It wasn't as though we had won the war – far from it. Caspian Prye was still in charge of Tumblewater. Maria was still in deadly peril. I couldn't relax until she was free, so this jollity felt wrong. I was desperate to get the Apothecary on his own and ask him about the key – but if I asked him here in the middle of a crowd and they got wind of who we were, we could be swamped by well-wishers and I could be separated from him for precious hours.

As we reached the bottom of the tunnel, beneath us spread out the site of the celebration. It was a cavern of huge size, larger than any building I'd ever seen above ground. It was perhaps the very centre of the sewer system, where the mouths of six or seven enormous tunnels opened on to a wide platform beneath a curved stone ceiling. There was a wide stone floor on which festivities were proceeding, and beyond that there was simply a drop into darkness, into which plunged powerful torrents from two giant bore-holes, one on either side.

On the stone floor was gathered a great spectacle of

celebration. As I had followed the crowds in the tunnels it seemed crazy to me for them to celebrate such an empty victory. But now I saw it, I understood: even if they didn't live out the night, they were going to enjoy themselves, and that made perfect sense.

If ever I had wondered who made up the population of the Underground, here was the answer. People of every type were moving among each other, talking, shouting and exchanging stories. In every direction there was much drinking, smoking, eating and dancing. From the torches on the walls and the bonfires scattered around the huge stone platform, I could see that most if not all of them were in torn and dirty clothes. There were people hobbling on sticks and lying on makeshift stretchers, but they joined in as much as anyone else, invalids smiling and laughing as they had drinks tipped to their lips, one-legged men good-naturedly playing the ogre for groups of shrieking children. And the 'pupils' from the school were there too, hundreds of boys and girls, handing out rations from the boxes and baskets they'd looted, and joining in the revelry.

And then there was food. The scattering of fast-burning fires was not just for warmth: each was being used to cook a dozen or more foods that were being handed out from hampers. Baked potatoes on skewers, big cauldrons of bubbling stew, haunches of pork and lamb with the leaking fat spitting up jets of flame around them, hot acorns, pans of eggs and bacon. In the corner nearest me two Indian ladies carefully tended a deep pot in which they stirred a rich, tantalizing curry. A third woman rolled out discs of dough with her hands and tenderly placed them on the surface of a stone among the embers, where they suddenly puffed up into little breads in a matter of seconds.

'My God!' said Rambull from behind me, sounding thunderstruck. I turned and looked up into his face and saw all its grave authority had vanished, replaced by the look of an excited schoolboy.

'*Curry!* I haven't had a good curry for fifteen YEARS! Out of my way, boy!' And, nearly toppling me over the edge of the tunnel into the crowd twenty feet below, he scampered down the metal rungs that were hammered into the stone, and launched through the crowd to make friends with the Indian women.

The others went past me and climbed down eagerly to enjoy their feast, until only the Apothecary remained. The smell of food and sound of revelry, the sight of people dancing on a stage, and others performing comedy acts, the sight of sparklers and fireworks and the sound of cheap guitars and violins and whistles and drums sending up a horrible but joyous medley, had no effect on me whatsoever.

'We need to talk,' said the man standing next to me, through the long hair that masked his face. I saw Uncle mingling in the crowd below, accepting a tin cup of ale from someone, having a joke whispered in his ear and laughing – at once he looked twenty years younger, and that made me smile, at least. I looked up at the Apothecary.

'First things first,' I said. 'I've known you as the Apothecary all this time. But now you're here it seems rude to call you that.'

Unexpectedly he bowed, and holding out one of his bony hands he knelt in front of me and said with a noble air, 'I am Arch-Apothecair Elect to the now deceased Lords of the Northlands. My family name is Wallsam Guthric-Earch Hannibar of the Sannovites, son of Hanric.'

I blinked, and looked around awkwardly while he raised himself back to his full height. 'OK,' I said. 'Then I might call you, er . . . Wally?'

He itched his nose. 'I'd rather not that, actually. That was what they called me at school. Call me Guthric.'

'Of course,' I said.

He sat down on a wooden crate. 'Now, all I know, young man, is that there is an evil here and – well, brace yourself, because this is going to sound pretty vague – that you and I are pieces of the puzzle. I know we are connected by Gora the witch, who is dead. And that I am supposed to help you. But that's all I know.'

'It's all right, I think I know,' I said. 'It's got something to do with this.' Pulling the key from around my neck, I handed it to him.

He hefted it in his hand once or twice and handed it back to me. 'I have the answer.' He smiled.

'And . . . ?' I gasped.

'It's a key.'

I kicked him about as hard as I could, just below the knee.

'OWWWW!' he shouted, hopping away from me.

'Sorry,' I said, not very apologetically.

'I was only joking. *God!*' He hopped around for a few seconds before settling down on a stool, taking his knee in one hand and holding the key up in the other. He frowned and turned it around in his hands for a few moments, as though he was suspicious of it.

After a while I was too nervous to watch him deliberate, so I concentrated on the throng below. At least *they* were laughing, singing, and dancing like they were—

My thoughts were cut off by a most expected sound. A deep boom, like that of a giant door slamming shut. More booms echoed down into the chamber below from each of the holes in the walls, one by one, brother-and-sister echoes of the same blast. For a moment the crowd hushed, and heads looked up. But it would take more to distract them on this night of nights, and quickly they began talking again, the musicians started up, someone laughed, and a firework was set off, scorching up into the air and making some young children scream with delighted fear.

The original noise was forgotten, but Guthric and I looked at each other fearfully. 'What was that?' he asked.

'I don't know . . .' I said. His fear was worse than mine – he'd never been trapped in tunnels so deep before, and didn't like not knowing the way out. But it affected me too. The sound was full of menace. It had travelled possibly all the way down from the surface, and who knew what explosion had caused it. It worried me that the Undergrounders were too distracted to investigate it.

'I'll tell you what,' he commented, holding up the key. 'I think I've remembered what this is.'

'*What?*' I asked desperately.

'I haven't seen one for a long, long time, and it took me a minute to recognize it. But it's no good telling you,' he said. 'I have to show you. Take me back to the surface, to the banks of the river, by Blackstone Bridge.'

We set off at once towards the surface. It was a cheerless and ghostly trek back through the passages that so recently had been crammed with life. For the first time we saw them, in the light of the occasional torch or lamp, as they were meant to be. Quiet, dripping, empty, full of silence. Mud and stones on the floor, walls covered with moss and lichen, broken only by the stalls and huts that humans had put up on either side.

It was a long walk, yet my excitement made light work of it.

'So you have no idea where my sister might be?' I asked. 'After all, you knew Gora the witch better than anyone.'

He shook his head. 'She did not allow people to know her. If she hid something it would remain hidden no matter what – unless she deliberately left some personal token. That's why the key's so important. No one knew

this place like her, or had been here so long . . . except . . .'
He trailed off, as though surprised by a sudden memory.

'Except the Monk?'

He flinched. 'Please, Daniel, don't be silly. The
Monk is just a silly story to scare children. Even people
who have practised magic for hundreds of years like
me don't think he exists, or ever did. Come on, let's
keep moving . . .'

He set off up the tunnel again ahead of me. 'It almost
feels as though someone called the Apothecary is being
superstitious,' I muttered. 'Talking of which, don't
turn right. That leads eventually to the Sharp-Toothed-
Rat-Ridden Cave of Absolutely Certain Death, if I'm
not mistaken. Straight on!'

We still had a way to go, and as we walked we
discussed the tales I had gathered in Tumblewater, and
told each other a few stories.

'I've remembered another one!' said Guthric
excitedly. 'It's a cracker.'

'Go on!' I said, gasping slightly as I clambered over
some rocks. I could tell he wouldn't be rushed into
giving me any more information until we arrived at our
destination, so it wouldn't hurt to hear his addition to
my collection of grisly tales in the meantime. 'I'd love
to hear it,' I said.

'All right,' he said. 'You might have heard another
version of this tale, but I was told this by an eighty-
year-old woman with a taste for wine. I hope you like it
as much as I do. It's called . . .'

THE MISER

While it is true to say that the continuing rain upon Tumblewater Hill, its perpetual soddenness, sogginess and the smell of mould, depressed most people, this wasn't true for everyone. Some liked it, even revelled in it, for whatever reasons of their own, and none liked it more than Zephaniah Crump.

For Zephaniah Crump was a miser. You may not know exactly what a miser is, because they are an uncommon sort of creature, but Zephaniah was as good an example of one as could be found.

Firstly, he hated spending money. He guarded what money he had with his life (keeping it in a locked steel box behind the bath) and hated spending it so much that whenever he paid anyone so much as a penny he would screw his eyes shut as though it caused him physical pain. Secondly, and more importantly, he hated pretty much everything and everyone. Nothing afforded him more happiness than seeing someone fall over in the street, or a poor family being thrown out of their house into the rain. This meant that his life was a very solitary one, which was all right by him. And thirdly, of course, he adored the rain, and the gloom and despondency that had settled in the grey streets ever since it had started.

As a miser loathes surprises above all things, over the years Zephaniah had settled into a routine with which he was very comfortable, and from which he never wavered in the tiniest detail. So, one Monday morning, as always, he set out with his dog, a nervous Dalmatian called Cheapcold, from his rooms on the ground floor of a shady and neglected tenement. He walked down a few short streets, enduring as he did insincere greetings from local nincompoops – the Lazenby sisters, a dribbling imbecile by the name of Albert Koney and some woman with curly hair and a fine new cape at whom he stared rudely to show that they didn't know each other. When he reached the newspaper seller he screwed his eyes shut as he paid for his copy of the *Bugle*, a weekly newspaper whose old-fashioned views offended him less than any other publication.

When he returned home he read it from cover to cover, making notes in a black leather notebook as he went, and circling certain articles and notices with his thin, scratchy pen.

Then, when he had finished, he opened his desk and, with the newspaper folded in front of him, he set about writing the letters which would take up the rest of the day.

'Dear Mr Bastable,' read the first. 'I read today that the sensible plans to close Tumblewater's post office have been shelved. This is an OUTRAGE. It is a haven for despicable layabouts of the lowest order, a breeding-ground for disease and an appalling threat to public order and health. It must be destroyed! As my local Member of Parliament, abandoning this admirable scheme marks you out for what you are. A blackguard! A scoundrel! And a charlatan! Your immediate resignation and exile would hardly heal the wound of this offence. Yours, as ever, Z. Crump.'

When he had finished, an hour later (for he was a very slow writer and picked his words carefully), Zephaniah stretched his arms and let out a long, satisfied sigh. Then he settled to write his second letter.

'Dear Mr Purlikew,' it read. 'I discover in today's newspaper that you plan to install a "soup kitchen" (hateful phrase!) to serve the poor and destitute in our neighbourhood. As an upstanding resident I speak for all of Slipstream Lane when I say that we are beyond speech with horror at the thought of hundreds of vaga-bonds queuing, spitting, stealing things, making lewd remarks and poisoning our air with their repulsive odour. We do not want our street becoming a home for tramps, drunkards and decadents. As you are the town mayor, I insist you cease this plan at once, or GOD WILL BE YOUR JUDGE! Yours, as ever, Z. Crump.'

He saved his favourite letter for last.

'Dear Madame Ornaldo,' it read. 'I have read this morning that you intend to bring your opera company to our great city. I feel I must warn you that this will be a catastrophe.' Here Zephaniah broke off to reach for his dictionary (which was tattered from use and almost as old as he was) to check how to spell 'catastrophe'. 'Our citizens,' he went on, when he had corrected it, 'are entirely indifferent to this ridiculous warbly-voiced music, and would probably rather throw themselves into the river than ever go to one of your concerts. With affectionate concern, Yours, Z. Crump.'

*

On the Wednesday, as he always did, he set out for a walk with Cheapcold shortly after lunch. First he found a trustworthy local lad who was nice enough to post his letters for him without expecting a penny as reward, and then he kept walking until he reached the Courts of Justice. He climbed the steps of the magnificent and imposing building with its giant pillars of stone, passed through the great arched doors and found his way to Court Number One.

'Just in time,' he muttered, as the policeman on guard opened the door for him, and he went in to find himself a seat in the front row of the public gallery, while Cheapcold nestled underneath to sleep.

Several winters ago Zephaniah had been told in grave tones by his doctor that his heart was beating too slowly, and that unless he was careful, one day it would stop entirely. The only thing to remedy this, the doctor said, was to find some vigorous and regular activity to keep the blood flowing around his old bones. Zephaniah had quickly found a solution that fitted his purposes wonderfully, which was to come to the courts each week and witness local criminals being convicted and sentenced. As a regular spectator he soon found that the most exciting sentencing took place in the court of Mr Justice Striker, a tiny old man who wore little glasses and a gentle, meek expression that blossomed into red-hot rage whenever faced with any type of defendant, even (and this satisfied Zephaniah especially) if they were very obviously innocent.

The first case today was a typical one. A lad arrested for stealing a loaf of bread from the nearby market was led into the court. His cap barely came over the side of the dock, and although he was bodily invisible the cap trembled, as if he were crying.

'Now,' said the judge. 'Your name is Tommy Groffin?'

'Yes, sir,' piped the boy, standing on tiptoes to show his face, 'I—'

'BE QUIET. And Officer Stanley caught you stealing this loaf?'

'Yes, sir, but I—'

'BE QUIET. You understand the punishment doled out to little thieves?'

'I do, sir – but, please, sir, I –'

'BE *QUIET*!' snapped the judge. 'There is clearly no need to involve a jury. I find you guilty. You shall pay a fine of three pounds or return for sentencing next week. You can expect at least a year's imprisonment. What have you to say?'

Had young Master Groffin been well-nourished enough to have any colour in his cheeks (which were only just visible even with him standing on tiptoes), it would have vanished completely at this moment. Trembling violently, he struggled to find any words at all. Finally he managed to speak.

'Please, sir,' he said, 'the baker said we could have it and pay next time. Then when I stepped out of his door he called for a policeman! My father is sick and we have no money. My mother needs the shillings I earn to feed my sisters, sir.'

'Then,' said the judge in a bored voice, without looking up from his papers, 'you will have a full calendar year to think about that. Count yourself lucky I do not increase your sentence for your disgusting lies. Take him down!' And he snapped his gavel down with such a crack that everyone in the gallery jumped, Cheapcold raised his head to look around, and Zephaniah felt an agreeable shiver run along his spine. He clapped furiously, his heart swelling with pride at this fine example of jurisprudence, and the blood flowing up and down his body like a young man's.

Shuffling his papers around, the judge's face returned to that of a humble and contented old man while Master Groffin was being led out, and remained like that until the next defendant took the dock, when it clouded over again at once. The court heard the case of Mr Richard Upwitch, a humble tailor's assistant who had found himself unable to pay the bills he owed to his butcher. This time the Hon. Mr Justice Striker was even more severe.

'Men who think the rules do not apply to them are the most dangerous of all!' he bellowed, his face a rich ruby colour. 'You deserve the worst that this court can give you! Presenting your case in front of a jury would be a waste of everyone's time. Guilty!'

Zephaniah could not contain his admiration for the

judge any longer and jumped up, shouting, 'Too right, judge! He's as bad as a murderer! Hang the brute!' and Cheapcold let out a bark of support. As he stood there, his fists clenched in righteous anger and spittle bubbling on his lips, it occurred to Zephaniah that he might have gone too far. The room had hushed, and Judge Striker peered upward over his spectacles to the public gallery.

'I shall be grateful,' said the judge quietly, 'if members of the public keep their thoughts to themselves.' In terror, Zephaniah threw himself back on to the hard bench and started coughing violently, and pointing accusingly at a rather fat, wide-eyed man to his right.

And so the day progressed. Zephaniah saw all sorts of terrible criminals sentenced and taken away for the safety of society, and he left with his heart beating as happily as a miser's heart could.

It was on the Friday that Zephaniah Crump encountered the first disturbance to his routine.

He rose early, as usual, and crept out to the stairwell holding a knife smeared with some butter. The little boy from upstairs, who was a cheeky little pest and deserved to be brought down a peg or two, was due to go to school any minute. With two quick swipes Zephaniah coated the seventh step with the butter, retreated to his apartment and watched through the crack in the door. A few moments later he heard the upstairs door shutting and the boy clattering downstairs. As Zephaniah caught sight of him, the boy's feet slipped and he tumbled like a sack of potatoes to the foot of the staircase.

Zephaniah put his hand over his mouth to stifle his giggles as the boy got to his feet, crying, and made off for school, leaving his packed lunch on the floor behind him. Closing the door, Zephaniah went to find his little notebook and beneath the inscription for last Friday (which read, 'Poured soot all over Mrs Mackery's washing. She very angry and upset!'), he scrawled, 'Slipped the little Bradbury boy up with butter. He burst into tears and dropped his lunch!'

There were inscriptions in his notebook going back many years, detailing all the practical jokes he had played on members of the public for his own amusement. Next to each was a number of ticks showing how satisfied he was with his work. Mrs Mackery's washing was worth two, but he could still hear the boy's sobs and they filled him with such delight that he placed three tidy little marks next to today's message. Then he went out to fetch the boy's lunch, and brought it inside. It was still Friday, after all, and that was practical joke day, so there was no reason he couldn't play another trick.

Untying the string from the brown paper package he saw an apple, a sandwich and a hunk of cheese. Good, he thought. Now I don't have to prepare my own lunch. He took out the food and went to his window to clip a tall sprig of holly from the bush that grew outside. He placed it inside the paper and bent it round carefully so it would spring out at the boy when he opened it, then retied the string. He put the package back exactly where it had landed, and retired to his apartment again to look forward to his lunch, have a little nap in his favourite chair, and wait for the boy to return.

While we watch him waiting for the boy, eating the sandwich with evident satisfaction, we might ask ourselves why people end up as misers. It is, after all, such a horrible thing to be.

Well, some of them are unhappy because they've only had bad luck and they think that's all others should have. And some are disappointed because they have always failed at things through their own fault, so they take happiness in other people being *un*happy. And still others are, simply, bad through and through – they always have been, and always will be. Which of these explained Zephaniah's predicament, we shall never know, only the sad fact that this was how he chose to live his life, and that is that.

Zephaniah did not in any way reflect on these matters as he waited for the boy to come home, but rather stared at the ceiling, which had been painted black (by him, long ago) and was decorated with splotches of damp. He whistled the only merry tune he knew as he thought of that little rascal's face when he opened the parcel to find his surprise, and chuckled quietly to himself. Pleasant thoughts such as these entertained him until, several hours later, he heard the unmistakeable racket of the boy's arrival. He laid his hand upon the smooth leather book, congratulating himself for performing two pranks on the same day.

As he heard the front door shut he quietly unlatched his own door, allowing it to swing an inch backwards so he could have a good view.

The little boy walked slowly to the stairs (he's weak from hunger, thought Zephaniah) until he caught sight of the brown paper lunch parcel, when he rushed to it, untied the string and pulled it open. As something flew out at him, Zephaniah closed his eyes, unable to watch in case he made some guffaw and gave himself away.

He heard a gasp. Then the boy called, 'Mummy!'

'What is it, Georgie?' called the boy's mother, appearing at the banisters above.

'A flower!' called the boy. 'My lunch turned into a flower!'

Zephaniah opened his eyes and stared. The boy was now holding up a beautiful yellow snapdragon.

Zephaniah stood back from the door, distrusting his eyes, as he heard the boy thump up the stairs and his mother saying faintly, 'Where on earth . . . ?'

He closed the door and sat down, feeling dizzy. After the unhappiness and upset the boy had felt this morning, his discovery of the flower seemed to make him *more* happy than he would have been otherwise. This troubled Zephaniah deeply, and he rested on his chair for a long time before he lifted the notebook to record his failure. Then he jumped up as though a scorpion had dropped in his lap, and the book fell to the floor with a thump. He stared at it, his hands, his legs, his lungs – even his very blood shaking.

For what lay in the dust in front of him was a Holy Bible. He rubbed his hands nervously against his trousers to get the touch of holiness off him. He thought: But I haven't had a copy of the Holy Bible for over fifty years! How did it get there?

He could not sit back in the chair, or rest in any way, he was so disturbed. He gingerly picked up the Holy Book and placed it high on a bookshelf that was otherwise completely bare except for his dictionary. Then he walked up and down his rooms for a few minutes, thinking anxiously, while Cheapcold watched him from in front of the cold fireplace. When his thoughts brought him to no conclusion, Crump threw himself into bed without taking off any of his clothes, and pulled the sheets over his head.

Huh! he thought, when he had slept for about fifteen hours, and felt a lot calmer. What nonsense! I have simply misplaced my notebook and accidentally put a bible (which I had forgotten I owned) in its place. And as for the flower, that is a stupid trick played by the boy to please his mother.

So he went about his business more grumpily than usual, and took Cheapcold out to visit a few other misers he knew. They would be spending Saturday sitting around a table in the Gun and Ferret pub, exchanging miserable stories.

As he closed the front door behind him, however, he heard Mrs Mackery's voice coming down the stairs, and stopped to listen.

'Last week I hung out the only two sheets I had,' she was saying, 'and when I came down they was ruined with soot. Ruined! So I took 'em up and washed 'em again – in a black and foul mood, I can tell you, exhausted so as I didn't know what day it was, with the six kids running around – and today I hang 'em out, and I go back, and there's two extra sheets there, clean and dried and folded in me washing basket! What do you think of that?'

When he reached the Gun and Ferret he could not enjoy his friends' miserable stories and was so distracted that he even forgot to cheat in the game of cards that followed. Time and again his thoughts fell to the sound of joy in the boy's voice after his trick failed, and the news he had overheard from Mrs Mackery. Each time he thought of them he felt a twinge of pain in his stomach, and an urge never to return to his house, which he ignored.

Zephaniah managed to banish these strange apparitions from his thoughts for the rest of the weekend. At the Sovereign Tavern he ate a roasted pigeon for Sunday lunch, with beetroot and broccoli (while Cheapcold ate the scraps), and enjoyed the rest of Sunday, his favourite day, chatting to his good friend Mr Grum, the local gravedigger.

On the Monday, he got up in good time to go and get his newspaper and to begin the week's regime. But on his way out he was met by the postman.

'Three letters for you, sir!' said the lad, handing them over. Zephaniah usually received two or three letters per year. They were always to inform him that an old acquaintance was sick, or had died, or was about to be buried. Looking at these envelopes, each written in a handwriting that he did not recognize, he felt instantly that something was up. Noticing that the boy was hanging around for a tip, Zephaniah was about to yell, 'Clear off!' when he saw a lady walking on the other side of the street.

It was the same one with the curly hair and the smart cloak who had waved at him the other day, and she was giving him a wide, friendly smile once more. Pretending not to see her, and yanking Cheapcold back on the leash (because the dog had seen her too, and darted towards her), he waited until she passed out of sight and then boxed the postboy on the ears, and tugged Cheapcold back inside the house.

He tore open and read the three letters in quick succession.

'Dear Mr Crump,' read the first. 'I appreciate your support in trying to keep the post office open. I also thank you for your promise of a vote in the forthcoming election! With gratitude, B. Bastable MP.'

'Dear Mr Crump,' began the second. 'If only all the inhabitants of Tumblewater were as public-spirited as you! Alas, many of them *oppose* the idea of free soup for the poor, in the ignorant belief that they will become swamped by homeless people. I accept your offer to help out in the kitchen with many thanks, and look forward to making your acquaintance! Yours, Q. Purlikew, Mayor.'

The last was worst of all.

The paper was perfumed with a sickly-sweet scent and written in huge, flowery handwriting which he found not only deeply aggravating, but very hard to read. It began: *Darling Zephy-woo!*'

Zephaniah put a hand to his head as the blood rushed from it, and had to wait a few moments for it to clear. Never, but *never* in his life, had anyone called him anything so utterly insulting.

Darling Zephy-woo!' he read, when he had the strength.

How I simply adored your wonderful letter and all the kind words in it. Facing the cruel public is so much easier when I know there are people in the audience like you – who THRILL to every note and are driven to a wondrous ECSTASY by the music. I, too, have gone without food for a week so that I might sit in the cheapest seat and simply melt at the sound of the opera. How can I resist enclosing two tickets for our performance

215

next week – for you and some lucky sweetheart!
With deepest fondness,
You dear darling dove,
Olivietta Ornaldo XXXX!!!

The note fell from Zephaniah's hand as though he had been struck dead. But the tickets remained between his fingers. For a long time he stared at them with a morbid terror, as though it might be his own death warrant, printed in duplicate. He moved his hands to tear them in half, and felt a resurgence of anger and energy. No! he thought. I shall *go along* to the opera and pinch the ears of the people in front of me. I'll take rotten eggs to throw and a tin whistle to blow during the quiet bits. I'll find a copy of the libretto and shout out the lines before they sing them! *Hah!*

For if I am going mad, he thought – I am sure I'm not, but if I *am* – then I shall make a proper spectacle of it, and have the time of my life!

Two days later, he stepped out of his house looking more pale and hollow than usual, and walked with a quick, mechanical tread towards the courthouse.

Mr Justice Striker sat behind his high pulpit seeming quite out of sorts – every bit as impatient and ratty, in fact, as Zephaniah felt himself. He dithered, dropped his papers and banged his gavel so hard it split in half right down the middle.

'Good old Judge Striker,' muttered Zephaniah to

himself, settling into his seat. 'At least I can rely on him.'

It did not take long for the judge's bad temper to be explained. Once he had given his replacement gavel (hastily fetched by a nervous court underling) a few raps to test its strength, and his papers had been put back in the right order, and he had banged for silence even louder than before, the judge peered out over his tiny spectacles and in a clear but chillingly quiet voice, said:

'Before we get down to this week's list of villains, there are a few small matters to attend to. Firstly, in the case of the Crown versus Thomas Groffin, it pains me greatly to announce that the baker whom the little ruffian stole from has dropped all charges.' Here the judge broke off and made a face as though a particularly disgusting taste had entered his mouth. The courtroom hung in utter silence, wondering what he would say. 'It would seem,' he went on, 'that the baker was persuaded by a "kind local gentleman" who paid for the loaf. A gentleman by the name of Zephaniah Crump.'

As the judge broke off to sneeze violently, Zephaniah shrank into his seat with horror. What was going on? Had he *really* done this, in some fit he could not remember? He felt pinned in his seat as the judge blew his nose raspingly on the sleeve of his judicial gown, and continued:

'And in the case of the Crown versus Richard Upwitch, a tailor's assistant, prosecution is powerless to pursue the case as the defendant's debts have all been settled by a Mr . . .' The judge stopped, frowning, and compared the two pieces of paper from which he had just been reading. 'It would seem by the same man. A Mr Crump. If Mr Crump finds himself in the courtroom today, and I believe *do-gooders* such as he are likely to want to see the effect of their sticking their nose in where it isn't wanted, he should be ready for *his* bread to be stolen and *his* money not to be repaid. Then perhaps he will appreciate the consequences of his actions and fully understand the MAJESTY OF THE LAW!'

The judge had begun speaking at a normal level but his temper, perhaps provoked by his obvious case of flu, soon reached a pitch that made the windows rattle nervously, and his voice rose to a volume that should not have been possible for human speech.

His final sentence was delivered with the strength and ferocity of a tornado. It swept Zephaniah bodily off his chair, into the corridor and out into the street so fast that he found he had been scurrying along for a full ten minutes before his legs were moving by their own effort and the judge's words had stopped ringing in his ears. He was almost surprised to find Cheapcold happily trotting alongside him.

Then he felt a pull on the leash and looked up. There was a familiar silhouette standing in the middle of the road far ahead: it was that cape-wearing, curly-haired woman again, whom he had seen on his own street. Staring at him with the same flat smile.

With a cry he dashed to his left, dragging Cheapcold

with him, down a tiny crack between two enormous buildings. Why this apparently harmless figure's appearance caused him so much fear he didn't know, but he was beginning to dread it like a mortal enemy. He slipped and tripped on rubbish and slime in the near-dark alleyway, and stumbled on loose cobbles as he came into the street at the other end, nearly falling beneath the hoofs of two horses pulling a carriage that reared up before him.

A black-eyed man with ferociously bushy eyebrows and a whip leaned down and yelled, 'What are you doing? Trying to get yourself killed?'

Zephaniah was on his feet and at the man's side in an instant.

'I'm sorry!' he said. 'But let me get on board. I've got money – I'll pay!'

'We're full,' the driver said, nodding back to a carriage packed with hats and impatient faces.

'Then let me get up there with you. A sovereign – no, a *guinea*! Go! I'll only ride for half a mile.'

No driver in the country could afford to say no to such an offer.

'Just in time,' whispered Zephaniah, looking down from the driver's seat to see the strangely smiling woman only ten yards behind, walking calmly towards him. He let out a cool sigh as her figure retreated. Her eyes grew more distant, and eventually vanished, but they never stopped staring at his.

*

As the river swung into view at the bottom of a hill, Zephaniah called loudly for the driver to stop. He hopped free of the vehicle, pressing the guinea into the driver's hand as gaily as a child paying a penny to the fairground man. The driver didn't meet his eye but snatched his hand shut and with the same movement twitched the whip, and the coach jumped forward and was gone.

The violent locomotion of the carriage and the rapidity of his escape had left Zephaniah with a sense of excitement as he walked along the bank of the river. He came to a large, busy bridge and darted across it. On reaching the other side he felt a sharp tug on the leash. He looked back over the road, thinking: This can't be happening.

But there she was. That same curly hair, that same placid smile, that same calm walk, coming towards him.

No matter that he was in the middle of a loud rushing street and surrounded by a thousand people going about their ordinary lives. Only the leash nearly slipping from his hands brought him round and he heaved Cheapcold with a mighty yank (which might have snapped the dog's neck if he wasn't used to such treatment) and pulled him back.

A few feet away he saw a stone staircase leading to the river and sped down it, running for the first time in over thirty years. Cheapcold trotted at his side as though this was a merry game and when they reached the water's edge, happily sprang into a wooden boat which was moored to the jetty.

Looking up, Zephaniah could see that the woman had not yet reached the staircase, so he unwound the rope in six quick loops, leaped aboard and pushed off into the current. As the boat moved away from the wooden platform he caught sight of a swish of cloth with the corner of his eye and turned to see the lady stepping on to his boat just as the gap became too wide for her to step off again.

He lay back against the prow of the boat and watched her in sheer desperation for a few seconds.

'Who are you?' he finally cried out.

She watched him quite calmly and seemed perfectly steady on her feet despite the boat rocking as the current took hold of it.

'I'm Grace,' she said.

'You follow me everywhere like a ghost! What do you want of me?'

'I simply wanted to make your acquaintance,' she said demurely, with a small smile. It was as though she knew everything that he was going to say. 'You seem like a very unhappy man.'

'I am!' he shouted in misery. 'I am an unhappy man, because someone is dogging my steps and writin' letters that they're pretending came from me, and – and – STAY BACK!'

She came forward and knelt, and Cheapcold licked her hands and nuzzled against her. 'I've been watching you,' she said. 'And I am convinced that you want to be a good man, really. It's just you won't admit it.'

Zephaniah was now perched right at the edge of the boat, nearly falling into the river. The woman was pretty, and her voice soothing, and persuasive.

'Mr Crump,' she said sadly, 'I have been alone for many years since my last husband died. I could look after you, and we could live a quiet and happy life.'

As a bridge cast them into darkness, Zephaniah felt as though he was being swallowed up and even the lights of the city disappeared for a moment.

'It was all you!' he shouted. 'The Holy Bible and the letters and everything!'

She could not meet his eyes, and he saw in the bend of her head a guilty acknowledgement. Still the same mysterious curl of a smile remained on her lips.

'I admit it,' she said. 'I was sure, when you saw the happiness you could bring, and the good things you could do, that you would change. That you would feel the warmth of goodness in your heart, and learn to love . . .' As the bridge above them passed, what light there was fell on them again, and her hand crept out from her sleeve towards his.

He trembled fiercely, not from the cold, nor the deep enveloping damp, but from an unquenchable anger. He saw that hand of hers creeping forward into his life, opening his door with a secret key, signing his name to a dozen damaging letters, unlocking his moneybox to see what he and only he knew – that he had hoarded a fortune, that he was in secret an immensely rich man.

He saw that hand distributing his wealth to a thousand undeserving villains.

'*Witch!*' he screamed, and leaping forward, grabbed her by the throat.

Now, whatever we may have discussed about misers, we found it was impossible to reach a conclusion because they are shut away, and never speak about themselves (should anyone care to ask), and largely remain a mystery.

But when it comes to murderers, we may say almost exactly the same thing. For if they are at large, they are hardly likely to boast about what they've done, and once they are caught they tend to be severely disinclined to discuss their actions – except if it's with a priest, who is himself condemned to silence. Even so, I will here risk telling you my theory about murderers: that many of them kill out of hunger, anger, avarice or greed, but that most men kill out of fear. Thus I suspect it was fear that made Zephaniah Crump throttle the woman's neck with all his might until the smile had slipped from it for good, and fear that made him hold her head under the water until long after anyone could have still been taking breath. And afterwards it was another kind of fear – at the realization of what he had done – that made him walk to the other end of the little dinghy and, insensible to the pleading whimpers that came from Cheapcold's throat, throw himself in.

*

He had lost all consciousness of his crimes, and the crimes against him, and indeed all consciousness of anything whatsoever, when long afterwards the steel finger of a boathook pulled him roughly up from the water and he was manhandled on to the deck of a coal barge, with much commotion and shouting.

When he had coughed most of the water from his lungs he found himself surrounded by a crew of the most hard-faced, brutish-looking men, now all transformed into the most caring nursemaids. They had covered him in blankets, and poured rum down his throat, and were now feeding him endless worried questions, asking if he was comfortable and so on. He gave them no answers however, but sat there, seeing in his mind's eye the little boat he had abandoned, and which by now had disappeared far into the distance.

At the first bridge, the men on the coal barge put Zephaniah ashore at his insistence. After several re-tellings in riverside taverns, the story would no doubt make him out to be the ghost of a drowned man. He could almost have believed that himself as he reached the main road without any idea where he was. He plodded onward, wet and cold, along the side of the river, waiting to recognize a road, or a sign, or a building.

It was something longer than an hour and shorter than a day later when he turned into Slipstream Lane, and approached his own door. He had walked past the courthouse, and the baker's where that boy had stolen;

he had passed the post office whose closure he had adamantly supported but which stood open, filled with a bustling crowd, and followed, in reverse, much of the path he had taken in running away from the strange woman. But not one of these things had elicited in him any of his old reactions: he did not snarl or scowl, or spit or snort. He did not feel angry. He was an old man. There wasn't left in him the energy to feel anything at all, save the teeth which clanked against each other in his head like empty bottles, and clothes so wet against his skin that walking was like swimming through cold water. He only wanted warmth, a fire, a hot drink – and he didn't care about anything else.

So when he reached his building and let himself in, and unlocked the door to his apartment and saw Cheapcold there warming himself in front of a new fire, he said nothing. And when he heard Grace's voice singing quietly in the kitchen he said nothing, but went and sat down in his chair. And when she saw him, and brought him a tot of warming brandy, and said she was preparing a huge pot of soup to be given out at the local soup kitchen, and that they could take it there tomorrow, and wouldn't that be nice, he said nothing, but nodded slightly. He thought he heard her saying something about opera tickets too, but he failed to make it out exactly.

He felt the warmth of the fire, and the comfort of the blanket on his lap, and listened for a noise he could barely make out, the soft booming of his heart growing slower after all its exertions, a sound which he could barely hear, a sound growing fainter with every passing moment.

s Guthric the Apothecary finished the story we stopped for a moment to catch our breath. I was fascinated by the tale and was about to ask him a question, when another loud blast from above was followed by a huge gust of wind that came rushing down towards us. Guthric tottered sideways and I turned my face away from the dust. It subsided after a second and Guthric opened his mouth to say 'What on earth was th—' when a second huge blast came, louder than the first.

It carried with it a huge cloud of dust and smoke that blinded us both, and threw me on my back. I clutched my hands to my ears and buried my face in the floor as the roar cascaded over us, too loud to bear.

After a few seconds the sound died and I sat up, my head ringing, as smoke slowly settled around us. Guthric was a full ten yards away up the tunnel. We looked at each other in bewilderment.

'Gunpowder,' said Guthric. 'These tunnels are becoming more dangerous by the minute! And with me down here it's even worse. Come on, I only meant this to be a short trip to show you something, Daniel. Let's get to the river.'

'Good,' I said, hiking on ahead of him. 'We're nearly there.'

Finding ourselves at a backstreet exit from the Underground a few minutes later, we slipped out into the fresh air and drizzle, and on to streets which were as empty as the tunnels below them. From here it was a short walk to the river, Guthric claimed, but as we turned a corner I found myself gazing ahead of us with a kind of transfixed horror.

Not fifty yards away stood a gaunt-looking church, its crumbling remains about to collapse any minute. In front of the church the hill fell away steeply, and on this lumpy slope were scattered hundreds of graves, all covered with wispy dead grass, the headstones cracked or standing at crazy angles. Exposed coffins stuck out of the earth, and one almost expected to see skulls and ribcages bobbing around in the graveyard's nasty-looking puddles.

'St Elsifer's Church,' muttered Guthric. 'Or it was, long ago – no churchman would set foot in it now.' He tugged me after him between a gap in the railings.

One enormous and magnificent tree grew beside the church, spreading its branches so it almost hid the building entirely.

'Don't look too long,' warned Guthric. 'There's something weird about that tree. This was once a thriving village church, hundreds of years ago. The tree is the only thing that survived, almost as though it sucked

the life out of the . . .' He tutted. 'I'm being superstitious again. Come on!'

As I followed him I couldn't help casting a look over
my shoulder. It was just a normal, healthy-looking tree
to me, with purple-russet leaves that shimmered in the
wind and crackled slightly from the rain. And then I
caught my breath. Looking at the earth in the graveyard,
washed away by decades of rain, I saw the exposed
roots of the tree, crawling down the hill like dozens
of spindly fingers, threading in and out of the earth,
through countless graves. They scaled gravestones
and slithered between railings into the street; they even
reappeared on the other side of the street, clambering
up the walls and leaving cracks where they'd found
their way between the stones and into people's houses.

Paying attention to the tree's roots and not looking
where I was going, I stupidly sank my leg up to the
knee in a gulping puddle filled with pale, almost flesh-
coloured mud and had to close my eyes as I pulled it
back out, bracing myself in case I caught sight of a
bone or a skull. Tearing myself free, I followed Guthric
more carefully, and didn't deviate from his path.

'Where are we going?' I asked. 'Will it take long?'

He shushed me. 'We're nearly there,' he whispered.
'Keep up!'

When we had finally squelched through the dismal
graveyard, we found ourselves at the river. By way of
a tiny staircase that no casual passer-by would give a
second glance, we found our way down to the water's

228

edge. The tide was out and we stood on a narrow bar of muddy sand with thick mooring posts standing high over our heads. The other side of the river was hidden by a low mist, and we could hear bells and voices ringing out from passing vessels. We reached the end of the sandbank and stood beneath a huge iron hook, green with moss, that hung from a stone in the wall.

'Here,' said Guthric. 'Now where's that key of yours?'

I reached up to put my hand inside my shirt but saw to my confusion that the key was already in my fist. I realized I had been clutching it since the graveyard, without noticing. I wondered for a moment why I was holding it up for all to see, but my curiosity was wholly distracted by Guthric. What were we supposed to find in this barren place?

'Stick it in the mud,' he said. Bewildered, I leaned down and pressed it into the brown, sludgy sand, as though to leave an imprint of its shape. 'No!' He laughed. 'Properly, like a key.' Feeling slightly stupid, I pushed it tip-first into the mud.

'Turn it,' instructed Guthric.

I twisted it clockwise, my mind reeling. The key stuck in the sandy mud as I had expected it to, and made my fingers hurt, but I twisted until it had slowly made its way all the way round. 'Now what?' I muttered. 'Are you having me on aga—' I stopped.

Almost invisible to see at first, the sand around the shaft of the key had begun to fall inwards, as though

229

a burrowing insect was about to appear. This quickly developed into a wider, deeper swirling motion and I plucked the key out of the hole that was rapidly appearing.

'Better stand back,' said Guthric.

I took three steps back, without taking my eyes off the ever-deepening whirlpool in the sand that presently fell all the way out of sight, leaving a perfect cylinder that drove deep into the ground.

'Unbelievable,' I whispered, staring anew at the key.

'It's a Mineral Key,' said Guthric. 'It's a magic tool for a very specific purpose – to open up (or lock behind you) hidden spaces inside solid objects. Spaces that would never appear to be there if you looked for them in a normal way. For instance, look how the tide is almost lapping at the edge of the hole. Water should seep right through the sand and flood it. But everything inside is perfectly dry.'

Peering down over the edge, I saw what looked like a stone well, but with walls of sand. At the bottom was an old wooden chair, a chest covered with dozens of burnt-down candles, a stack of books, and a basket of forgotten foodscraps.

'It belonged to a friend of mine,' he said. 'She was accused of witchcraft and had to hide.'

'How awful,' I said. 'Why did they accuse her?'

'Well, because she was a witch, I suppose,' he said, shrugging. 'I used to bring her food and candles and new books when I could. At night she used to swim in the river in quiet seclusion, and came to know the wildlife and plant life well, and the ghosts and secrets that are drowned under the river. She came to love this place.' He went quiet for a moment and I wondered whether he had perhaps loved her.

'Anyway, she's dead now,' he said cheerfully, clapping his hands together. 'And this is just to show you: that key will open up a place hidden in stone, wood, rock, iron; in a chalk cliff, a clay pit or a slate quarry – wherever Maria is hidden.'

'But how do I know where to put the key?'

'Trust the key. It will tell you when you're near a lock that can be opened – you will suddenly find that it is in your hand and you don't remember putting it there.'

'I see,' I said. 'And does the hidden place have to be the same size as what it's hidden in? Could I find a whole room hidden inside a house brick?'

'It depends on the power of the person who sets the spell. The two things have to be *roughly* the same size, I would say.'

'But Gora the witch was powerful . . .' I suggested.

'She couldn't hide a castle inside a pebble – it's just not possible,' he explained. 'The pebble would crack and shatter. Perhaps for someone very powerful it might be possible to have . . . let's say, a railway engine fitting inside an ordinary horse-drawn carriage. A grapefruit inside an egg. Do you see?'

'Er – sort of . . .'

'Good. And there's one final thing to remember.'

'What's that?'

'These spells don't last forever. Gora the witch is dead, and her magic is going with her. It is weakening all the time. At some point it will ebb away and be gone, and the hidden place will be lost forever.'

He gestured to the secret hole in the sand, which had silently filled itself up again without our noticing.

'Keeping someone *alive* in these places requires serious magic,' he said. 'And that's what your sister's hiding place is not getting.'

I didn't want to ask, but I had to. 'What actually happens if the magic runs out?'

He looked out at the ebbing tide, and the voices crying out to each other in the fog. 'Just don't let it happen,' he said quietly.

I nodded. His words had given me a new boost of urgency, and for all that I had made great friends at Ridley Garnet's school, once again I felt stupid for letting myself be distracted from looking for Maria for so long. As I led Guthric back to the nearest entry to the Underground, I knew what I had to do.

We soon found ourselves at a secret entrance in the cellar of an abandoned building. Guthric went on ahead of me before turning back. I felt cowardly as I saw the concern in his face.

'Daniel?' he asked. 'You aren't coming?'

'After this next turning, keep on straight ahead and there's a wayfarer's cottage,' I said. 'I've got no choice. I can't go back down there. I have to look for

Maria. She might already be dead . . .'

'I understand,' he nodded. 'Don't worry, I've survived in stranger places than this. I'll find my way back.' He took my hand in his. 'Daniel, *good luck*,' he said. And with that, he took a candle from the wall, turned right a few paces ahead and became nothing more than a diminishing glimmer of light, vanishing in the darkness.

I went back up the stairs and looked out at the empty road.

This was it. I was alone now. It was just me, the key, and Caspian Prye.

Tumblewater is such a twisty-turny place, it has so many different parts, that you can never know all of them at one time without some of them slipping out of your mind and surprising you the next time you are there. Although it's just one crammed little district in the centre of a much bigger metropolis, sometimes it seems to be a whole city. So it was that now I found myself wandering through a tiny part of town known for its humble few streets of dressmakers' and shoemakers' shops, a place that for a few days had entirely slipped my mind.

The place was dead. I passed a single shop that was open, from which the shopkeeper looked out nervously. A dozen other shops on the same road were shut. The very few individuals I saw on the street cast anxious looks at me, and families kept to themselves, whether they were sitting glumly on the steps of their house or rushing along on the other side of the street to get home safely.

I walked quickly, with my collar turned up and my head down. My hands fidgeted in my coat pockets, and I waited to feel the key magicking itself into either one of them. I strode through the docks, past the abandoned financial district, I explored the forgotten museums with their big blocks of stone, and wove my way between the warehouses with their pulleys that reminded me of the gallows.

Nothing. The key didn't stir.

I walked fast along the riverside piers with their clinking chains and creaking ropes, I darted through the shanty town of wooden huts at the top of the hill that looked like it could be knocked down by a badly timed sneeze, I climbed cobbled streets and ran down muddy tracks ...

And then I felt it. There was the key, in my hand.

I was in a dark, winding lane overhung with roofs and I looked around desperately for anything the key might fit into. Eventually I saw a huge old millstone lying disused in a sidestreet. It looked perhaps too small, but my hands were still shaking as I held the key to its side, and saw it slide in. I turned the key, and a chunk of rock slid from the side of the stone as easily as a safe door.

Within was a paper package, bound up with string. I grabbed it out and tore it open, still thinking that it might be somehow connected to Maria, and give some clue to her whereabouts.

They were love letters.

Love letters written hundreds of years ago in a language I found hard to make out, from a miller to his girl, and from her to him. Disgusted, I threw them on the floor, where they scattered among puddles, and kept walking.

I walked and walked, and waited for the key to come into my hand once more. Rain soaked through my clothes and the sky darkened behind the clouds. I walked and walked . . .

'Dross, poppycock, balderdash . . .'

In my meanderings I had found myself outside the door of Jaspers & Periwether Publishers. I was feeling hopeless and alone – and what's more was wet and cold to the bone. A friendly face was what I needed, so I had stepped inside.

I saw immediately that there was one place in Tumblewater, at least, that hadn't changed. Huge piles of mildewed paper sprawled in every direction, and piles of books were crammed wherever I turned my eye.

'Piffle, nonsense, cretinous waffle . . .'

Horatio Jaspers leaned back in his chair, flicking through a manuscript in his hand. His eyebrows were arched in disdain.

'The *rubbish* these authors come up with!' he was chuckling to himself. I had a moment of discomfort as it occurred to me that the manuscript in his hand might be mine. I noticed that there was a slightly awkward atmosphere in the office, and no one else was saying anything. I coughed politely and Jaspers looked up.

'Ah! Dear boy!' he bellowed. 'My favourite author!' I felt a curious mixture of emotions to be spoken to in that way. I was pretty sure that he spoke to everyone like this, out of sheer habit – possibly even people who weren't authors.

'How is the publishing industry?' I asked politely. This question threw him back in his chair, with a look of greatest anguish.

'Daniel, what can I say? It's diabolical. Quite diabolical. We are beset on all sides by the forces of stupidity and ignorance. We publish great books but the public refuses to buy them! All of our effort and energies are for nought!'

I opted not to say that the most energetic thing I'd ever seen him do in his office was attempt to swat a fly, or take a sip from his cup of tea (which was made for him by the nervous office boy, Cravus) and chose instead to change the subject. I tentatively asked whether he had had a chance to read my manuscript.

'READ it?' he asked. 'My dear boy I LOVE it! It's funny, sad, delightful, delicious! It made me see the world in a completely new light!'

'But it's a collection of . . . horror stories,' I said. 'Was it – you know – scary?'

He leaned forward and fixed me with a deadly earnest look. 'My . . . blood . . . *froze*.'

'Oh good,' I replied.

'It's so good that I've had it sent off to be typeset and proofread, ready for publication.'

I couldn't hide my relief. 'That's wonderful!' I said.

'Please see my editorial notes. CRAVUS! When you're ready.' He waved a hand and Cravus came forward, blinking nervously behind his spectacles, and handed me a letter. It read simply:

Grisly Tales from Tumblewater, by Daniel Dorey
Editorial notes by Mr Horatio P. Jaspers, Esq.
1. I have deleted the story 'The Boy Who Farted'.
   It is most offensive.
2. Otherwise, manuscript fine.
   Yours sincerely,

The letter finished with an indecipherable squiggle, which I presumed to be Jaspers's signature. As I finished reading it, somewhat nonplussed, there was a rather horrible farting noise from Jaspers's side of the desk. I looked up to see Cravus and the young blond man who worked silently at a desk on the other side of the room flinching in disgust.

'Cravus!' shouted Jaspers. 'I've warned you a thousand times not to do that. It's revolting.'

'You don't want me to include the story called "The Boy Who Farted"?' I asked.

237

'No. Of course not. It's a disgusting topic. Not even the most mindless nincompoop could enjoy reading such a story.'

I rubbed my chin, not sure how to respond. Jaspers noticed my uncertainty and all of a sudden bowed to me, and took on a servile and obsequious air.

'Of course, my notes are only suggestions. *You* are the *author*.'

'You mean, if I insisted, then I could include it?'

He made a circular motion of his head, as though he was trying to work out some other way of saying no, which did not involve the word 'no'. Gradually the motion turned into a reluctant nod. 'If you *insisted* . . . then yes.'

'Even though you think it's a bad idea?'

'Even though I strongly recommend that you don't include it, yes.'

'So if I *really wanted* it, you'd allow me to include it?'

He regarded me somewhat stiffly for a moment.

Then he nodded.

'Good,' I said.

THE BOY
WHO FARTED

Once upon a time there was a boy who lived in a very poor part of a very poor town, whose existence was one of suffering and hardship, and who nevertheless possessed a quite miraculous talent.

His mother was a frail, thin creature clothed in rags. She dragged herself to the river every day to wash clothes for richer folk, and received such a pittance for her trouble that she could only afford to feed her poor son gruel.

Do not mistake this word 'gruel' for its recent meaning – a nutritious paste made from fruit extract and mashed grain which came to popularity a few hundred years ago as a cheap, and to some palates delicious, alternative to starvation. No, this was in a time long before such an invention, when a poor woman knew very well that a son's stomach had to be filled with anything to hand, whether it was mud, gravel or wood shavings, and if the occasional mouse's tail or crushed bone crept into the mix he could consider himself lucky. (The mother herself dined quite modestly on one of the pigeons which would often became stuck in the hole in the roof of their mud hovel and flap themselves to death. She would boil one of these each week and make a stew which would last her all week. If it ran out before the week was up, she would suck the bird's feet for nutrition.)

This boy's name was Willem, and his poor diet caused him all sorts of trouble and embarrassment. His mother packed him off to a tiny schoolroom of the poorest kind each day in the hope that he might grow up to have a better life than her, and here his miraculous gift began to show itself, a few weeks after his seventh birthday.

One morning, as the short-sighted teacher bent low over a parchment, reciting words the children could not understand, Willem felt a sudden rumbling in his belly and all of a sudden, with no warning and no chance to stop it, he broke wind. To his amazement, no one seemed to notice. That was, not until the room started to fill with the most delicious smell of peaches. Then the boys began to look around, and to hunt up and down the length of the room to discover the source of this smell, even if it was only the stone of a single peach, that they might suck on it. The teacher called weakly to try and control them, but, never having listened to him before, they weren't going to start now, not when this smell was driving them crazy.

Later, on the way home from school, as he passed one of the many poor shacks which lined the street, Willem found himself unable to resist breaking wind once more. At once the rich odour of roast boar wafted across the street, so strong that passers-by cocked their heads, as though they could almost taste the crackling flesh on their lips.

Before the smell could pass, a four-horsed coach came to a crashing stop and the furious lord of the manor, tall and well-dressed, jumped down and began running from house to house, shouting, 'Bloody poor people, poaching my animals!' Soon he reappeared from one house, dragging a woman out by her hair.

'Tell me who it is! Who's been eating my boar!'

'I don't know,' the woman screamed helplessly. 'Let go of me, you brute!' He threw her into an especially deep puddle before climbing back on board. 'Drive on!' he called. 'I shall be putting the rents up for this, you thieves!'

Willem ran home as fast as he could.

When he got there a pewter cup full of gruel waited on the place in the floor where these days a table would be.

'There's your dinner. Eat it up and shove off to bed!' bawled his affectionate mother.

'I really think I shouldn't, mother,' he warned. 'I don't know what's in it, but it seems to be having some very strange effects on me.'

'Be grateful, you ugly little lump!' she said, smacking him sharply on the head, 'or I'll throw you out once and for all!'

This made Willem so nervous that he sat and gobbled the meal at once, afraid to meet his mother's one working eye. He rested against the wall after forcing it down, relaxed for a moment and involuntarily let out a little fart.

His mother's face contorted as she realized that the smell which rose up from the boy was that of a freshly baked gooseberry tart, something far more delicious and sweet than anything she had never seen, let alone eaten, in her entire life. She twisted into a horrible shape; she jumped as though a soldier had bayoneted her backside; and finally she crumpled on the floor in a heap, quite dead.

After spending the night on his own, Willem didn't know what to do except go to school. He was quite wretched with fright, however, and had not slept a wink, so it was hardly surprising that, soon after lessons had started, he let go with another little trumpet. The aroma which spread across the classroom was that of frying bacon.

Now, the smell of frying bacon does funny things to people at the best of times, even on a relatively full stomach and if you have not suffered a day's starvation in your life. But these poor children, whose nostrils had never experienced anything so tantalizing, went quite mad with hunger. Some stopped their mouths with their fists or clawed the windows. Some ran from the room, never to return. Others simply pointed at Willem and shouted incoherently.

Grasping Willem by the larger of his two nostrils, the teacher pulled the hapless boy down the street. The shock of this was not good for Willem's bowels, of course, and odours of smoked venison, newly picked strawberries, poached salmon and fresh hot fudge trailed behind him, all the way through the town.

By the time they arrived at the Manor House half the townspeople were following behind them. The Lord of the Manor bad-temperedly opened his door and, seeing the crowd, asked, 'What's this?'

'Take the boy away!' they all cried. 'He's tormenting us!'

The landowner opened his mouth to tell them they were all fools and that if they did not leave he would set his horses and hounds among them (and put the rents up again), when Willem let out a final squeak. The smell of duck-liver pâté rose to the lord's nose. Ah, I see, he said to himself. This is quite a talent. It could be my chance to make my name at court and gain the king's favour. 'Fear not!' he shouted out at the crowd. 'I shall take this boy off your hands!' and with that, to relieved cheers and shouting, he ushered the boy inside and told his land manager to raise the rents anyway.

Willem was dragged inside and dropped in the centre of a rug in an enormous study lined with thousands of books. The Lord of the Manor (whose name, incidentally, was Alphonse) stood back to regard him from quite a considerable distance and, if someone can be said to bark orders with trepidation, then that is what he did.

'Do it again!' he hollered.

Owing to his nerves, Willem now had no difficulty at all in performing at will. He did so and produced a smell of lamb roasted with rosemary.

'Remarkable!' said Alphonse, and fell into a deep reverie, clearly considering what to do with the boy

244

next. At last, still undecided, he rang on a bell. A servant came in and Alphonse shouted, 'Fetch my wife!'

A minute later a very prim lady was shown in wearing clothes that had altogether too many frills, and so much face powder that she seemed almost ghostly. Willem was forced to perform his trick once more, and this time emitted a smell of rhubarb-and-apple crumble.

'Golly, what larks!' screamed the woman in a most undecorous and horselike manner. 'Peterson, fetch the children! Quick!'

Willem was now starting to feel somewhat weak and, if truth be told, rather emptied-out. But at last the children appeared, a young boy and girl who resembled their parents exactly, even down to the wispy little moustache shared by father and son. Willem had enough in him to provide one last peroration (if you will excuse the word, and I'm sure that you will), which resulted in the aroma of a beef-and-oyster pie, and sent the children into horselike paroxysms (if you will excuse that word as well). Then he fainted, and collapsed on the floor.

The family gathered round him at once and helped him to recover – the parents by splashing his face liberally with water and the children by pinching his ears. When Willem came round, smart clothes were fetched for him – a shirt, and a tie forced round his neck – and an enormous feast laid on for his benefit. It quickly became apparent that the family was fetching all their friends and relations from near and far.

The Lord of the Manor's imperious manner had quite vanished and he kept rushing in and out of the room in a state of great excitement.

'The boy will make us famous,' he was muttering, 'across the length and breadth of the land. Riches! He will bring us riches – we'll afford a home that makes this place look like a pigsty . . .' He eventually worked himself into such a state that his family had to apply some cold water and pinches to bring him to his sense too.

Soon carriages started to arrive, and guests were shown into the ballroom at the back of the house. Meanwhile all the richest food from the larder was being gathered for Willem to devour. Troops of servants brought roasted and peppered guinea fowl and set them on silver dishes in front of him; these were replaced by curried kidneys and terrines of a multitude of rare and exquisite birds. Then they plied him with puddings stuffed with ripe berries and swathed in cream; pastries dipped in syrup; sweet and rich wines from far-flung, sun-drenched countries. It was a feast far beyond Willem's most daring fantasies, and he devoured it all until he felt as though he had turned into a ball and could simply be rolled into the next room rather than walking.

While Alphonse's children prepared Willem for his appearance, in the next room dozens of the local nobility leaned eagerly forward in their seats to catch a glimpse of the miracle child, and every one of the estate's servants – farmhands, stable boys and all – squeezed themselves into the back of the room to get a look.

However, as he was about to make his appearance Willem started to notice that something was wrong. His body was completely unused to any of the rich food he had just consumed, and the usual agreeable rumbling of his stomach was replaced by something altogether more strange and unpleasant. There was a groaning noise and a deeply painful sequence of minor explosions within him. He started to become afraid. It felt as though his belly was on fire – it was certainly filling rapidly with gas. But now he was suddenly desperate to keep it in, for he was sure that something terrible was going to happen if he relaxed and let go.

As he was led in front of the crowd, Willem's eyes were turning blue from the effort of clenching. But there they all were: ancient white-haired duchesses peering through ivory opera glasses; rows of boys and girls in shorts and dresses, hugging each other and giggling with excitement; handsome lords chatting to their ladies, glancing over their shoulders towards Willem with pretended reluctance.

Eventually the whole crowd quietened and stared at him, seeming content to wait for as long as it took to see what would happen next.

'Ladies and gentlemen, I am proud to present the new curiosity who shall be the talk of the whole continent before the year is out!' declared Alphonse, stepping aside to leave Willem quite alone in front of the crowd. There was a smattering of confused applause.

There was nothing Willem could do. The door was twenty feet away and guarded by a trio of tall bewigged butlers, who all refused to take their eyes off him. All his energy was taken up in controlling an enormous fart that was fighting to be released from his bowels.

He closed his eyes. Tears of effort streamed down his face. He turned his back to the audience from shame. People started to mutter.

Then it began.

Perhaps the sound was audible only to dogs at first, for a great howling went up from the courtyard. Then a sound like the squeal of a trapped mouse began to ring out from his trousers, and the lords and ladies exchanged glances. This high note continued for some seconds, and then minutes, getting louder and deeper, until it seemed to have no end. Willem kept his eyes tight shut but imagined their faces changing from delighted expectation to dawning horror.

He heard a bump as someone fell, then another; then a loud chorus of bodies falling and furniture being tipped over; then silence. Not a word or a breath from anyone.

Covering his eyes with his hands he turned round and peeped through as much as he dared. His worst fears were realized – everywhere around the room people were lolling, their tongues hanging out of their mouths, their eyes open. The lords and ladies, the servants and stable lads – they were all dead.

As ever after one of his farts, Willem was completely unable to smell anything odd in the air at all and could detect no trace of it. He was too terrified to do anything except run from the room, into the hall, then out through the nearest door. Coming out from the indoor light, he blinked as he blundered forward in the dark, and found that he was in the courtyard.

He saw some objects glinting ahead of him and he stood still, trying to get his whereabouts. He paid no heed to the door he had left open behind him, from which spilled an incredibly pungent odour that filled the courtyard. An odour disgusting to humans – repulsive enough to cause a fatal attack – and yet not so to animals. To animals it was an inviting smell, a smell that made them hungry. And so they came forward out from their pens where the farmhands and stable boys had been in too much of a rush to secure them properly.

Horses and enormous bulls and pigs shuffled forward out of the darkness, devilishly hungry.

And Willem, temporarily blinded, wandered out into the darkness, towards the glimmering lights of their eyes and their bared teeth.

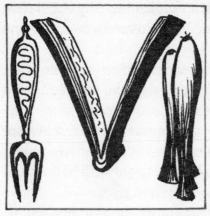aria was once more on my mind, and it was time to leave this warm and welcoming (if slightly smelly) cocoon.

I thanked Mr Jaspers for his time and as he rose (after offering me a glass of sherry, and one of port, and brandy, and schnapps) Mr Jaspers noticed something sticking out of my pocket.

'Dear me!' he said, becoming all a-fluster. 'You're reading that, are you?' I looked down and was surprised to see the copy of *The Junior Ornithologist's Guide to the Dietary Requirements of Subtropical Birds of Prey in Temperate Climes*. He plucked it from my hands, flicking through the pages with a nostalgic air.

'This was the first book I ever published! Terrific bestseller. Author was a dreadful bore but at least he accepted my title suggestion. Didn't take any of my editorial notes, of course,' he sniffed. 'Just like you. Damn fool died before we could get him to write a sequel.'

'I promise I'll try not to keep up the tradition,' I said quietly, accepting the book back.

'Where are you off to?' he enquired in a semi-interested tone, clearly thinking about inviting me for a late lunch, even though evidence of the one he had already eaten was freshly spattered over his tie and waistcoat.

'Well,' I said, sighing in anticipation of his response, 'I'm going to try and rescue my sister before Caspian Prye gets his hands on her.'

'I love it,' he said, narrowing his eyes. 'I just love the way you *live* your stories!'

Sighing again, I waved to poor, put-upon Cravus and the mysterious blond boy and, pulling my collar up so it hid my face, I left.

I found the streets no less daunting and unhappy, and sticking to the shadows, I walked the dark, quiet alleyways. I had a lot of thinking to do, to try and work out where Maria's hiding place might be. More than ever, I wished the others were here with me – Tusk, Mayrick and Sally. But I had left too suddenly to enlist their help and for now had to do without them.

I knew one thing for sure: Gora the witch had not set foot outside of Tumblewater for decades, perhaps even hundreds of years. When she died she was extremely old and wanted to remain where she knew the territory. That was why she used Guthric the Apothecary to bring her supplies. That was one consolation: Maria must be somewhere in the streets and houses nearby.

Only the sound of my footsteps accompanied me. Swirls of smoke came down from the occasional chimney pot and the rain, of course, pattered down as ever.

I passed ancient timber buildings overhanging

gloomy little lanes, I crossed iron bridges over the narrow canals. I saw a waterway crossing overhead in a makeshift wooden aqueduct held up by sturdy posts. I saw hundreds upon hundreds of crows perching on the washing lines stretching across an abandoned street, fluttering occasionally to shake the rain off their wings. In the flooded basement of a collapsed factory I saw trout and carp, swimming in slow circles among tables and hatstands.

Evening came on, and the rain took on a dark blue hue.

As I walked, I thought. Everything around me was in bits and pieces – bricks, rivets, cobbles, glass, slates. Nowhere could I find (or think of) anything whole enough to hide Maria inside. I suspected wherever it was it would be either a very secret place, or a very obvious one – hidden in plain sight, to thwart Prye's attention. This was what I could not riddle out. But I walked, and I thought, and even though I went in circles, every second I convinced myself I was getting closer.

Because of the constant cloud-cover, shadows in Tumblewater never had distinct shapes as shadows from the sun do, but instead gathered in the corners and invisibly swallowed things up. As evening drew on they began to grow and creep out into the street. My hands were fidgety in my pockets – but there was nothing I could do except walk, and wait for the key to appear in one of them, telling me I was close.

And then, walking through the encroaching dusk, I came across my first gunpowder-destroyed building. It appeared suddenly in a quiet street of workmen's cottages, as ugly and unexpected as a shout in the night. Where three of the humble little houses had been, was now a huge scorched hole. The buildings on either side were charred at the edges and decorated by splashes of soot that had smudged in the rain and dripped down them, looking as dismal and appalling as could be. Nothing remained except shattered brick and glass, and splinters of timbers and slate.

I huddled into a doorway opposite the remains of this act of violence, feeling the cold sneaking in through my clothes. So it was true, after all – Prye was destroying houses now in his search for Maria. But there was one relief: if she was indeed hidden inside a single large piece of rock or iron or wood, as Guthric had suggested, then Prye would never find her this way. Yet his anger knew no bounds – where would this stop? When every house lay in rubble?

'Daniel!' said a voice behind me. I jumped, and darted into a side alley. The voice came from the shadows, but it was muffled and suspicious, as though the speaker held a cloth over their mouth. 'Daniel! I can't hear you, come back out!'

The side alley was a dead end. Ignoring the voice I looked along the street for an escape. The nearest Underground passage was not too far, hidden beneath a fake panel in the fireplace of an abandoned villa in the next street. I might make it if I sprinted. But no one came forward to apprehend me and there was something familiar about the voice that made me pause. I waited for a moment to see what he would say next.

'*Daniel!*' said the voice, getting quite desperate. 'It's me, Lapiday, you suffering little fool! You came to visit me in my tower not three days ago!' Without hesitation I darted back out into the street.

No one was there, just the rain, dust and those shadows, still creeping slowly from their hiding places. For a moment I was disorientated, thinking it was a trick. 'Where are you?' I whispered.

'What's that? Speak up, lad!' I spun around, more confused than ever. I still couldn't tell where he was hidden, but the voice somehow seemed to be coming from somewhere in the air above me.

'Where *are* you?' I asked again, louder.

'I'm at home! I'm speaking to you through this voice contraption of mine, a devilish clever thing it is too. It doesn't have a name as such. I was going to call it a voice-thrower, but you see it also *receives* sound, so—'

'Mr Lapiday, please!' I said loudly up into the dingy mist above the rooftops.

'Ah yes, of course, sorry. I get carried away talking about my contraptions. Now, Daniel, listen up! I have something I must tell you. Do you know the way to my tower? It's the third left after the second right from Laburnum Terrace, which you get to after the museum.'

'Yes, I remember,' I said, 'But that seems like the

long way round. Surely I can take a left after the water-works and go behind Gamwells's Brewery?'

'Huh! If you've got a *day* or two to spare,' came back the voice. 'Then you've got to follow the one-way system all the way over the canal and back! You might as well come via the North Pole!'

'But what about the Vesuvius Street shortcut behind the Carfax Theatre?'

'That's not a shortcut!'

'*What?!*' I said. Then I caught myself. 'OK,' I said more quietly, 'I'm not sure this is quite the time or the place. I'll find my way and be with you within half an hour.'

'Come quickly! It's most urgent.' There was a brief squeaking noise and then silence.

How this bizarre machine worked – how it had found me in the first place, and how he threw his voice in that way, without magnifying it so everyone in the district could hear it – I couldn't begin to fathom. But I didn't mind that now – I wanted to hear what he had to say to me. I slipped into a nearby alley and was grateful to be swallowed by the shadows again, and find my way towards Lapiday's tower.

In a few minutes I was at the side of the deserted factory, where the staircase up to Mr Lapiday's house began, and in a few more I was crossing the rusted iron gangway towards his front door, not panting and struggling for breath this time, but swiftly and without pause.

As I knocked and waited for him to answer, and looked down into the thick fog that blanketed the rooftops, a sudden yellow flash burst out in the middle of the murky darkness. Then came the rumble of an explosion, and I heard stones rattling down on the rooftops.

'First one of the night,' muttered Lapiday from the open door. 'There'll be more. Come in, dear boy, quickly.'

Inside Lapiday's cave of artistic and scientific delights, I found it wasn't as welcoming as it had been before. He was studying, and just a little candlelight glittered off the metal artefacts, making the animals' heads on the wall cast flickering shadows that were quite spooky.

'Here,' he said, climbing the stairs to his raised platform. There was his home-made rocket Doctor Whizzbang, propped against the wall beside the enormous brass horn that I'd seen before. He presently pulled the cover off the latter object, and positioned it at the window so it was pointing in a certain direction. 'This is what I spoke to you through,' he explained. 'I didn't invent it, you know. I found it in a charming antiques shop on Ampersand Street. Wonderful contraption. Come forward, come forward. Depending where I aim it, we can hear specifically from through people's open windows, you see? Even if they're half a mile away. Like a telescope, but for the ears!

'Now, I was worried about all these explosions and

(although it took me hours and hours) I stumbled across a conversation among the police. Here we are . . .' Checking his notes for the coordinates, he moved the instrument by adjusting three separate pulleys that he twisted in different directions, one degree here, one degree there, until after applying himself to the earpiece seven or eight times and making further adjustments, he found what he wanted. 'It's now pointed directly at a second-storey window in police headquarters. I've heard lots of interesting titbits, although I don't always understand all of them.' He gestured to me to put my ear to it.

At first it was impossible to believe I was not listening to a conversation that was happening right here in the room with me. Two or three times I had to remove myself and look around before returning my ear to the instrument, as Lapiday watched, silently chuckling. When I got used to the sensation I realized what I was hearing was some chat between three men somewhere distant in the city. I listened in with a smile on my face, hearing them joking among each other, until the conversation turned to business.

'He's a meddler . . . friends with the troublemakers. Fat old fool . . . they . . . wizard . . . him right.'

'I can't hear,' I complained to Lapiday. 'It's fading out.'

'Could be the wind,' he said. 'Keep listening, your ears are younger than mine.'

'. . . tower, set for the second explos . . .'

I looked round at him again, feeling a little uneasy. He looked quizzically at me but I didn't want to scare him, so I listened again. The wind must have calmed because this time the voice came through clearly.

'They say he never sets foot outside of his tower.'

'Now he never will,' said a second voice.

My heart skipped a beat. I tapped my wrist and Lapiday showed me his pocket watch.

'When's it due to go off?' said the first voice.

Lapiday's watch showed eight o'clock exactly.

'Eight o'clock. Listen out, it should be going off right n—'

'They're talking about us. It's *us* they're targeting! There's no time! RUN!' I shouted, grabbing him by the collar.

Terror was beating inside me like a fast drum, terror that we would be caught in the collapsing tower and crushed alive. Even the tiniest delay might mean death. Sprinting with all my strength, I reached the door and pulled it open, but saw the old man still six paces behind me. I rushed back, grabbed him by the shoulder, and at the same moment felt the stones under my feet shaking.

As I dragged Lapiday with me towards the door the sound of a huge explosion reached us from below and the shaking turned into a shivering, as though the stones beneath my feet were turning to water. We fell out of the door on to the iron bridge but I knew there was no way we could survive – the bridge would be pulled downward too, and we would be cut to pieces by the twisting metal.

The bridge convulsed, and stones and shards of brick that had been showered upward by the blast smashed against the underside, jolting us.

I grabbed the rails, closed my eyes tight, prayed and waited.

Now stones that had been blown high up above us began to rain down, and I heard myself coughing in the smoke and dust.

I should be dead, I thought. What's happening? Still coughing, I sat up and saw Lapiday still lying nearby, his eyes wide open, looking up at the dark sky. I thought for a moment he was dead, but his eyes swivelled to me and he smiled like a schoolboy who'd just got away with something.

'The spell worked, then,' he said. 'I wasn't sure it would.'

'What spell?'

He stood up, wiped the soot from his spectacle lenses with his tie, put them back on and pointed over the railing.

'I hate moving house, you see,' he said. 'And it always worried me what I would do if they demolished this tower.'

About ten feet below Lapiday's front door there was a ragged edge of bricks all the way round the tower, sticking out irregularly like bad teeth. Below that, nothing. The base of the tower had fallen away into the mist below and Lapiday's residence remained in mid-air, only attached to the earth by this frail iron bridge.

The sight was so bizarre, so outrageous, that I laughed hysterically at it – at the sight, and at having survived. I patted Lapiday on the shoulder and leaned my head in my hands for a moment.

'Well now,' he said. 'This would seem like a moment for a cup of tea, wouldn't you say?'

'No,' I said sharply, following him inside. 'Tea can wait. If you can help me with the key, as you said you could, then that's more important right now.'

'There's gratitude for you. And after you made us run outside into the smoke for no reason!' Then he turned to face me. 'How did you know they were going to attack us?'

'That's what the police were talking about!' I said. 'It was you they were after all along, not someone else from the Underground.'

He shook his head. 'It wasn't me they were talking about earlier, it was something else entirely. There is an arrest happening at midnight, which is still an hour away, and Prye's underlings are very excited and nervous about it. They seem to think the whole game is up if this fellow is caught. So I had to warn you – *on no account* must you go to the main square at midnight.'

'But I wasn't going to. Why on earth would I?'

He was surprised. 'You mean you haven't been told to go there to meet someone? Even by someone you really trust, who told you to keep it secret?'

I shook my head.

'But if it's not you, Daniel, who could it be?'

I had no idea – all the Undergrounders were still busy with the celebrations as far as I knew and would be for hours still. The Apothecary would be far beneath the surface by now. During this speech Lapiday had retreated down the steps to a little side parlour where he was preparing our tea and crumpets, which not only involved a lot of banging and clattering of pots and bottles, but took a long time. He could never be dissuaded from making a cup of tea.

As I waited for him to reappear, I tried to distract myself from my impatience by looking over the exotic paintings and decorated mirrors that hung on the walls.

'What are these things you have here?' I called out to him.

His voice came back from the next room. 'They're from dead cultures mostly, but all of them are to do with my art – with magic of some kind. Be careful, some of them are still alive, and could do you a mischief if you're not sure what you're dealing with.'

In the low glimmer of the candlelight I saw the head of a mighty horse-like creature with horns, mounted on the wall above me. As I watched, it turned on its neck to look down at me, its mouth chewing emptily, and the red of the candlelight blinked back at me in its glass eyes.

I gulped and turned away to another wall. Here I

261

saw oil paintings, fabulous rugs with whole battles told in their intricate weavings, and in one corner I recognized the mirror that I had seen last time I was here, still covered with a crushed velvet cloth. It was quite high up the wall, but Lapiday had left his portable ladder-on-wheels nearby and it slid silently over the carpet to where I wanted, letting me climb up and look more closely.

'I'm not joking, Daniel,' came the voice behind me, between clinkings of cups and the whistle of the kettle. 'Don't touch anything, it could be dangerous!'

I barely heard him, because I had experienced this magic myself already, and knew it was quite safe. I climbed until I was level with the picture and pulled back the cloth. Just like before, it was hard to see at first, and I stepped inside, feeling a shimmering of reality shifting around me as I did so, and the cloth fell back across the hole.

I was in a different place from before, but I didn't worry at first. It was very quiet, dark and peaceful. I could hardly see anything except a bed close by, and a table near it, covered with overturned bottles, tubes and jars. They were dirty and contained lumpy residues and cloudy mixtures. There was something of a disused chemistry set about it, accompanied by a sharp and nasty smell.

When I was quite close I noticed that the bed was not just unmade as I had first thought, but there was a thin figure beneath the sheets of a wasted-away old man, turning uncomfortably in his sleep. He awoke suddenly, and stared at me from where he lay, perhaps thinking I was a servant. He seemed malnourished, with his patchy beard and dark bulges beneath the bloodshot eyes.

Getting up on his elbows he mumbled and pointed at the table, as though he wanted me to fetch something. For half a second I thought perhaps I knew him somehow, and then in a flash I saw the real horror of who this was. It was the same man I had seen when I stepped through the mirror the first time, the man who was trapped alone working peacefully over his ledgers. Now here he was, reduced to a rag of a man, with all those years past, and nothing to show for it.

It was only then I began to wonder whether it was safe to be here. The mirror had chosen to show me these sights for some reason. The room I found myself in was enormous, as wide and high as a cathedral or a banqueting hall.

The old man climbed from the bed and leaned on a stick, staring at me glassily. He tried to speak, but only a garbled mumble came out, so he shouted loudly instead, as though calling for help.

Footsteps came from far away. I heard the snap of bolts being pulled back, then saw shapes emerging from the corners as the old man drank a draught of cloudy liquid, and strength seemed to come back to him.

I stepped back to the mirror from which I had

emerged, and which was propped near the bedside. He walked towards me. Now I realized there was something else in this old creature I knew from somewhere else. I couldn't put my finger on it, but the people coming to help him were close and, seeing me, they began to call out.

He pointed at me, and finally it dawned on me that I had seen his figure before, long ago, as a shape outside the window of a shop I was hiding in. I was struck motionless with fear, and at the last moment when the servants were almost within reach of me, a strong arm came from behind, grabbed me by the waist and pulled me back through the mirror.

'Are you all right, are you all right, boy?' Lapiday asked. I nodded. My head was spinning and over his shoulder I could see the whole tea service, buttered crumpets, jam pots and all, smashed and scattered on the floor. He clambered to the floor and allowed me to collapse into a chair nearby, taking deep breaths. He sat opposite me.

'What did you see?' he asked.

'It doesn't matter,' I said, avoiding his eye and trying to get my breath back. 'There's no time. Please, Mr Lapiday, excuse me. I may only have a few hours to find my sister's hiding place. I thought that was what you were going to tell me about.'

He didn't try to stop me, but helped me on with my coat and walked me to the door.

'I'm sorry I made you drop the tea things,' I said.

'I'd stay and help you clear up but . . .'

Without even looking behind him, Lapiday clicked his fingers and the whole service – pot, cups, saucers and tray – swept themselves up in a loud clattering movement and disappeared into the kitchen.

'I can have the tea make itself if I want to,' he explained, opening the door. 'I just enjoy the routine. Daniel, I won't ask you to tell me what you saw inside the mirror, but assure me of something: you'll stay away from the main square, at midnight?'

Standing on the iron bridge, with the mist around me, I buttoned up my coat. I nodded again. 'Of course,' I said. 'But as for the mirror, it told me that things are worse than I had thought. I thought Caspian Prye was some kind of fairytale villain – strong, demonic, wielding a sword perhaps. But he's just an ordinary man, weak and insane, drugged so he barely knows where he is. For some reason that makes me more afraid.'

He watched solemnly as I walked away over the bridge and closed his door quietly behind me. I began the long, cold descent down towards the street.

This was the darkest, coldest hour of my journey. I was alone with the rain, the streets and the possibility of Caspian Prye's police, who wanted to kill me, around every corner. All I could do was walk, and hope and wait for the key to pop into my hand.

The metal steps rang out beneath my feet and as I often did when walking alone, I began to think of one of the grisly tales I'd been told, running through it in my head to make sure I had the story straight for the next book of tales. I tried to think of the boys and girls at the Circus, and being gathered around that table once more. I told myself I would have the chance to tell it and, as I ran through it in my head, imagined the crowd (with Tusk and Mayrick, and Sally and Cook, with Boggins the dog farting in the background and a cup of hot chocolate in my hand) and smiled to myself at what their reaction would be. It was an audacious tale, called . . .

THE THING
IN THE
CHIMNEY

Number 34 Hester Street was not a quiet house. The family who lived there were poor, and what they lacked in money, they more than made up for in noise. There were at least seven children in the Poulter household (for that was the family's name), although no one was ever entirely sure, as disease had taken several of the less noisy ones, and Mrs Poulter always seemed to be giving birth to another.

But let's say there were, for the sake of argument, seven. The eldest, who was called Robert, was the strongest and the loudest of the boys, and the second eldest, who was called Sarah, was the loudest and the strongest of the girls. On the whole it was these two whose voices could be heard above the rest of the children, although the younger ones did their best to live up to their siblings' example.

For some months now, whenever they lit a fire smoke had poured back down the chimney into their house. This gave the impression of cannon fire on a battlefield, and not the sort of children to waste this opportunity, they had taken to having intense and noisy wars in and around the beds and chairs. But they quickly got tired of how the smoke made them cough (and made the younger ones faint) so they began moaning about it to their mother, and pulling her skirts, and going on and on until she thought she would lose her mind.

It wasn't exactly as though the children moaning at her was anything new to Mrs Poulter. They were forever complaining about being hungry, or not receiving presents, or about the horrible smell which came from one corner of the room (where sat their two uncles, Uncle Clare who was deaf and Uncle Osbourne who was mad, and their grandmother). In fact they usually made so much noise that hearing them moan made a pleasant change. This time, however, they went too far and their father raised himself from his chair and bellowed as loudly as a foghorn until they hushed, at which point he slumped back exhausted in his chair, and then the children's voices slowly started up again, and grew louder, until they were as bad as before.

'What did he say?' shouted Uncle Clare to Uncle Osbourne.

'Did you see that?' replied Uncle Osbourne, pointing. 'The wall. It moved!'

'WHAT?' bellowed Uncle Clare, straining to hear.

And so life went on.

Today, as it happened, the children were quite subdued, for now, and continued playing quietly until teatime. When I say quietly, I mean with about the noise level of a bunch of lunatics playing in a brass band. But that *was* quiet for the family, and so a peace of sorts descended.

Soon enough Mrs Poulter had managed to get the food ready and on the table and Mr Poulter unslumped himself from the chair once more to unleash the foghorn calling everyone to eat, as loudly as if they were scattered in the far wings of a great mansion. Roughly they jumbled into chairs and picked up their knives and forks and the children (along with mad Uncle Osbourne) rattled them loudly against the table in a chorus of impatience.

The noise and the food distracted the assembled family momentarily from the heavy fog which hung over the table. Uncle Clare secretly hoped that one of the children had caught fire, and would burn to a crisp, so there would be more food to go round. Soon, though, the smoke grew so thick that they could hardly see what was in front of them but even then they ate quietly, knowing that if they looked away for a second, their food was likely to go missing.

Finally Uncle Osbourne raised his head and cleared his throat.

'Excuse me?' he said. A little hand reached out and plucked a morsel of mutton from the point of his fork.

'Excuse me,' he said again, timidly, this time catching the hand which shot out and giving it a little slap. One by one the others looked at him and when he had all of their attention (with many hands quietly grabbing left and right from the plates), he opened his mouth as wide as it would go, took a deep breath, and yelled, '*FIRE!*'

Everyone jumped including Father, who was amazed to discover that anyone in the family had a voice louder than his. When they landed back on their chairs, everyone seemed to wake from a stupor and saw great churning gusts of smoke pouring in every direction. They all looked around and then returned to their food, finding that they were too hungry not to eat their dinner, even though they couldn't see it.

'We know there's a *fire*, Uncle Osbourne,' said Uncle Clare, happy that for once he had been able to hear something. 'We like the fire. It's the *smoke* we don't want.'

'We'll have to call the chimney sweep,' said Mrs Poulter sadly, glancing at the spot in the gloom where a little pot rested on a high shelf, containing their meagre savings. All of the heads simultaneously turned to look in the same direction (even though the pot itself, and the shelf, were quite invisible). Then they turned miserably back to their meals, and in the smoke could be heard the hungry chewing of twelve (or thirteen, no one could ever be sure) hungry mouths, broken only by the occasional cough.

When the chimney sweep arrived, three days later, the family were at dinner once more. There was nothing especially odd in his appearance, but nevertheless from the moment he appeared, he struck an uncanny fear into the family.

He was tall, true – but Father was tall, and broader around the shoulders. He was dark as well, but lots of people were dark who weren't at all frightening. He had bright eyes which shone almost madly from the middle of his wild mop of black bristly hair – yet none could match Uncle Clare for mad eyes (his were practically popping out of his head). Even so, at his appearance in

271

the doorway, something strange happened: every one of them instantly went silent.

The sweep watched them for a few moments before walking to the table and pulling up a chair which one of the children hurriedly jumped off to avoid being sat on. Then, tucking into the food on the plate in front of him and drinking tea from the cup in front of Grandma, he said, 'My name's Brisket.' He said it with a brittle hardness, as though not referring to himself but to an inhospitable splint of rock sticking out of a dark sea. 'Gabriel George Selsey Brisket the Second. Not that "the Second" is my surname,' he continued, turning his gaze down to the tiniest child who was on the seat next to him, 'but because my father was the First.' The little girl nodded dumbly.

He turned his eyes slowly around the entire family and unsettled each of them in turn with his cold, certain eyes. They looked back at him and saw the black moustache which stuck out over his lip as heavy as a thatched roof, and the two eyebrows as bristly as new boot brushes, and also as black. They looked at the sack he had brought, which clanked with equipment as he picked it up again (the unlucky child's meal being finished in two mouthfuls and Grandma's tea disappearing in one monster gulp) and walked to the fire.

The whole family knew at once that they were at the mercy of Mr Brisket, and could only watch as he now fastened a brush to the end of a short pole and pushed it up the chimney, then began fitting short lengths on the end as he pushed it further up. Some of the children came to watch, and such was the faith inspired by this curious man's confidence, they began to think that all their problems might be over in a matter of seconds.

As he watched the silent Brisket get to work, Mr Poulter wandered up behind him and coughed politely.

'You don't . . . er . . . you don't ever use children, Mr Brisket, in your line of work?' he asked in a casual voice, and gave a nervous little chuckle as with his eyes he took a headcount of his own little ones. He had tried to keep his voice low, but the chorus of tutting and 'dear oh dear's and shaking of heads that came from the other adults at the dinner table made him turn crimson with shame.

Brisket looked over his shoulder. Mr Poulter retreated a step, as though he was afraid of the sweep's reaction. But Brisket answered as matter-of-factly.

'Children?' he said, turning back to his work. 'The trouble with children is they're not economical.'

'You're telling me,' muttered Mr Poulter.

'You have to pay them a few pence each day. And they get sick, and die, or they get stuck in the chimneys, and you've got to get a new one. Which is a right pain, you know,' he said. 'Aah!' He shouted suddenly and the whole family (especially the children) jumped again, at least as high as they had before. Mr Brisket turned round, his face lit up and the bristles of his moustache and eyebrows shimmering like pine needles.

'A blockage!' he said, as though this came as some kind of surprise, considering it was he who had been called. 'A definite blockage, towards the top of the chimney.' He struggled for a few minutes trying to loosen it, but for some reason it wouldn't shift.

After getting no result except for little piles of ash and black dust all around him on the floor, he said he was going on to the roof. 'To try from another angle,' he explained. They all watched him go out and then stared at each other for a moment before Grandma said what they were all thinking.

'How's he going to get up there?' she asked. The answer came at once from the rhythmic squeaking of the drainpipe and as they tumbled over one another to the door they saw the chimney sweep clambering up the side of their house, already near the top. As they watched he stopped and looked down.

'It's rude to stare, you know!' he said, so they shuffled back inside and waited there to see what would happen. They all stared at the fireplace. After a little while they heard a *whumpf* sound, and a trickle of soot came down, lumps of it making a musical sound against the metal grate. They could hear Mr Brisket's voice far above, very faint and muffled, talking to himself between downward thrusts of his brush. 'It's a heavy blockage, that's for sure,' he said.

Whumpf. Another trickle of dust.

'Harder work than I expected!'

Whumpf. Trickle.

274

'Oh dear oh dear.'

Foomf. Trickle.

'This is getting a little bit frustrat—'

FUMMF!

Soot began to pour down in little torrents as though a black stream had been unblocked. It filled up the corners of the fireplace and gathered in silty piles on the stone floor. But Brisket didn't seem to get any closer to dislodging whatever was in the chimney and as the family stared at the fireplace he hammered away more and more aggressively.

Up above, Mr Brisket was struggling terribly with his desire not to swear. He was perched on the top of a steep roof, at an uncomfortable angle. His legs and feet ached. He knew that what he said could be heard by the family down the chimney because he could hear their voices filtering up from below. And with every push of the brush (which might make him lose his balance and hurtle into the street) he let out a grunt and an involuntary curse. Whatever was stuck down there (and it definitely wasn't just soot), it was large, heavy and almost impossible to move.

'*Drat* it,' he muttered, smashing down with the rod again. He imagined the blockage as a bulging sack of potatoes, stupidly lying there for no reason and waiting to be moved. He smashed it again.

'Blast it! Curse it!' he said, picturing a bag of books or cricket balls lodged there, or some collection of other articles which should never find themselves in a chimney. He started to wonder whether it had been put there to drive him mad.

His arms were tired, and the rain, as rain pretty much always will do, was making his temper worse. 'Wretched thing!' he cried, trying again, and finding he was almost at the end of his strength. He hung limply over the chimney's mouth, breathing in fine black dust in great deep lungfuls. He only had the strength left for one or two more tries, and he had never been defeated by a blocked chimney before. He was exhausted, miserable, soaked, and if anyone spotted him there, he would look pretty stupid into the bargain.

Once more he tried stuffing the pole down with his hurting arms. The object was stuck firm as concrete. Oaths and curses of the most abysmal rudeness writhed on the end of his tongue, desperate to be spoken. He bit his lip tightly and let out a little whine at the effort to keep them in.

The problem with swearing, you understand, is not that it's bad, and nasty, and a horrible thing to do. Because it is obviously all of those things. No, the *problem* with swearing (and keep this to yourself because adults won't admit it to you) is that if you are especially angry or upset or appalled or whatever-you-like, it does actually make you feel better. It gets rid of the bit of anger or upsettedness into the air, never to return. So while Mr Brisket struggled with his black hands on the black brush in the soot-encrusted chimney, he struggled just as hard against his darkening temper, and finally, raising his arms over his head, he lost. Thrusting the brush down one final time, he screamed out with anger: 'Oh *BLOODY HELL*!'

At the same time with this last push he felt the bulk of the thing in the chimney shift, sending the pole plummeting straight down with it and threatening to suck him clean into the chimney too. He nearly lost his footing, and his feet scrabbled on the wet slates as he hugged the chimney stack for dear life. When he was able to stand again he gingerly moved his head over the hole. Darkness: something was still blocking the light. But he could hear a lot of shouting and wailing from the room below, and worried the family had heard him swear and were angry with him, he called down to them.

'Is it OK?' he asked.

No answer came for a while, then he heard Mr Poulter's voice. 'I think you'd better come down and see for yourself,' it said.

In the main room of the Poulters' abode (which served, as such rooms did for all poor families, as kitchen, playroom, dining room, pantry and bathroom) all the players in this story sat very quietly in their usual places. Mr and Mrs Poulter sat at the table with Gabriel Brisket, the children on the floor at their feet. Grandma reclined on her threadbare rocker in the far corner, and Uncle Osbourne sat in his favourite chair, swinging his feet and smiling, and enjoying the first prolonged silence that this house had ever seen in his memory. Everyone else stared at the fireplace.

'Take it away,' Mr Poulter pleaded, without moving his gaze from the fireplace. 'Please. It's nothing to do with us, I promise. We'll pay you anything! Just take it away!' As if to illustrate what a fee of 'anything' might add up to, Mrs Poulter poured out the rest of their savings from the bowl on to the table. It amounted to no more than a miserable little heap of pennies.

Brisket stared back at them, his grave and serious face completely unreadable. The family, who had found him formidable to start with, now looked at him with undisguised terror. He might report them at once to the police. They might all end up in prison, or in the workhouse – or at the end of the hangman's rope!

Brisket's gaze turned to the fireplace, where in the middle of a pile of ashes stood the object of their discussion: a pair of stout leather boots, above which rose a pair of trousers and, just visible, the hem of a coat.

'Is he dead, do you think?' asked Uncle Clare, nervously.

'He'd probably tell us if he wasn't,' said Brisket, getting up, and walking over to the fire. 'Now, this is what I'm thinking. You lot can't be responsible for 'im, or else why would you have asked me round here?' They all nodded eagerly, encouraging his train of thought. 'And heaven knows what the law will make of it,' he went on. They all shook their heads as one – heaven

278

knew! 'So, although it's not traditionally in my line of work, I'll make an exception and get rid of this thing for you. On one condition: we keep this absolutely secret. Understood?'

It was hardly likely that the Poulter family were going to go around telling people of the special service Brisket was about to perform for them. Nevertheless, they promised him that the need for secrecy was indeed understood, and between them came to a further understanding over his fee for doing this. (Quite understandably, it had never occurred to Brisket to fix a fee for getting rid of dead bodies, but he reflected that it wasn't likely to be more difficult than dislodging the body from the chimney in the first place, so he requested double his original fee, and they shook hands on it.)

Once this was agreed, the family sighed sweetly, their shoulders fell in relief, and all at once Mr Brisket rose in their eyes from a feared stranger to a saviour of sorts, perhaps one even to be worshipped. Without a moment's delay he was at the fireplace and wrestling the awkward bulk of the body down from the chimney, with much more splashing of soot, and a good deal of grunting and sighing from Mr Brisket. When it came to the level of the shoulders, perhaps out of superstition that, after all that, the man *might* still be alive, Mr Brisket eased the body out as gently as he could. Rigor mortis had passed long ago, and the body was as floppy as that of someone who was just asleep, or in the middle of a faint.

He laid out the corpse, which was that of a man, on the floor in front of the fire, with its arms stretched above it, looking as though he had died in the middle of diving into the sea. The children couldn't keep their eyes off it, and Mr Poulter said something quietly into Brisket's ear which made him lay the arms back at the man's side. They all stood back to look at it.

The dead man was not young. He was thin, his cheeks were drawn and his face wrinkled terribly about the mouth and eyes. In his last unhappy moments he had fixed upon his face a look of horror – his mouth was open in a gasp – and every tiniest bit of his face and enormous beard was utterly covered in soot, giving his open blue eyes a penetrating clarity. His hair, which was long and splayed everywhere in a haphazard way, was coated so thickly it was like black string, and his clothes were so densely matted that they looked as though the colour black had been growing on them like a fungus. Everyone who looked at the aghast face supposed that he must have been a poor tramp, trying the chimney out of desperation to get out of the cold and wet outside, and they felt terribly sorrowful at the idea this had happened just a few feet away from them.

Mr Brisket, however, with a double fee in his sights, was not so sentimental. After staring at the body for a moment, he pulled a canvas sack out from his big bag and shook it open. 'If we could get on with the business at hand,' he snapped, and Mr Poulter helped Brisket force the bag over the corpse's head and down to his waist. Then Brisket produced another (these were sacks he used to collect the soot that fell from his customers' chimneys) and forced it up over the feet to the waist again. Where the two bags met he ran a rope through holes round the rim of both bags, which were usually used to tighten them shut, and tied the ends to each other to make one big package. He hoisted it up over his shoulder and bounced it a couple of times, testing the weight. It seemed fine, so he picked up his leather bag with all his equipment safely stashed in it, placed his fee in an inside pocket, and looked them all over once more in a secretive way as though to say, 'Now you can forget that I was ever here.' Then he stepped out into the street.

'So, what to do with it?' he thought to himself when he had been walking for a few minutes. 'The river will be the best place, but I'd best make sure it falls from the middle of a bridge – if it's near the bank it might be swept straight on to the shore, and I might get caught.'

As he walked, he staggered a little to the left because of the huge weight, and in trying to correct himself, went sprawling in front of a huge coach coming up behind him. Startled, he dropped the body right under its wheels and leaped for safety. The hoofs and wheels pounded the sack with a great thumping, crunching sound that made Mr Brisket look away feeling sick, only to find there was another coach riding up right behind it. Six more horses (and twenty-four more hoofs) and another four wheels made a jaunty little jump as they pounded over it, leaving their prints clearly on the soft, squidged mess.

Running into the traffic, he darted between the vehicles and yanked the package back to the side of the road. It was now covered in mud and giving off a rather offensive smell, but was still just about in one piece.

Sighing, and cursing the moment he'd ever set foot inside the Poulters' house, he hoicked the heavy weight over his shoulder again, shaking a little now. What if someone asked what was inside it? Then he'd be done for. He had to move fast. He decided not to take any more risks and to sacrifice a few pennies of his fee by taking the next coach which would drive him straight to the river.

Within a few minutes it came and Brisket got on board gratefully, tossing his mysterious package up on to the roof before the driver had a chance to examine it.

In the meantime the Poulter family were settling round the fire once more. In the tradition of thoughtful and helpful men throughout the ages, all the gentlemen present had decided to sit back and watch Mrs Poulter do all the work as she swept out the fireplace, threw the soot into the street, laid a new fire, lit it, cut some bread, buttered it, handed it to them and sat down. Then they all watched as the flames began to nibble cautiously around the sticks of wood, and then catch and burn with a soothing steadiness. They were cold to their bones, so just watching those first little teeth of flame made them feel warmer. After the discomfort and horror of the day a quiet air of contentment, settled in the room. Puffs of smoke curled up the chimney – and a few seconds later, curled right back down again.

'Who was that man?' said Uncle Osbourne, rather suddenly, as though the thought had only just occurred to him.

'That is it!' shouted Mr Poulter in fury, leaping out of his seat. 'That ... is ... IT! It's an OUTRAGE! Still blocked! Charlie! Lucy! Amy! Matthew! You're going up the chimney!' And throwing his tea into the fire, he kicked at it until it was truly out, and ordered all the littlest children who were big enough to walk up the chimney one by one.

Charlie, who was the smallest, thought it was wonderful fun. He stood on Lucy's shoulders. Lucy protested violently, and was completely ignored, and forced to stand on the shoulders of Amy (who was afraid of the dark, and squeezed her eyes shut), who in turn was propped up by Matthew.

'What was that dead fellow *doing* up there?' asked Uncle Osbourne, but no one listened to him.

'You are an infernal bellyache, you know that?' muttered Uncle Clare to him. 'And I can't even hear you.'

'I mean, how did he *get up there*?' shouted Uncle Osbourne.

'Have you found anything?' called Mr Poulter to his children up the chimney.

'I fink so!' called Charlie. 'It's quite big!'

'"Think", darling, say "think"! It's *so* important to speak properly,' called his mother, over her husband's shoulder.

'There's a time and a place, my dear,' muttered Mr Poulter. Then bending down to the fireplace he called upward again, 'Grab hold of it and pull it down, if you can. Quick sharp, come on!' And with military precision he counted them, blackened, tumbling and giggly, as they came back out of the chimney. 'Matthew! Amy! Lucy! Charlie!'

After Charlie a great heaving black shape fell into the fireplace, and a cloud of soot exploded into the room again. The family stared, wondering who would have the nerve to approach it first.

The coach placed Mr Brisket down a few hundred yards away from the nearest bridge. In throwing down the package to him the driver had aimed badly and accidentally thrown it on to the railing spikes that ran up the street, where it landed with a sickening splat.

'Oops, sorry, guv'nor,' said the driver.

'Not to worry,' said Brisket cheerfully. His black eyebrows and thick moustache quivered with anger because he was in no position to argue with the stupid man. He levered the body up off the spike with difficulty and threw it over his shoulder one last time. Now it was oozing some sort of unpleasant slime over his shoulder, but there was only one last little stretch to walk until he reached the river and then all this would be over with.

It seemed to take longer than all of the rest of the trip put together. The package was unbearably heavy now, and Brisket felt terribly guilty-looking. At every step his feet slipped a little and his legs felt a little weaker. As he reached the bridge a strolling policeman nodded at him, and in response Mr Brisket (who had until now always been a God-fearing man who followed the last letter of the law) smiled in a way he was sure made him look like an unscrupulous crook and murderer.

At last, he found himself in the middle of the bridge. Traffic was passing back and forth, making its blessed clatter and roar that would cover his sin.

'Quickly now,' he thought, and leaned the package against the wall ready to go over into the river. Then, as he balanced it on the edge ready to fall in, his breath caught in his throat and he let out a cry of horror. For the package started to wriggle, like an enormous black maggot. A coughing sound came from within, and a tremulous voice.

'Oh dear, oh dear, where am I?' the voice said.

Brisket screamed again, and out of fright gave one last mighty shove, pushed the thing over the parapet and down into the fast-racing water below, before he had a chance to think what he was doing.

He watched the mighty splash, saw the package consumed by the river and vanish completely. He stared after it for a long time, unable to move his eyes from the water.

In the Poulter household, Uncle Osbourne stooped over the sack in the middle of the floor. 'Why has everyone gone so quiet?' he asked. 'What's going on?'

They had indeed gone quiet. The noise of number 34 Hester Street had gone, and it would never return. Getting no reply, Uncle Osbourne reached into the black sack which they had dragged from the fireplace (and in which a fire now smoked with a quiet crackle). He pulled out of it a little black box, and rubbed the soot from it to reveal a covering of bright, attractive wrapping paper. Then he reached in and saw another and another, all different sizes, and as he rubbed the soot off, he saw they were all addressed to children with different names.

'How lovely!' he said, delighted. 'How utterly lovely! A bag of presents! Is it Christmas, then?'

No one answered him. They couldn't. Uncle Osbourne grew confused at their serious faces, and instead turned his attention to the sack of parcels and carried on pulling more and more little gifts from it, wiping the dust from each one as he went, and lining them up in a row.

nce I had told the story to my imaginary audience, I was alone again in the dark streets. A deep sense of danger hugged me like a cloak, and I hunched my shoulders. It wasn't to do with the explosions, or the police – it was something else, creepier and more instinctive, that made me look over my shoulder.

Even now I saw no sign of the police, or even heard the hoofs of their horses. Maybe there were so few people left that they didn't need to patrol so often at night. Yet I almost wished for the threat of their presence – they were at least human. The route away from Lapiday's tower (or the rubble where his tower had been) led gently downhill. The only sound was my feet on the cobbles, the rain too soft to make a noise except for a quiet dripping from the gutters. I felt that something was watching me and looked over my shoulders again.

Stay calm, I thought. It's just the city streets at night. They're creepy. You're used to this.

The road curved as it went downward and I could only catch a glimpse of something I thought I saw moving in the distance, but it struck a fresh chill into me. It was no ordinary person, but a figure in a monk's habit, walking at a gentle pace. I even thought I saw his glow, but it was hard to make anything out distinctly.

I needed no more warning – I ran, sprinted as hard as I could, not caring what noise I made, until I had put hundreds of yards behind me, and rested in a shady doorway, breathing hard. Who knew what danger would take me first – Prye, his policemen, or the Monk? Something was definitely coming to a head this evening, and I had precious little time to search the streets and wait for the key to appear in my hand. Who was expected to appear in the main square tonight, and why?

I walked hard, and pushed the danger out of my head. There were near-misses with policemen passing on horseback as I darted between streets, but I kept going, searching out areas I didn't know well, going by every one of the doors which had been secret entrances to the witch's house (she had many doors so she could get into her cosy home from almost anywhere in Tumblewater). I went in wide circles until I was almost sure I had covered every street in the district.

Nothing.

Nearly midnight, and the key hung by its string and bumped against my chest as ever it had. I was nearly out of choices, out of possible ideas, and as I found myself at a crossroads, and saw that whichever road I chose I would be retracing my earlier steps, I began to fear it was true.

There was nothing I could do. Maria was lost, there was nothing and no one to help me find her in this enormous, endless city. With unbearable dread I looked the fact of her death in the face. It made me walk faster, run – that was something I wasn't going to accept.

Then the clock struck a quarter to midnight, and it made me think.

The one place I *hadn't* tried was the main square, because it was so dangerous, and because I had been warned away. Stupid! Now I was nearly out of time to try it. And it was nearby. I remembered that there was a statue of Caspian Prye in the centre of the square carved from an enormous block of stone. I began to get excited. What if she could be there – hidden, as I had supposed she might be, in plain sight, and inside his very own emblem? It all seemed to make sense.

Despite a nagging doubt that Lapiday's knowledge and learning were vast, and his advice not to be taken lightly, I planned a route through the Underground that would get me there quickly and invisibly: I could enter a house nearby, follow a tunnel from a hidden entryway under the street and into a row of abandoned dwellings. Then the path was easy, through a sequence of hidden doors that went all the way to the square. It would bring me out of a basement door whose staircase was hugely overgrown with ivy. This would make the perfect vantage point. Whatever happened at midnight, I would wait for my chance to approach the statue. I set off at once.

As I hurried along my journey I became more and more puzzled by who it might be the police were due to ambush. No one from the Underground was stupid enough to come up to a rendezvous in such an obvious place: they would be too suspicious. Even someone as new to the place as the Apothecary – after so lately escaping the gallows, what could possibly entice him above ground? And the same could surely be said for ex-Inspector Rambull? That left only me, but that didn't make sense either! No one could possibly know where I was going to be, if I hadn't known myself a short while before.

I had to think of other people who might be totally unexpected. Perhaps Gora the witch had somehow survived, or perhaps they *had* discovered Maria after all and found some way of having her released and handed over to them. It all sounded so preposterous that when I took up my hiding place I was hardly able to concentrate due to the anticipation. On the stairs leading up from the basement to the street I found a spot just above ground level, where I could peek out but escape quickly if anything happened. I looked in every direction around the square with a burning curiosity.

There was nothing to see, but from the first moment of looking out into the square I sensed something was gravely wrong. There was a silence that was stretched with tension, as though people were waiting in each shadow, invisibly – the shadows themselves seemed deep and seething. I tricked myself into thinking I could detect the whispering of strangers from every corner.

The minutes ticked past and I sat and looked from side to side, trying to keep an eye on every part of the square. Then, just before the clock struck midnight, a horse-drawn carriage appeared at the east end, to my left, and drew to a halt. Then, to my astonishment, I heard my name.

'Daniel?' called out a voice. My heart leaped into my throat. Uncle! How could he be so stupid as to come here? Had he gone mad?

He appeared from the right side, and as he walked across the cobbles towards the carriage I thought I could see shapes stirring in the shadows, figures moving, ready to pounce. I wanted more than anything to shout out, because surely this was a trap. But that would mean certain death for both of us. Somehow I kept my mouth shut and watched that slow, steady tread as Uncle walked towards his doom. Of *all* people, why would he be here?

I stood and pulled the ivy back from head height so I could jump over the fence if need be.

I could definitely hear sounds now, footsteps and rustling movements, from different corners of the square. It was impossible that Uncle didn't hear them too, and I saw a grim determination in his face as he kept walking without turning his head. Although his figure appeared unhealthily thin, his gait seemed extra-heavy and burdened, as though he knew he was sacrificing himself.

'Daniel?' he called out, but I was sure he didn't expect me to appear. He knew what was going to happen next. Four shapes ran from the shadows on the other side and surrounded him. As I had anticipated, he showed no surprise, and once they took hold of him, only struggled when their grip on him was severe and painful.

They brought him to his knees with brute force, and for a sickening moment I thought they were going to execute him there and then. But then they let go of him and one of the police officers unfurled a sheet of paper ready to read it out.

They paused, relishing their victory, waiting for something. A door in the carriage opened and a slim figure stepped out, one whom I had very recently laid eyes on. Caspian Prye.

He walked with a stick until he was standing only a few feet away from Uncle. He nodded to the policeman, who began to speak.

'Augustus Prye, I hereby place you under arrest . . .'

I didn't hear the rest. My head span. Augustus Prye. So that was why I never knew Uncle's name. How could this be? It couldn't be true!

I regained my composure, and stupidly climbed over the top of the railing, determined to rescue Uncle if I humanly could. I was in plain sight as I dropped on to the street, hoping that I might even create a diversion.

Thanks to the drugs there was a strength in Caspian Prye. He had the hideous, manic energy of the potions that had lost him his mind, and instead of leaning on his stick he walked with perfect grace, as a gentleman might, tapping it happily on the floor, and then, raising it up, he pulled the handle from the shaft, revealing a wickedly sharp blade in his hand.

It wasn't clear that he even knew where he was as he whipped the blade through the air a few times, only that the blunt-faced men around him were going to allow him to do what he pleased, which meant, I was sure, running his own brother through with his sword.

'Oh dear,' said a voice behind me. It seemed to come from the air, and I spun round looking for it, but couldn't see anything, so I turned back to the Prye brothers. I raced towards them, taking no care to remain silent, and I knew that any second now I would be spotted.

Then everything happened at once.

I had been dimly aware of other figures stepping out of the shadows, from the far end of the square. Now someone else became visible, emerging from behind Prye's carriage and taking its place behind him – the chilling vision of the red-haired creature, whom we had thought as dead as could be, its mask still intact, and a slight dragging limp in its gait.

The sight of this was met with a blistering roar of anger from the other end of the court, and a large group came running forward with what looked like weapons in their hands. At the head of the group was ex-Inspector Rambull, brandishing a pistol. Around him were people from the Underground – Mr Shallows was there, Silas Crone and Miss Slade – but best of all, my friends from the school. All together and armed, they looked as well-trained and fearsome as an army.

'I've killed you once!' Rambull shouted, confronting the red-haired creature, who still refused to speak. 'Damnit, I'll do it again!' He aimed his gun and fired it at her. The bullet hit her square in the forehead, splayed the skin and splintered the bone. Her head jerked back for a second and then with a painful-looking shrug she twisted it back into place and ran at him.

Other teachers and pupils fell against the line of policemen, hacking with their swords, making a great crashing sound. A knife clattered to the floor near me and, picking it up, I jumped into the fray, ducking beneath blades and parrying blows. But there was one more noise I could hear. I turned round.

'Get stuck in, chaps! Good show!' It was that voice coming from the air above me again. In the back of my head I distantly recognized it was Lapiday, using his contraption again. 'By the way,' the voice went on, 'I thought you might need some help, Daniel. Here goes!' This, too, took me a second to take in. Then I stumbled out of the fighting crowd, and looked. There was an orange light in the sky, like a flame. A flame that seemed to be growing larger.

'Oh my God,' I said. 'It's Doctor Whizzbang! Get down!'

The orange flame grew larger in the sky above as the rocket approached, and at my words Caspian Prye's head snapped in my direction. Instantly he completely forgot about Rambull's men, and even his brother. I was the prize.

'Get him!' he shouted. 'All of you, get that boy!'

Everyone suddenly turned and looked at me – and came straight towards me, the policemen trying to grab and the Undergrounders rushing to protect me. The sight of them all was too terrifying to behold without running. I turned and sprinted to the nearest side street, seeing the orange glow get bigger in the sky, and when I got to the corner I stopped and looked back. Ten or fifteen of Prye's men were just twenty yards behind, with Prye himself, who with the chemical poison in his blood was now made as agile and athletic as any of them.

As I watched, the orange flame tore down from above and landed in the middle of the square. The Under-grounders had heard my voice, and seen it coming, and had retreated to safety or thrown themselves on to the ground. But there were two figures who didn't move, trapped in a desperate clutch of hate-fuelled strength. Rambull and the flame-haired creature stayed in the middle of the square as the rocket exploded and they vanished in a bright, intense, billowing plume of fire, both of them incinerated in less than a second.

It was a deafening, shattering blast. Every window in sight exploded and chunks of rock smashed into the sides of houses. All the men were knocked off their feet and I was thrown far backwards, down the side street.

When I struggled to my feet I saw figures surrounding me and jumped up, shouting, 'Get back!'

'We shall do no such thing,' said Sally. 'We're here to protect you, idiot!'

There she was, with Mayrick and Tusk, and all the others from our class.

'This is the uprising, Daniel!' said Tusk. 'It's actually happening!'

Sally grabbed me by the collar. 'The one thing Prye mustn't get now is that key, for your sake. We'll hold them back, but get away. Run!'

I didn't need to be told twice. I ran, clattering down the empty cobbled streets, glancing back over my shoulder only when I found an alley to dart down.

The others did an incredible job of holding back the men. I heard gunshots, saw sickening plunges of blades turned red, but one man, Caspian Prye himself, fought with a desperate slashing nastiness and broke through the line, sprinting after me.

I vanished into the alley, and ran in the darkness.

Soon I found an even smaller turning, and ducked into it, never slowing. I turned right at the end, then left again, pushing every muscle and stretching every tendon, twisting with all the skill at hiding and escaping I had learned, until there was . . .

I stopped. Was there quiet behind me? I ran again, down a short lane, turned right, stopped and listened once more.

The streets seemed perfectly empty, I couldn't hear

a thing. I decided to keep following my route westerly through the little lanes, walking quietly so I could hear anyone behind me as I made my way down the hill, and wiping the rain from my face.

Now it was several minutes since I had lost sight of Prye, but looking back up the hill I thought I glimpsed a shape coming towards me. I couldn't be sure, but at first glance it didn't look like Prye, but seemed to be someone dressed in old-fashioned clothes. I quickly darted through a courtyard to the next street along, and kept walking, but when I turned, a figure in the corner of my vision slipped out of sight slickly, almost as fast as my eyes could look. It was closer than last time.

I decided to run, and made a sudden burst, expecting to hear footsteps behind me. I put thirty fast yards between me and whatever was behind before I reached one of the lopsided crossroads in Tumblewater where lots of streets all converged at once and then went off in different angles. Without stopping, I couldn't help a quick glance over my shoulder again. Something caught my toe and I went sprawling, scraping my knees across the cobbles and tumbling over before I could regain myself. Disorientated for a second, I couldn't tell which of two streets I had come sprinting out of, until I saw someone high up the slope above me, walking slowly downward. For a moment I stayed on my knees, watching him approach. This was no ordinary person.

As hard as it was to be sure in the dark, I thought I saw the shape of a monk, his face hidden by his hood. And he didn't seem to walk, more to float. I even thought I saw the dim glow of his teeth, but it was impossible to be sure of anything.

I got up and sprinted again, harder than ever, not caring what noise I made, not caring if any of the last remaining policemen came now, because they might scare him away. I looked down and saw what had made me trip: it was the tiny roots of that tree that Guthric had shown me, growing between the cobbles. The roots spread like creeping fingers along this whole street, down the hill. They were the roots of the tree from the graveyard at St Elsifer's. Suddenly thinking of a plan, I followed them.

I didn't look back any more, but only ran like the wind, following the roots towards the churchyard. The Monk, that ancient evil spirit who was supposed to be not a monk at all, might not be afraid of anything, I thought, except a church. I didn't take breath until I turned a corner and saw the forgotten, mouldering graveyard and tumbledown chapel not fifty feet away.

I looked back again, and thought I heard pattering footsteps, so I ran the last few yards to the churchyard and leaped between two broken railings. I slithered on the mud to get my feet and tried to make no noise. I was still too close to the street, so I wormed my way between two graves, into the darkness. I felt my foot slip into a cold pool of liquid and it crunched against what could have been gravel or bones, but I didn't care – I felt a raw fear that I was still in plain sight to whoever was chasing me. Putting both feet into the muddy grave, I waded quietly through it to the other side, and slipped out behind a mournful marble angel. There was a large family gravestone leaning against it, which I dived behind, using it for cover. Now I allowed myself a cautious peep over the top into the street.

Up at the corner, where I'd been less than a minute before, was the unmistakeable shape of Caspian Prye. My eyes had deceived me – it looked nothing like a monk at all, but a slim, wasted-away man, whose strength-enhancing drugs were wearing off, and who was starting to look wild in the eyes. Although he couldn't see me, and couldn't know for sure I was there, when he walked along the railings looking in, he did it with calm assurance. A chilling sensation struck me still, unable to move.

He *doesn't* know I'm here, I thought, as I crawled backwards in the dark, still in the cover of that large stone. He *can't* see me. I clambered over some roots and the stump of a broken gravestone, and slithered through a trickling stream that spilt over what might or might not have been a grave. Everywhere I caught my hands and feet on the spindly roots of the tree that had grown into every last nook of the place. I was terrified I would slip and make a noise. Then I saw ahead of me a small marble mausoleum, not much larger than a broom cupboard. Its front door had been cracked open by the moving of the earth over time, leaving a hole just wide enough for me to squeeze in. I slithered inside almost silently, clambered on top of a rotting coffin that was covered in weeds, and turned around so I could see back through the crack in the door.

I was only afforded a narrow view from my vantage point. There were muddy, puddle-strewn graves in the foreground, then a few large headstones and beyond that all I could see was a section of railing, nothing more. I couldn't tell whether Prye might appear at the railings, or whether he had already moved on.

I held my breath, and wondered how long I would wait before it was safe to look outside again. I'd stay here all night, and all day, and all year if it meant not setting eyes on Caspian Prye once more.

My breathing was just starting to calm when I saw his face, right up close, outside the mausoleum door. My heart juddered to a stop. I thought it would never start again. He was looking right towards where I was hidden. Only now did I think that he must have acquired occult abilities from the magicians in his employ.

But it was too late now. There was no other way out of this tiny stone prison. I had trapped myself. I could do nothing but watch from the darkness, hating every step he took closer, hoping that something, anything would happen.

All at once he brandished his blade and stuck it in through the crack in the door, whittling the air around my head. I shrank back desperately and the coffin cracked beneath me. I fell half into it and as I clutched for a grip felt my fingers close around bones. The sword

300

angled inwards again, closer to me this time, chipping the stone beside my shoulder. I flinched, knowing the next time it would slice through my skin, and he would be able to reach in and pluck the key from around my neck.

Instead, he moved his face close to the crack, and stared into the darkness where I hid. I couldn't tell whether he saw me, but at last I got to look at his face close up. I saw that the quiet, mild, hard-working young man I had seen through the mirror was still there, in the lines around his mouth, and the shape of his cheekbones. But it was into the eyes themselves that one couldn't help staring. They seemed quite empty, like holes through which his human soul had long ago drained.

He was not a man, just an animal, and he looked at me like I was an animal too, waiting to be slaughtered.

I saw all this, and then realized that he had ceased to move, and was quite still. I wondered whether this was some slowing of time, that in my last moments before death perhaps one had longer to come to an appreciation of one's life and to make peace.

Then I saw there was a glow all around him, a soft light that grew in strength. I slithered to the furthest corner, the lid of the coffin snapping into shards, and squeezed myself against the marble to try to disappear. But he didn't move, and the light grew stronger.

His face seemed to shake slightly. It looked almost as though he couldn't move. The shaking spread to his shoulders, then his whole body, and he jolted as if struck by lightning, throwing his head back. His sword clattered to the ground.

Then I noticed two hands, that were not his but belonged to someone standing behind him. The glowing seemed to come from them, and they were outstretched, as though in blessing. Prye was no longer in control of his body.

I didn't even think. In a flash, I leaped forward and picked up the sword. Standing there, paralysed and transfixed, there was something in his eyes, at last. It was fear. With all my strength I jabbed the blade upward, into his chest, through his body and out the other side.

Then I fell back, and watched.

It was impossible to tell whether I had killed him or if he was already dead. Still fixed in his rigid posture, he rose until his feet left the ground, jerking from the sheer power coursing through his body. His arms and chest and neck twisted as though in agony – although he was clearly no longer alive.

There he hovered for a few seconds, and then he was lowered back down to the ground and the arms closed around him, as gently as in a brotherly embrace, and I saw the veins stand out on his head. His eyes started open and his mouth gaped, as though he felt a terrible pain but could not scream. Then, very fast, his skin shrivelled as though he aged fifty years and passed through death to a state far beyond; his hair shimmered bright white, the bones stood out from his skin. He shrank in an instant to an ancient corpse, sucked of life and crumpled into a dry shell.

The glowing figure removed its arms, and what had been Caspian Prye fell to the earth.

My breath whispered shakily out of my mouth. I tried to make no sound at all.

In front of me, serene and still, stood the figure of a monk, his hood hiding all of his face except a gentle smile that revealed his glowing teeth.

He slowly clasped his hands peacefully in front of him, and remained standing there in perfect calm as the shining light was absorbed back into him and became a dim glow.

Just as slowly, a realization began to dawn on me. I knew this must be the Monk whom the boy ghosts had told me of, older than any religion or language that we knew. There was only one difference from how they had described him: now I was alone in his presence there was no feeling of threat or menace of any kind. Only peace. I wondered if this was the truth of him, that he was in fact a guardian of this place. If he had spirited away people's souls it was because they were going to do something terrible – whether they had murder on their minds, or were innocently transporting the plague in their bodies, and risking the spread of it. Perhaps he appeared on the streets only late at night because that was where the very worst characters were to be found.

Very slowly I stood up. Nothing pierced the air of quiet serenity. I squeezed through the gap and stood in front him, wondering what he truly was, or who he had been. With no idea what else to do, I knelt in front of him and bowed my head, to show thanks. I wanted it to be a solemn gesture that he would understand, but even there in the graveyard I felt a bit foolish. When I looked back up his hands were not clasped in front of him any more – he was pointing over my shoulder, back up the slope.

I couldn't see to the top of the graveyard where he seemed to be pointing, so I scrambled up the knobbly roots and over muddy ledges, grabbing handfuls of slippery wet grass until I was close to the looming shapes of the chapel and the tree. Trying to clamber up the last bit of slope I was momentarily distracted by an annoying obstruction in my hand that had made it harder to climb. As I turned back to look down at him, I felt it.

The key.

I opened my fingers and saw it there, like magic. An instant ago it had been banging against my chest as I climbed, and my hands had been full of mud and grass as I pulled myself up. I hadn't made any move to put it in my hand. And I suddenly realized how stupid I had been. The clues had been in front of me all along, from the moment Guthric explained the key to me! He had said that the key would find its way into my hand unexpectedly, when I was close to something that was hidden. And I realized I had been walking through this graveyard with him, on my way to the river, when it had found itself there. I just hadn't put two and two together.

Seeing the abandoned church in front of me, I walked straight to the great tree, which had for so long unnaturally thrived in this sickly place, and pushed the key into a cleft in its ancient hardened skin. The key sank in easily, as deeply as into a lock. I took a very long, deep breath before trying to twist it.

No well-oiled lock ever turned as easily. I stood back, and pulled the key gently. Hundreds upon hundreds of years' worth of rings in the wood were revealed as a section of wood swung outward like a door – a door which by some optical illusion was thicker than it was wide. Standing back, it was as though the enormous tree had just grown a mouth, and now it hung open in astonishment.

I didn't need a candle to look inside, because a faint light issued from the hole, deep in the middle of the enormous tree. The light was soft, and the hole was tiny, hardly big enough to fit a person, yet a small body was somehow curled up on the floor in there.

I did not stop to feel relief, or happiness or gratitude. I could only rush forward to her, to pull her up, and carry her carefully back through the doorway until she was outside of the tree's influence. Then I laid her down tenderly on the ground.

I murmured quietly to her, and shook her gently.

Although she was more than ten years older than me, she had been frozen in time, and we seemed almost the same age. I marvelled at how similar we looked. At first her face was utterly still, as though she was actually frozen, but then she started to have irregular breaths, and even let out a little cough.

'That's it!' I said. 'That's it, Maria! Come on!' I was light-headed after all I'd been through the last few days – explosions, celebrations, ghosts, everything – and I felt that she was so close to coming back to me I was laughing and crying at the same time, as though I was cheering her on. She blinked.

'Yes!' I laughed, and rocked her back and forth in my arms. 'You're here!'

She opened her eyes, and looked lost, and I suddenly realized that she couldn't know who I was. It didn't matter – I could explain later. I kissed her cheek and her forehead and rocked her harder. She looked up at me.

'You're alive again,' I said, smiling. 'You're safe!'

She didn't seem to see me, but gazed at something behind me.

'My friends . . .' she said.

I looked up and saw standing several little figures standing around us. I knew them as Oates and Wrigglesworth and Featherstone, and all the other little ghosts. I had never expected I could see them acting so well-behaved. Featherstone had even removed his ghost cap, and was holding it in his hands.

'You're her friends?' I asked.

Oates slowly looked from her face to mine. 'We've visited her, yes, over the years. She was so nice to us, it was like having a kindly aunt. How could we know that you knew her?'

'This is my sister!' I said. 'This is who . . .' I didn't want to say the name, and curse the moment. 'This is who *he* was looking for.'

'We had no idea,' said Wrigglesworth. But the boys weren't really talking to me, they were just staring at Maria. It filled my heart that I had met these boys and loved them, and she had too. It was the first thing I ever knew about her that we had both done, independently of each other. It was the first glimmer that my sister and I truly were alike, and I was unspeakably grateful to know it.

Before the little ghosts or I or Maria could say anything, we were all struck silent by something that none of us had expected. In front of the door which had been opened in the tree, four or five other children were standing, looking dazed. They looked from one another to the chapel, and then to us, and the graveyard below, not knowing where they were. Another boy came out behind them, and then two more, a boy with his little sister in tow, holding his hand.

'My friends!' said Maria quietly, still smiling.

'But how did they *fit* in there?' I wondered.

She hardly had the strength to speak. 'I don't know how I knew it was you, but somehow I did, Daniel.'

307

She rested her head on my arm and looked back at the children appearing out of the tree. There were more than a dozen of them now, and without speaking they were walking carefully in single file down through the graveyard to the gate.

'They're not alive,' she whispered softly to me, almost as though she didn't want them to hear, and have their feelings hurt. 'They are spirits, who died long ago and were trapped there long, long before I was. Before we were born, Daniel.' She closed her eyes for a second and put her hand to her forehead, as if dizzy.

'Come on,' I said. 'We'll have you in a bed in no time, safe and away from the streets.' I made to try and get her to her feet, but she held my wrist.

'No,' she said. 'I want to see this. We must watch.'

The line now spread from the hole in the tree all the way into the street, where it split to go in three different directions. People kept coming, children and adults, blinking as they came out, as though using their eyes for the first time. Now the ghost boys recognized some of the friends they had told me about, missing at the time of the plague, and called them forward. The spirit children came over as though in a daze, and Oates and his friends gathered them in with love and attention, asking them nothing, just accepting them into the group as though they hadn't been gone a day.

Still they kept pouring out, and now I saw that a change had come over the neighbouring streets: houses that had stood empty for years were opening their doors, and whole families were standing on their doorsteps.

'They've been waiting a long, long time for this moment,' said Maria. We saw people hugging, embracing, laughing, the streets alive again – with dead people. Four brothers, hand in hand in a little row and the eldest barely six years old, were all met by their mother, who picked them up in one huge bundle and squeezed them close. All around them other ghosts were walking to similar welcomes, streaming out of sight to find doors in the streets beyond.

Oates and Wrigglesworth sat playing and talking with the boys they had just rescued from the tree, filling them in on hundreds of years' worth of gossip, news, jokes and tall tales. Now I slowly helped Maria to her feet. She was weak, but happy. We knew it was time to go, and leave this scene to play out on its own.

Very carefully we walked down through the graveyard towards the rusted gate. When we had nearly reached the bottom there was a rushing sound like a sudden wind ripping through a forest. We looked up and saw that the last ghost had come out of the tree, and instantly all the life had gone from it. The light had disappeared from the hole, the door had withered into nothing more than a thick piece of bark that had peeled away from the trunk. All of the leaves were falling from the tree in one huge rattling wave, dead and brown and dried already, covering the graveyard in an autumnal cloak. Even the branches themselves seemed to curl inwards as we watched, and a few minutes later as we walked through the streets we saw the roots between the cobbles were gone, or broken up already and turning into flakes and shards of driftwood in the rain.

She leaned heavily on my shoulder, and seemed to be about to pass out, and as I walked and the excitement of the last few hours ebbed from me I felt an exhaustion of my own. That's when another arm fell around my shoulder, and another around hers. It was Sally Dolton and Tusk. Mayrick was walking ahead of us. I felt as if I hadn't slept for weeks, but the only important thing was that Maria was alive, and I had to see her to safety. The presence of my friends meant that there might be good news, but I was too tired to even think of a way of asking. It was Mayrick who turned to me and said, 'It's OK, Daniel! It's safe! Once Prye was gone, they ran! They fled! Tumblewater is ours again!'

I felt the rain falling on my grateful face, and turned to share the good news with Maria, who was already deep in the sleep of one who is recovering.

EPILOGUE

t was three weeks after we moved back above ground, when people were still finding their feet, still moving back into their own houses and dragging their possessions above ground, when the first burglary occurred. Uncle found me a backstreet cottage to stay in, where I tended my sister, who was making a quick recovery. Uncle's injuries were rapidly healing too, and he was sipping his morning coffee when he heard the news. It threw him into a terrible depression.

But not me. I didn't try to explain it to him that moment, but when I heard that a crime had been committed, no doubt by a member of the Underground community, I knew that things were on their way back to normal. It was a signal that at some point, relatively soon, things would be the way they had been, before all this had started. Soon we would have police, and criminals, and markets, and schools, and streets that were dangerous or safe, and dirty or clean, and posh or poor. Then we would be a real place again. But as I say, I didn't tell Uncle my theory at once, and I just waited, content that I would be proved right.

He was healed in a month; Maria took much longer. She didn't understand things entirely at first, and I spent a lot of time tending her, of which I did not resent a single minute, but instead loved watching her getting better, degree by degree, getting used to the world around her, and going on gradually increasing walks. She was funny, and scatterbrained, and impatient with her own recovery – often to the point of tears. I had to bring her dozens upon dozens of books, which she read voraciously, and which, when she was too tired, I read to her. But not *The Junior Ornithologist's Guide to the Dietary Requirements of Subtropical Birds of Prey in Temperate Climes*, though. Somewhere on that dark night I had dropped my copy of that famous bestseller. Thank God.

I was visited by Tusk and Mayrick and Sally, who were enrolling at a new local school despite being too old, at Sally's insistence, so they could continue a less violent education than that they had received under-ground. The boys grumbled, but knew she was right. I looked forward to them visiting me frequently, and staying friends for a long time to come.

There was a knock at my door one day and I found Mr Jaspers standing there with a copy of *Grisly Tales from Tumblewater* in his hand. He held it out with a proud smile.

312

'Thank you!' I said. 'And in return I have this . . .' And going back into the room I fetched the manuscript of the second Tumblewater book (which is this one that you have in your hands).

'Dear boy,' he muttered, showing no especial pleasure at being given another pile of paper to read. I invited him in, and poured him a cup of coffee.

'I've been thinking about this,' he said grandly. 'You've worked devilish hard, and I think you need a break from grisly tales.'

'I think you're right,' I said.

'Of course!' he answered. 'Write about something else next time. A historical story perhaps – maybe something set in the Middle Ages.' And then he farted, as was his habit, and looked around for someone to blame. There wasn't anyone, so he simply grinned.

Many months later there was another knock at my door, and I found a humble-looking Uncle standing there.

'Augustus,' I said. He looked suitably abashed at being addressed by his birth name.

'I've come to tell you that I'm not staying here,' he said. He spoke quickly, as though he wanted to get it off his chest rather than talk about it. 'I'm going abroad. I've given all Caspian's property back to its original owners. Or those who are still alive,' he acknowledged with a haunted look. 'I've taken as much money as I need, no more. The rest will go to helping rebuild the parts of Tumblewater that were destroyed. After being under the ground for so long I want to see other parts of the globe, Daniel. I'll be gone for several years, but I'll look you up when I return, you can be certain of that.' He faltered, looking unexpectedly emotional. 'I want to say thank you. When you came along I was almost despairing. I think you saw that towards the end. But you helped me carry on, and pull through at last. Thank you, Daniel.'

And he suddenly leaned forward and grabbed me in a tight hug. I was startled and didn't know how to respond. Before I knew what was happening, he'd let go, and walked off up the street. I stepped out to watch him leave, with a great heaving happy sadness in my chest, and feeling a terrible loss and a great gain, that though he was gone, I would have this friend forever. As I turned to go back into the house and check on Maria, something blinded me.

I blinked and covered my eyes briefly, and felt a pleasant warmth on my face, as though from a nearby fire. It took a few seconds before I realized I was standing in a narrow shaft of sunshine, and turned my face up to the light so I could feel it. Before I knew it, it had faded. I blinked again, and looked round to see if anyone else had noticed it. There were people all the way up and down the street, costermongers counting out onions, people gossiping and arguing and laughing. No one had noticed a thing. I went back inside with a ludicrous grin on my face, as rain spattered into the mud behind me.